all I ever
wanted

BOOKS BY KATE HEWITT

STANDALONE NOVELS

A Mother's Goodbye

The Secrets We Keep

Not My Daughter

No Time to Say Goodbye

A Hope for Emily

Into the Darkest Day

When You Were Mine

The Girl from Berlin

The Edelweiss Sisters

Beyond the Olive Grove

My Daughter's Mistake

The Child I Never Had

The Angel of Vienna

When We Were Innocent

That Night at the Beach

The Mother's Secret

In the Blink of an Eye

FAR HORIZONS TRILOGY

The Heart Goes On

Her Rebel Heart

This Fragile Heart

AMHERST ISLAND SERIES

The Orphan's Island

Dreams of the Island

Return to the Island

The Island We Left Behind

An Island Far from Home

The Last Orphan

THE GOSWELL QUARTET

The Wife's Promise

The Daughter's Garden

The Bride's Sister

The Widow's Secret

THE INN ON BLUEBELL LANE SERIES

The Inn on Bluebell Lane

Christmas at the Inn on Bluebell Lane

THE EMERALD SISTERS SERIES

The Girl on the Boat

The Girl with a Secret

The Girl Who Risked It All

The Girl Who Never Gave Up

The Other Mother

And Then He Fell

Rainy Day Sisters

Now and Then Friends

A Mother like Mine

all I ever
wanted

KATE HEWITT

bookouture

Published by Bookouture in 2025

An imprint of Storyfire Ltd.
Carmelite House
50 Victoria Embankment
London EC4Y 0DZ

www.bookouture.com

The authorised representative in the EEA is Hachette Ireland
8 Castlecourt Centre
Dublin 15 D15 XTP3
Ireland
(email: info@hbgi.ie)

ISBN: 978-1-83525-271-0
eBook ISBN: 978-1-83525-270-3

Dedicated to Anna, for being amazing.

PROLOGUE

At first, I'm afraid to look. I hold my breath, angling my gaze away from the screen. The mood in the darkened room is tense, the air taut with expectation. No one speaks, and the only sound is the hum of the ultrasound machine, the catch of my breath as I try to stay calm.

Part of me still can't believe I'm here, that I made it this far, that I agreed to all this. Part of me is still looking around in blank surprise, a tangled mix of wonder and alarm surging through me, a dazed shock that this is actually happening.

"Now you should be able to see something," the technician tells the three of us with a smile in her voice. Three people are in this room, besides the technician; three people, when in almost every other case there should only be two. Three people, all of whom are meant to be invested in what's there on the screen.

But I'm still refusing to look. Then I hear a soft gasp, and it didn't come from me. Almost unwillingly, I turn my head, lift my gaze to the black and white image moving on the screen. The initial splodgy blobs reform into something recognizable, something human and real. A baby.

A baby.

My breath escapes me in a dazed rush.

This changes everything.

PART ONE

ONE

ASHLEY

"I'm sorry."

Two words, I reflect, my hands clasped tightly together in my lap, that you never want to hear from your doctor. You certainly don't want to hear them spoken in the kind of hushed tone usually reserved for a cathedral or a museum. As I force myself to meet Dr. Bryant's gaze, the gynecologist's expression an unsettling mix of matter-of-fact briskness and a grimacing kind of sympathy, I'm simply grateful that in this moment I feel too numb to cry. I don't want to break down in front of a woman I've only met twice.

My husband Mark was the one who wanted me to see a fertility specialist. He offered to see one as well; he is, if anything, relentlessly fair and determined. If medical science improves to the point that men can carry babies, I'm pretty sure Mark would jump at the chance. As it is, science hasn't moved on that much and I'm the one learning that I have as much chance of carrying a baby as my husband currently does.

Those two words, said in that grave whisper, still reverberate through me with all their devastating repercussions.

"Ashley?" Dr. Bryant's voice is gentle. "Do you have any questions?"

I stare at her mutely. I have no idea what the expression on my face is, and I feel too shocked and dazed to attempt to regulate it. I have so many questions, and yet at the same time none at all. After all, what more is there to say?

Dr. Bryant has just explained to me that I can't possibly get pregnant because I have no eggs left in my poor, withered ovaries. I imagine them tucked away in my uterus, shriveled little raisins dying on the proverbial vine. I never even suspected something was amiss. I am, at the age of thirty-eight, in premature menopause. It's like my whole life has taken a giant, lurching step into a future I wasn't even aware of, and here I am, gormlessly standing still, staring into space. I don't know how to catch up. I don't want to.

"I'm not sure I know what to ask," I say finally. I give a little, light laugh, which doesn't feel like the right response for this situation. But the truth is, I don't know how to be, or even how to feel, in this moment. Should I be sad? Stoic? Quietly, nobly accepting my fate? Or maybe Dr. Bryant expects me to break down and weep into my hands, sobbing over the baby I'll now never have.

If I had a script, I'd read from it, but I don't, and so I force myself to meet the doctor's gaze, which *seems* compassionate, her eyes and mouth both drooping downward. But then I see her, very discreetly, check her watch before her gaze swiftly flicks back to mine.

"That's understandable," she murmurs as she recrosses her legs. "But there is a lot of really helpful information about early-onset menopause out there. I can give you a leaflet, and there's also plenty of useful websites online. There are ways to manage your symptoms..."

"I don't think I have any symptoms." None that I noticed, anyway. I'm not the classic case of a woman waving her hands in front of her face, good-naturedly bemoaning the embarrassing inconvenience of hot flashes. And I don't think I am particularly tired or moody, and while I haven't had a period in a few months—hence one of the reasons for this appointment—they have been a little hit or miss since I was in my twenties. This has really come out of left field...

And yet, at the same time, it hasn't.

Didn't I always know this—*us*—was too good to be true? Mark and me, nine months of marriage, my longed-for happily-ever-after to be tied with the bright pink or blue bow of parenthood. Part of me has been waiting for something to go wrong ever since I met him. Why not in this way?

"So, just to be clear," I ask Dr. Bryant, "there's no way I can become pregnant?"

"Not with your own biological child," she replies. "I'm afraid your stage of menopause is too advanced for that. But there are other options when it comes to starting a family. You could look into surrogacy, or an egg donor, if you wanted to try to carry a pregnancy to term yourself... we can discuss those as and when, and with your husband, as well."

I shake my head; I'm not sure why. Maybe I'm just not ready to think about all those intimidating possibilities quite yet. I only learned I was infertile five minutes ago, after all. I need to absorb this news before I can think about anything else.

"There's time," Dr. Bryant murmurs, and I almost laugh, even though I feel hollow inside. *Is there?* I'm thirty-eight; Mark is forty-one. It doesn't feel like there is very much time at all, and yet I know I don't want to rush into anything. I'd already felt like we were rushing, when, after only three months of marriage, Mark suggested we try for a baby, as I'd suspected he would. Six months on, and that dream is already dead.

"Thank you," I tell Dr. Bryant, and then I gather my purse and coat.

I came from work, and my low, sensible heels pinch my toes.

The neck of my blouse feels constricting; the waistband of my skirt is digging into my middle. I want nothing more than to go home and step into a scalding-hot shower for at least twenty minutes. But first I know I'm going to have to face Mark. How can I tell him what I've just learned? He won't just be disappointed, he'll be *devastated*.

And all because of me.

"Let me give you one of those leaflets," Dr. Bryant says, opening a drawer. I murmur my thanks as she hands it to me. *Living with Premature or Early Menopause* is written across the front in flowing, purple script. There's a photo of a woman in her forties, looking both reflective and determined as she gazes out at a field of waving wildflowers, her hands clasped in front of her. It makes me think of a brochure for a yoga retreat or a health spa.

"Thank you," I say again, and then I slip it into my purse.

I don't meet her eye as I leave the room and stand numbly at the front desk, waiting to hear how much my copay is. Nothing comes free when it comes to health insurance. Then I meekly hand over my credit card while my mind whirls. Mark will want to know how the appointment went as soon as I step into the house. In fact, he'll probably call me even before I get home, eager for news. He was disappointed when I told him I wanted to go to this appointment alone, but I knew I couldn't deal with his kindly concern, the well-meaning but insistent questions he would undoubtedly ask the doctor, whose answers I wasn't ready for. My husband wants a baby more than anything in the world. A baby I can no longer give him.

Blindly, I turn away from the reception desk and head outside. I squint in the glare of the June sunshine that reflects off the endless expanse of the medical center's parking lot, making the hot tarmac glitter. For a few seconds, I can only stand there, unable to perform the simple steps that will take me back home. Get out my keys. Unlock my car. Drive three miles to our townhouse in the suburbs of Hartford, Connecticut. Go inside, slip off my heels, kiss Mark's cheek, get out the vegetables we prepped for dinner last night. Turn on some jazz while we make dinner together, chatting about our day. Maybe open a bottle of wine, sip it slowly as I stir the pasta sauce. Mark will light a candle, smile at me over the flickering flame. Contentment will steal through me, a self-satisfaction tempered by wonder and gratitude. Some days, most days, I feel so lucky that, *finally*, this is my life.

This, however, is not one of those days. I dig in my purse for my keys. I am on autopilot, my mind determinedly blank as I get in my car and drive home. I barely notice the blur of suburban sprawl—big box stores and restaurant chains, billboards and traffic lights. I am only thinking about the look on Mark's face when I tell him what I've learned.

A sigh escapes me, a lonely gust of sound, before I straighten my shoulders and stare straight ahead. I hate disappointing people, and I know I'll be disappointing Mark more than either of us can bear, and there's nothing I can do about it.

He'll do his best to act like I haven't, but I'll still know. I'll see it in the faraway look in his eyes, I'll sense it in those moments of silence that feel like falling into a well. I'll feel it in myself, in the knowledge that now sits in my stomach like a stone, that the one thing Mark has wanted more than anything was a child of his own.

Sure enough, as I drive home, my phone buzzes twice with texts from Mark. I see them flash up on the car's screen and I ignore them. Then he calls, and I don't answer. My stomach has started to churn, and dread pools like acid in its bottom. I do not want to have the conversation I know we are going to have to have. I don't *know* how to have it, what tone to take, whether I should be upbeat and determined—"Dr. Bryant said there are other options"—or just let us both wallow in the sadness for a while.

Mark is a relentlessly cheerful person; in the year we have known each other, we have never argued, although, to be fair, that might be as much down to my fear of confrontation as to his good humor. But we have a good marriage, we love each other, and while it all still feels so new, that doesn't mean it is fragile.

At least I hope it doesn't.

The air is soft, the sun still warm, as I park my car in front of our townhouse and climb out. It made a lot of sense once we were married to move into Mark's modern place, everything sleek and custom built, with smart appliances and a gently flickering gas fireplace that looks like something you'd see in a hotel lobby.

Everything in it is a cool, dove gray—the walls, the floors, the curtains, the countertops, even the dishes and linens. My Fiestaware pieces and vibrant modern art prints look incongruous against all that cool-toned sophistication, but Mark insists he likes the splashes of color.

"You've brought color into my life, Ash," he always tells me. "It was all so boring and bland before."

I know he means it, but nine months into our marriage I still find it hard to believe.

I've always liked color, even though my entire wardrobe is a palette of black, gray, brown and beige. For Christmas, Mark bought me a gorgeous scarf of scarlet silk. I'm too timid to wear it out, but I love that he bought it for me. I wish I could be the person he seems to think I am, who could wear that sort of thing with self-assured flair. But now I can't even be the person I thought I could, who can give him a baby. How can I tell him?

As I unlock the front door, I breathe in the smell of garlic and basil; Mark has already started making dinner. I take off my heels and drop my bag onto the chest in the hall, longing to postpone this moment and knowing I can't. As I close the door behind me with the softest of clicks, Mark, ears undoubtedly pricked, comes out of the kitchen, holding a glass of wine, which he passes to me with an expectant smile. The wine is a sign of his gratitude, that I went to the appointment at all; he advised me to go off alcohol, as he has, while we were trying to conceive, and since he doesn't yet know that I can't, this is a truly gracious concession.

"Well?" he asks, and I hear the eagerness in his voice. "How did it go?"

I take a sip of wine to avoid answering, but he must see something in my face because his smile slips, and his dark eyebrows draw together.

"Ash?"

I stare at him over the rim of the wineglass. Mark has the kindest face of anyone I know. It's round—some might say a little chubby—with full lips, soft brown eyes, and long, curly lashes that any woman would covet. His hair is thin on top, and he chose to forgo a regrettable comb-over to embrace baldness, which somehow just makes him look kinder, a little bit like a young Santa. I can't disappoint him like this. I just can't.

"Ashley..." His eyes and mouth both turn down with concern and sympathy, but even so, I can sense the fear lurking behind those more honorable emotions. "What happened? What did Dr. Bryant say?"

"It isn't good news," I manage to squeeze out through a throat that has become too tight.

I walk past him into the living room and curl up on one corner of the gray leather sofa, taking another sip of wine, simply to have something to do. Mark comes to stand in the doorway. He's wearing his apron with the cartoonish "An Apron is Just A Cape On Backwards" logo, and his face is flushed from cooking, his fringe of dark hair forming little curls by his ears. I gaze down at my wine, because I can't bear to see the unhappy confusion I know must be on his face that makes me think of a kicked puppy.

"It is?" he asks, his voice turning soft, and then he comes to sit next to me. "Ash? What did she say? Talk to me." He reaches for my hand, and I let it lie limply in his. The silence stretches between us, and I know I'm the one who has to break it.

"I'm in premature menopause," I finally tell him, my voice low. "I have been for a while, apparently, without realizing it. That's why I haven't had my period in the last couple of months. It's more common than anyone realizes, she said."

"*Menopause...*" He sounds mystified. After being a bachelor all his life, Mark has taken living with the vagaries of womanhood in his equable stride. He doesn't blink at buying tampons —not that he's had to buy those recently—or having our bathroom taken over by my toiletries and cosmetics. He doesn't understand the devastation of a bad haircut or why you cannot wear orange with green, but he is gamely willing to be instructed in such matters. Still, the concept of menopause is a mystery to him, as it was to me, because I didn't think I'd even have to think about it for at least a decade. "So what does that mean *exactly*?" he asks.

I shake my head slowly. I'm too tired to go into all the details right now because I know Mark will want to forensically dissect everything I've learned today, and then some. He'll be on his laptop within minutes, researching websites and jotting down notes. By tomorrow morning, he'll be sending me articles on managing symptoms and inspiring blog posts about women who triumphed through early menopause. He'll find the one-in-a-million case where a woman in premature menopause was able to get pregnant and went on to have six children of her own. I don't need the brochure Dr. Bryant gave me because I'll be living with an entire encyclopedia.

I know this, because this is how Mark has been since we decided to try for a baby. He bought four different kinds of prenatal vitamins; he sent me articles on fertility-boosting foods and the importance of sleep and exercise. He did the same for himself, too—limited hot baths and bike rides to boost his sperm count, quit alcohol, save for the occasional glass of wine, and made sure to exercise. He did it all out of kindness as well as excitement, because there is not a mean or manipulative bone in his body, and while I appreciated it all very much, I'm not ready for another onslaught of relentless goodwill.

"Ash..."

"Basically, my eggs are dried up," I announce, a little abruptly. "So I'll never be able to have a baby of my own. *Our* own." I finally force myself to look at him. "I'm sorry, Mark."

He stares at me for a second, his face screwed up in confusion. "*Sorry...*"

"I know how much you want a baby," I whisper. I look down at my lap, so I don't have to see the disappointment on his face. I feel it in myself, the disappointment that I disappointed him, a curdling in my stomach.

Babies were something that came up, deliberately and matter-of-factly, on our very first date. We'd met on a dating app for commitment-minded people in their thirties and forties, and that night, over a shared charcuterie board, Mark explained, his voice calm and reverberating with certainty, that he'd been adopted and had never known any of his biological relatives. His adopted parents, both dead now, had been great, he told me, but he really wanted to have his own biological child.

"I know people say it doesn't matter, but the blood tie makes a difference to me," he'd explained then, with both dignity and determination. His expression was open, his smile affable, but there was a stubborn set to his rounded jaw that made me realize just how serious he was. "I've never known someone who has my eyes," he had continued, "or whose chin I share. I have no idea why I look or act or think the way I do. Sometimes it feels like I've just been... floating in space, alone, all this time." He'd laughed then, a little abashedly. "That probably sounds kind of overdramatic, but... it's how I've felt. And I know it is as much nurture as nature, but I've completely missed the nature part. It was a closed adoption, so I can't find out any information about my birth parents at all. I have no idea who either of them are, not even their names, and certainly not their personalities." His voice choked a little as he finished, "It's like I came from... *nowhere.*"

He'd paused then to compose himself, before continuing more calmly, "I want that connection, that sense of family, of... of knowing someone is truly part of you, right down to your bones, your *genes.* I want a baby." He gave a grimacing smile as he met my gaze resolutely. "I know this is just our first date," he added, "so it might seem like I'm seriously jumping the gun, but I just feel like I have to get it out there, because I want to be honest, and if it's not something that could be on the table for you, then we can end things right here, absolutely no hard feelings whatsoever. It would probably be easier for both of us."

He had ducked his head then, like an apology for his forthrightness, and I saw both the hope and fear in his soft, brown eyes. We'd known each other for less than an hour, although we'd been texting back and forth for a week, but already I'd felt that we both wanted to make this work. I certainly did.

As for a baby? I stared at him as he waited for my response, my mind whirling. I'd thought about having a family one day, as most women do, but in a far vaguer sense than he clearly had. When there's no Mr. Right on the horizon, dreaming of your own baby can feel kind of bleak, as well as pathetic. But I appreciated Mark's honesty; both of us were too old for playing games or pussyfooting around, even if it felt a little bizarre to be talking about babies when we'd only been chatting for about half an hour.

"I'd like to have a child," I had told him hesitantly. "One day." It might have seemed like something of a lukewarm reply, but it was enough to make Mark beam, and we had our second date just two days later and were engaged within three months.

And now, just a year later, we're here, and already it feels like the end of the road.

"Ashley," Mark says, squeezing my hand, his voice soft with sorrow, tender with concern. "You don't need to be *sorry*. This isn't your fault."

"I know it isn't my *fault*, but..." *It kind of is.* It's my problem, anyway.

I don't want to put into words how disappointed I know Mark is, how hard this will be for him, to say goodbye to the one dream that practically defined him.

And the other thing I can't begin to explain, not even to myself, is that when Dr. Bryant first told me, underneath the numbness... I felt a flicker of relief.

TWO

DANI

"I don't *have* out-of-network benefits. As I told you." I am trying to sound pleasant while speaking through gritted teeth about my health insurance, or lack thereof. My knuckles, clenched around my phone, ache with effort.

I have been on this call to AmeriMedical, my health insurance provider, for forty-five minutes, thirty-two of those minutes on hold listening to a muzak version of "Wind Beneath My Wings" played on repeat. I'm ready to scream.

"Yes, and as I've stated before, without out-of-network benefits, this surgery cannot be covered." The woman's voice is crisp, officious. "I appreciate your frustration, but I'm afraid there is nothing we can do on your current insurance plan."

We have been going around in circles for almost fifteen minutes. "But as *I've* stated before," I try yet again, "the surgery is an essential—"

"It's out of network," the woman cuts across me, now sounding impatient. It is the third time she has informed me of this, like I'm not understanding her, when the truth is, she's not understanding *me*. No matter how many reasoned arguments I make, faceless bureaucracy always seems to win. "AmeriMedical does not extend coverage to that surgeon *or* to that hospital, and therefore cannot offer any financial compensation if you choose to go ahead with this procedure. If you feel this surgery is truly essential, then I'm afraid you will have to find another insurance plan or provider, or pay for it out of pocket." She pauses for a millisecond before she asks very politely, "Is there anything else I can help you with today?"

"No," I snap, unable to keep myself from sounding bitchy. I'd slam the phone down, but I'm on my cell and so all I can do is jab at the screen to end the call.

I throw my phone onto the sofa as I lean back with a groan. My eyes are gritty with fatigue, and I am days behind in my work. I opted to teach a summer class in biostatistics for some extra money, and I have thirty lab reports to look over, as well as preparing my own research for a meeting with my supervisor. Welcome to the glamorous life of being a twenty-eight-year-old microbiology PhD student.

I stare at the ceiling for a few minutes as I try to rally myself. I've spent three months gathering all the information for AmeriMedical—X-rays, a doctor's report, even research and statistics trumpeting the success of this surgery. I've appealed their decision twice, and I am now officially at the end of the road. My sister Callie cannot have her back surgery unless I do something drastic.

As if on cue, my sixteen-year-old sister comes through the front door of our apartment. Looking at her, you wouldn't know that she has a debilitating condition, at least not at first. She walks with a spring in her step, a swish to her long, blond ponytail. Eighteen months ago, aged fourteen and a half, she cracked a vertebra during a track meet, and for six weeks afterward she couldn't even walk. An X-ray and ongoing pain led to the diagnosis of moderate pediatric spondylosis, which is when the soft discs between the vertebrae of the spinal cord become compressed. It led first to stiffening muscles and increasing pain, and then to numbness and tingling, and a resulting clumsiness that kept her from running competitively ever again, and sometimes has her struggling to complete simple tasks.

Thanks to months of physical therapy and exercise, she now can walk and, save for the way she sometimes moves stiffly and carefully, you might never know she had the condition at all. Most children who do have it manage fine with physical therapy, but a small percentage have cases which tip over into severe. Callie is right on that knife-edge.

Without surgery, not only is her promising career as a hundred-meter sprinter over, but she potentially faces a lifetime of chronic pain and limited mobility. Some days, she pops painkillers like they're M&Ms. According to one specialist we saw, her back pain is likely to get worse with time, unless she has a spinal fusion surgery that, despite its positive success rate, AmeriMedical has insisted, during my many phone calls to them, is "unnecessary", meaning they won't cover the cost.

"Why do you look like you want to tear someone's head off?" Callie asks lightly as she drops her backpack onto the kitchen floor before riffling through the kitchen cabinets for a snack.

"Because I do," I reply, trying to make my voice sound as light as hers does, and failing.

Callie and I are pretty much opposites in every way, even though we look practically identical, save for the twelve years between us. We're both tall, leggy, blond and blue-eyed. Typical California girls, which is as much a curse as it is a blessing. I've never really sought out male attention, and I certainly don't want it for my little sister, but, the truth is, Callie is a knockout.

Unlike me, she's also endlessly cheerful and deliberately kind, whereas I can sometimes be kind of a bitch. Or so my mother likes to tell me, although she never says it quite like that. "Why are you always so angry?" she asked me in exasperation, just last week, and I had the self-control not to remind her it was because she walked out on Callie and me after our dad died three years ago. I had just started my PhD; Callie was in eighth grade. We were both grieving, needing a parent, and she chose to just walk away. What kind of mother does that?

"So who is it this time?" Callie asks as she closes the cabinets and takes a banana from the fruit bowl on the table instead. "Some poor student who didn't show up to a tutoring session? Or your supervisor, postponing a meeting yet again?" She raises her eyebrows, smiling at me, as she takes the armchair opposite the sofa.

"No." I sigh and close my laptop. I had it out on the coffee table, with all the statistics and percentages I was ready to tell the AmeriMedical representative, if she had just let me.

"No?" Callie raises her eyebrows as she starts peeling the banana. "What is it, some secret?"

I hesitate because Callie can be a little touchy about the spinal surgery I want her to have. I'm the one who found out about it online, who called the doctor who offered it, who scheduled the consultation by Zoom. I'm the one who insisted on X-rays, who showed her how this surgery could transform her life... even if she isn't yet convinced.

"Just life," I say instead, as I get up from the sofa. There's no point mentioning the surgery at the moment as it's a no-go, as infuriating a reality as that is. If my lousy student health insurance won't cover it, I'll have to try to find another insurance plan during open enrollment in November, so there's no point even talking to Callie about it until then.

I walk into the kitchen and pour myself a glass of water. Outside, the sky is relentlessly blue, and if I stand on my tiptoes and squint a little, I can just make out Mission Bay. I know how lucky I am to have scored this apartment on Linda Vista Drive, right near the University of San Diego. There are only a few dozen units for grad students in Presidio Terrace, and I really am thankful I got one, even if the five-hundred-square-foot one-bedroom is cramped for Callie and me. My boyfriend Ryan kindly erected a partition in the bedroom so we each have our own space, but it's still tiny. Not that Callie complains, because she never complains about anything. I'm the one who always has to complain *for* her.

"How was camp today?" I ask as I turn around and lean against the sink.

Callie is a counselor at a local summer camp for disadvantaged kids, three hours every afternoon spent supervising crafts and snack time, which she enjoys even though it takes a lot out of her. Right now, she is eating her banana very carefully, but I still notice how her hands tremble a little bit, one of the symptoms of pediatric spondylosis. As the nerves in her spinal cord compress, her hand and leg movements can become weak. She tries to cover it, but I can always tell. I'm always looking for it, even as the knowledge cramps my stomach and makes me silently curse the faceless, heartless bureaucrats of AmeriMedical, and the student health insurance that hardly seems to cover anything.

"Fine." She finishes the banana and neatly folds the peel up into a perfect square. She's not looking at me, which makes me sense something happened.

"Callie?" I ask, my tone guarded.

"What?" She looks up, her expression clear and too guileless. Something definitely happened. I know it. "Just tell me," I say, and she sighs.

"I fell over at the park. It was no big deal."

"Fell over?" My voice sharpens with anxiety.

"My foot went numb. I didn't realize. It was just for a second." She shrugs. "It happens."

"Callie..."

"Don't, Dani, okay?" She raises her voice only a little, keeping it friendly but firm. Even when she's in a temper, Callie sounds like she's being nice. "I'm *fine*," she insists, and then she rises from the armchair.

I can't tell if I'm being paranoid as I watch her walk to the trash can to throw out her banana peel. Does she seem more stiff-legged than usual? A little off balance? Both are symptoms of severe spondylosis. So far, she's been hovering on the moderate side, but if she tips into severe, she'll *definitely* need the surgery... whether she agrees with me or not. And whether insurance covers it or not.

Somehow, I have to find a way.

Later that evening, while Callie is watching Netflix on her side of our divided bedroom, I meet my best friend Anna for a drink at a bar in Pacific Beach. We became friends during the first year of our undergrad at USD, living on the same hallway. Now I'm swimming in student debt and subsisting on grants, while Anna is making six figures for Milliman, an actuarial consulting group in La Jolla.

As we sip our drinks—beer for me, a vodka and tonic for her—I can't help but grouse about my call with AmeriMedical. Anna is sympathetic as well as pragmatic; as someone who does consulting work for health insurance companies, she can see it from both sides, which is both annoying and helpful.

"It's difficult," she says, "because so few pediatric spondylosis cases require surgery. Most kids can manage their pain with therapy and medication, and it can get better as they get older."

"But Callie *can't* do that," I remind her, even though I've said this a thousand times before.

"She seems to be doing okay right now," Anna ventures

cautiously. Her dark sharp-cut bob swings against her jaw as she takes a sip of her drink.

"She fell over today," I tell her flatly. "Her foot went numb. What's next? Do you know in severe cases, children can lose control of their *bowels*? They're ten or twelve years old and they're in diapers."

Anna winces in sympathy. "She's not there yet," she reminds me, keeping her voice gentle. "But I know it must be a difficult prospect to consider."

"I don't *want* her to ever get there," I snap.

I know I shouldn't take out my frustration on Anna, but I don't have many friends—taking care of my sister, trying to finish my PhD, and having a boyfriend has put paid to much of a social life—and Anna is someone who actually gets it. She knows how broken the system is, how someone can pay thousands in health insurance and still be slammed with a huge bill —and that's if they can have whatever procedure or medication they desperately need in the first place. Without insurance, Callie's surgery would cost close to half a million dollars. It's such an inconceivable amount, it might as well be Monopoly money. There's no way even to consider it without some kind of coverage.

"And your mom can't help?" Anna asks cautiously, far from the first time. She has loving parents who paid her tuition for all four years of college, plus a Master's. Considering I had the same middle-class upbringing she did, she can't understand how I can basically be broke, even though I've explained why, multiple times. Some things just don't compute.

"My mom is *not* going to help," I say flatly before taking a swig of my beer.

Three years ago, when my dad died of a heart attack, our family was thrown into a total tailspin, emotionally as well as financially. Without any of us knowing it, my dad had taken out a second mortgage on our split-level house in Visalia to cover the gambling debts we didn't know he had. After his death, we were left with basically nothing; the house was repossessed, the bank accounts emptied, and then my mother announced she was moving to Arizona, more or less abdicating all maternal duties, while Callie came to live with me, thirteen years old and overcome with grief. I'm still furious at my mom for abandoning her, even though I try to sound cordial when she calls on the phone, which isn't all that often. It's as if, when my dad died, the part of her that was a loving mom died, too. I'll never understand it. I don't even want to try.

Anna is silent, her lips pursed. "You could try for another insurance plan," she tells me. "One with out-of-network benefits. It will be more expensive, but at least the surgery would be possible then, even if you're hammered with a massive co-pay, which, let's face it, you probably will be."

"I've looked into that," I admit on a sigh. "And it *would* be possible, if I can find a plan that takes students, but even so, the surgeon requires a deposit of *fifty grand* just to do the surgery, and most people don't get that back, even with the coverage." Which is why I'd wanted to work with my current insurance. I've been paying into it for seven years, so you'd think they could give me *something* back. "Frankly," I tell Anna, "fifty grand feels the same as five hundred thousand. Both are totally impossible for me." I press my lips together, knowing Anna doesn't need to hear more of my diatribe, but it frustrates me so much that all that is keeping my sister from getting the care she needs is *money*.

"And Ryan—?" she begins, but I cut her off with a shake of my head. I'm not asking him for help. I can't live with that kind of indebtedness to anyone, not even him.

I've been dating Ryan Stewart, an audit manager for a local accountancy firm, for two years. I've kept it casual for Callie's sake, and also because I'm not sure I have it in me to consider what something serious would look like—marriage, children I'm not ready to have, the house, the picket fence, the station wagon, the dog. I'm pretty sure Ryan wants all that at some point. He's never said so directly, but he *hints*, and I pretend not to notice. It's not the healthiest framework for a relationship, but it works for now, and I keep telling myself that we have time for all that later.

"Okay, well then, you need to figure out a way to get fifty grand," Anna replies with a playful smile. "Then you can switch insurance and pay the surgeon's deposit. Easy, right?"

I know she's trying to lighten the mood, and I appreciate the effort, but I'm too far down in a funk. Callie *fell over* today. What's next?

Still, for my friend's sake, I do my best to match her levity. "I could become a social media influencer?" I muse. "Start posting artistic selfies with my matcha lattes on Instagram for millions of likes. *That's* easy."

"Totally." She smiles, and I see the relief in her eyes. Nobody likes to be around someone who can't do anything but complain. "Or, I don't know, you could do clinical trials? Hire yourself out for psychological studies? There's money in that."

"Now there's a thought. Or what about an artist's model?" I tap my chin reflectively. "I think I saw in the Student Union that the art department is hiring live nude models for twenty-five dollars an hour. So I'd only have to work for..." I pause, screwing up my face in mock concentration. "Two thousand hours."

"Twenty hours a week for two years and you'd be there," Anna quips. "Plus tax, so maybe two and a half years."

"Yeah, and I can fit twenty hours of modeling every single week into my schedule," I scoff, smiling. "No problemo."

"Why not just go to where the real money is?" Anna's dark eyes dance over the rim of her glass as she takes a sip, swallows, and then pronounces triumphantly, "OnlyFans."

I nearly spit out my beer. "Now *there's* a thought." I know

Anna is joking—at least I hope she is—but the very thought of selling photos of myself or writing lewd messages to anonymous guys makes my stomach roil. There is no way I am ever doing something like that, not even for Callie. There has to be another way.

"Okay, well..." Anna casts her gaze to the ceiling as she considers other money-making options. I can't tell how seriously she's taking this conversation; I'm already finding it hopeless. "Well, there's always surrogacy," Anna says, and now I can tell she's joking. "I read in *People* that Ronaldo paid his surrogate ten *million* dollars."

"How do I get in touch with him?" I joke back.

Anna pulls out her phone and starts swiping. "Even ordinary surrogates make something like sixty thousand, plus all medical expenses," she remarks as she scans whatever she's pulled up on Wikipedia. "I mean, it's nine months of your life, but whatever, right?" She looks up, smiling to share the joke as she puts her phone away.

Except I'm not smiling. Sixty thousand dollars for being a little inconvenienced for nine months? All right, I know that's probably not the best way to view a pregnancy, but it's *doable*. I could still work, research, take care of Callie. Now that *does* sound like easy money...

Anna's smile drops as she takes in my serious expression. "Dani, are you actually thinking about it?" she exclaims. "I mean, being *pregnant*? Not to mention giving away your baby?"

"It's a quick way to make money," I reply. "And nine months *is* only nine months."

"I think you should reconsider OnlyFans," she says, and once again I can't tell if she's joking. She's clearly horrified by the thought of me upending my life with a pregnancy.

In any case, *I'm* not joking. I don't say as much to Anna, though, because I want to do my own research. I don't know anything about surrogacy, but I can find out. But, for now, I just smile and switch the topic to what she's doing this weekend, and I nod and smile some more as she tells me about the 10K she's running along the coast, but all the while, my mind is racing, racing, because if there's *any* chance of making this surgery happen for Callie, I already know I'm going to take it.

Whatever it is.

THREE

ASHLEY

"Surrogacy?"

I say the word carefully, like I'm speaking a foreign language, because, in a way, I am. It's the middle of July, six weeks since my appointment with Dr. Bryant, and just as I knew he would, Mark's been doing research.

He gave me time to absorb the news and recover first, being extra-considerate about everything. There were candlelit dinners and bubble baths run for me after work, a gift certificate to a beauty spa for a massage and facial. He did the laundry and made dinner every single day and generally treated me like I was made of finespun glass. I've married an incredible guy, but when it comes to having a baby, he's like a dog with a bone.

And so here we are, having brunch on a Sunday afternoon at Red Rock Tavern in Hartford, sipping mimosas and digging into delicious plates of eggs Benedict. And talking about surrogacy.

"It's just a thought," Mark says, but I absolutely know for him it's more than that. He probably has a printout of practicalities in his blazer pocket. He's ready to sign on whatever dotted line there is.

I take a bite of my eggs Benedict, mainly to stall for time. This isn't the first time since my appointment we've talked about the baby issue. Mark mentioned the possibility of an egg donor a few weeks ago, and we both met with Dr. Bryant to discuss it, only to discover that despite what she'd said earlier, egg donation was "probably not the best course of action for our particular situation." That is, my menopause is advanced enough that there is an "unfortunately high percentage" of miscarriage or complications, and IVF is likely to be "challenging" and would require months of hormone treatments before we could even make our first attempt, which even then has only a small chance of succeeding. Not to mention it would all be disastrously expensive.

"I wouldn't shut the idea of IVF down completely," Dr. Bryant told us, "but as you can imagine, it would be both costly and time-consuming. With your particular case, Ashley, it might take several rounds of IVF before you were able to become pregnant and then, of course, there is the issue of *successfully* carrying the baby to term, which is not a guarantee by any means, all things considered."

I left the appointment feeling, more than ever, that *I* was the problem. Back when we'd first started trying, Mark had a full work-up done; his sperm count was fine, he was healthy and raring to go. Now, not only can I not produce an egg, but I can't even carry another woman's baby. I'm useless.

Mark must have sensed my discontent about the whole thing because we didn't mention babies or pregnancy possibilities for several weeks. And now we're here, on a sunny July afternoon, kicking back and sipping mimosas, and he's launched surrogacy at me like an earnest, well-meant grenade.

"I know it's not something we've wanted to think about," Mark tells me in the measured voice I've come to know well. He's a lawyer, and it's clear why. He knows how to construct an argument, and he uses a kindly, reasonable tone of voice to get you on his side. But then, I remind myself, I *am* on his side already. We're in this together. I just wish I didn't have to keep reminding myself of that.

"No," I agree slowly as I put down my drink. "And, truthfully," I admit, wanting to be fair, "I don't know much about it."

"I've done some research," he says, and I smile encouragingly, even as something in me wilts, just a little. Here we go with the facts and figures, the statistics and stories. But as I brace myself for him to launch into it all, Mark suddenly goes silent.

I focus on him and realize he's gazing at me with a somberness that unnerves me a little.

"We don't need to talk about this," he says quietly, "if you don't want to."

Which just makes me feel worse.

"Of *course* we can talk about it," I say. "It's just..." I'm not sure how to frame my thoughts, because, the truth is, I don't know what I'm thinking, and I haven't ever since Dr. Bryant sat me down in that chair and told me the news. I want to please Mark, of course I do, and I also want us to have a family, even if it all feels overwhelming. I just hate coming up against my deficiency again and again, this sense that this problem exists solely because of me. It's a truth I feel like I can never escape, even as Mark resolutely tries to find ways around it.

"Ash?" he prompts gently. "What is it? Why do you seem... reluctant?"

His tone is so kind and understanding that now I feel like a complete heel. I'm selfishly stewing in my own feelings rather than trying to approach this together.

"I'm not," I assure him. "It just feels overwhelming... and I can't help but feel like a failure." Tears gather in my eyes, and I blink them back, although one drips down my cheek anyway. "I hate that," I whisper. "I'm sorry."

He reaches for my hands across the table, squeezes them

gently. "Ashley, you don't ever need to apologize to me," he says firmly. "*Please*. I know you know how much I've wanted a baby, and I *do*, but I want one with *you*. And if you're not on board with this…" He lets the thought trail away, and I wonder how he meant to finish it.

If I'm not on board, then what? He'll forget the idea of surrogacy? Do I want that, and could I even ask it of him, when I barely know what surrogacy is? Would he really stop all of this if I wanted him to?

"No, no." I squeeze his hands back and manage a smile. "Tell me, Professor, what you've learned about surrogacy, because I really don't know the first thing about it."

I sit back as Mark launches into everything he's researched, and there is a lot. He tells me how there are two kinds of surrogacy: gestational and traditional. How it's about getting to know the woman involved, creating a relationship, making sure you're all on the same page with how to proceed. The baby would be his biologically, but with the egg from another woman, an anonymous egg donor. We could be at the birth, as well as supporting this unknown woman through her pregnancy, and we could create a pre-birth order, a legal document naming us as the parents, even before the baby—*our* baby, he emphasizes—is born, so there would never be any questions about custody.

I keep smiling and sipping my mimosa, because I don't know what else to do. This feels like a lot of information, and none of it really involves me. Not technically, anyway. Emotionally…? I'm not sure about that, either.

"Well," he finally says, running his hand over his bald patch as he gives me a smile that is hopeful, wry, and a little fearful all at once. "What do you think?"

"It's… a lot to take in," I say carefully. I've barely taken in any of it, but I know I need to come up with some thoughtful questions. "I mean… how do we even find a surrogate? And how much would it cost?"

"There are agencies to help us find the right match and navigate the whole process," Mark assures me, sounding like an expert already, which he probably is. "As for the cost..." He pauses, steeling himself, or maybe I am. Clearly it's going to be a lot. "I've made an initial budget, obviously only with estimates... but with the agency fees, the surrogate's payment, her insurance, the egg donation and IVF, as well as the legal fees and other potential contingencies and variables... we're looking at one hundred and fifty to two hundred."

"One hundred and fifty to two hundred *thousand?*" I say on a gasp, lurching forward. Obviously he's talking thousands, but I still struggle to get my head around that kind of figure.

Mark nods, solemn, resolute. "Yes."

I reach for my drink and take a sip without tasting anything. I'm a relatively lowly administrative assistant and make a modest salary. Mark makes at least four times as much as I do, but even so... we don't have that kind of savings. Does anyone? And even if we did, do we want to bankrupt ourselves for a baby? Mark's baby, and not mine?

"That's a lot," I finally say as I put down my drink with an unsteady hand.

"I know it is." He sounds accepting, unapologetic.

"Do we even have that kind of money?" Since our marriage, Mark has handled our finances. It made sense, since he had so much more than I did, and he's a corporate lawyer. He knows what he's doing.

"Sort of," he replies after a moment. "We've got maybe one hundred thousand in savings and the rest I could get out of my retirement IRA, although I'll be subject to more tax for taking it early. But it's definitely doable."

I shake my head slowly. Mark knows I grew up with a mother who lurched from paycheck to paycheck, and things like groceries were sometimes seen as a luxury. Financial stability is incredibly important to me, and I've always been a saver, not a spender, even on my small salary. "Mark, that's—"

"Please, Ashley." His voice is a quiet throb of emotion that has me falling silent, chastened and moved. "I know this is a lot to ask. I *know* it's a big deal. But... surrogacy is our only chance to have a baby of our own. I just want us to consider it seriously. Take our time if we have to, and really think about it."

"We could always adopt," I venture, and am surprised to see his face harden in a way I never have before, his jaw thrust out bullishly.

"You know how I feel about that."

"I know you want a biological child," I agree carefully, feeling as if I am stepping across a minefield I wasn't aware existed until this moment, "but, Mark, *you* were adopted. You must appreciate how amazing and important it is to give a new chance at life to a child in need. Instead of spending hundreds of thousands on a... a designer baby, we could help a needy child who's desperate for a home, a family..."

He stares at me for a moment, his face crumpled in hurt, and I fall silent, feeling chastened.

"Is that how you see it?" he finally asks. "Like to me a baby is just some *accessory*?"

I cringe, both at the tone of his voice and the implication of the word. That's not what I meant, at least I don't think it is. And we are perilously close to arguing, which we never do.

"No," I tell him. "Of course I don't think that. I understand why having a baby that is biologically related to you is important. Very important." I pause and then continue as gently as I can, "I just don't completely understand why you're so set against adoption."

"I told you my reasons," he replies, and now his voice sounds the tiniest bit cool, which makes me want to backtrack immediately. We've barely begun talking about this, and already it all feels so fraught, which I hate. "Yes, I want to be related to someone," he states fiercely. "Blood-related to my own baby. I thought you understood how important that was to me."

"I do, I really do..." Except, I am thinking, *I* won't be blood-related to this baby. Has Mark even realized that? What's so important to him now *can't* be important to me. It's not as if I've got a raft of biological relatives out there, either. There's my mother, whom I see almost every week. Her parents are dead, and my father has been completely out of the picture since I was a baby, although his mother stayed in touch until she died in my teens. But, I tell myself, that's more than Mark has. At least I know where I come from.

I am trying to frame some of my thoughts into words when Mark suddenly reaches over the table to take my hand again. "Ash, I'm sorry," he says, his voice quiet and heartfelt. "I don't mean to be so obsessive about this. It's just... hard to let go of the dream." He pauses, lacing his fingers through mine. His expression is troubled, his eyes shadowed, his lips pressed together. "The reality is, adoption is a difficult process for anyone. It's absolutely wonderful for so many children, I *know* that. It was for me, in many ways. But I remember someone at an adoption support group once saying that 'at the heart of adoption there's always brokenness,' and even though I loved my parents, even though I had it *great*, I got what she meant. A lot of adopted kids rebel at some point—not because they hate their adoptive parents or anything, usually far from it. But just because of the brokenness." He pauses, his fingers squeezing mine. "I did."

"You did?" This is news to me. Mark always painted his childhood as solid, if not absolutely idyllic. Loving parents, middle-class home, bit of a geek.

"Yeah, in high school. I lashed out at my parents. I was angry, and I didn't even know why. Classic stuff, but you don't realize that when you're in it. I ended up living with my friend's parents for the last six months of high school. I came around in college, and my parents always operated an open-door policy with me. They were great. But I'm telling you all this just to say... adoption is *hard*. It can be a long, hard road, and it's not for everyone."

"No," I agree quietly. Truth be told, I'm not sure it's for me. But two hundred thousand dollars for a baby simply so it can be blood-related to Mark?

"Can we just talk to an agency?" Mark asks, an ache in his voice that makes me ache in response, because, yet again, I'm the one holding him back. I'm the problem. "Get some more information? We can both be involved in every part of the process, Ash—picking the surrogate, having discussions, even being right there in the delivery room. This baby would be *ours*, Ash. He or she really would."

There is so much hope in my husband's face, as well as so much longing. I've already disappointed him once, terribly. Can I do it again, just because I have some formless reservations? All he's asking is to talk to an agency. Get some information... although already I suspect that once we get that ball rolling, it will only gather speed.

And yet, this is what Mark wants most of all, and I love him so much.

"Of course we can," I say, and I squeeze his hand back, determinedly ignoring the buzz of fear that is electrifying my insides. I don't even know what I'm afraid of, or what is making me so reluctant.

I owe it to Mark to keep going with this... despite the dread already swirling in my stomach at the thought.

FOUR

DANI

It's been two weeks since Anna mentioned surrogacy, and I am now connecting to a Zoom call with a surrogacy agency and holding my breath.

Nerves flutter in my stomach and I tuck my hair behind my ears, wondering if my button-down blouse and string of fake pearls is a little too Stepford wife, but when I completed the prescreening online, Creating Dreams seemed to be stringent about my lifestyle requirements. No smoking in the last twelve months, limited alcohol intake, a clean driver's license, no government assistance, a high-school education and preferably a college degree, as well. All that, plus the health requirements, suitable height and weight, and no history of diabetes or heart disease. And that was just to get to this, my first consultation, to decide if I can continue on the "surrogacy journey."

After my drink with Anna, I spent hours researching surrogacy, trying to avoid the flashing promises on various websites that I could earn over a hundred grand "making someone's dreams come true." I wanted the nitty-gritty, the *reality*, because after everything—my dad's death, my mom's abandonment, the current health insurance nightmare—I know better than to trust promises that sound too good to be true. But I don't need a hundred grand, I need fifty. And fast. When Creating Dreams promised intended parents they could find a match within ninety days, I figured that was the agency I wanted.

The call connects, and within a few seconds, the director of the surrogacy agency, Andrea Dreyfus, is on the screen, smiling at me. She is mid-fifties, African-American, with very short gray hair and a warm smile. She is wearing pale pastel separates, looking relaxed in an office chair, her background a cream wall with a bland watercolor print of the ocean.

I smile nervously. "Hi."

"Hello, Danielle." Her voice is warm and rich. "Is that what you go by?"

"Dani, usually."

"Okay, Dani." Her smile widens. "Thank you for completing our online prequalification screening, as that's an important part of our process. We don't want to waste anyone's time—yours, mine, or potential parents—so it helps to make sure we're only speaking to eligible surrogates."

I have to swallow because my throat has gone dry. It's almost like she knows I hedged a bit on my answers, but I'd told myself they were white lies that weren't hurting anybody. In fact, I was doing a lot of good, because I really, really wanted to give some desperate couple a baby of their own. For fifty grand.

"Of course," I tell her, my hands folded sedately in my lap, and then I smile, a stretching of my lips.

"So, tell me a little bit about yourself," Andrea encourages as she leans back in her chair, one hand pillowing her head. Her smile widens, invites me in. "I know from your form that you're a PhD student?"

"Yes, in microbiology."

"That sounds challenging."

"It can be." I let out a little laugh, thin and wavery. I love the detail involved in microbiology, the hope and possibility that can be found in such small things, but I'm not about to go into all that right now.

"And what made you consider being a surrogate, Dani?"

"Well..." I lick my lips.

A few nights ago, I did a deep-dive down the rabbit hole of surrogate message boards and learned that surrogates need to be *very* family-friendly. In reality, you may be no more than a rent-a-womb, but intended parents—as they're called—want someone they are able to not just work with or even trust, but love. Which is weird to me, because as soon as that baby is in their arms, I'm pretty sure they're not planning on keeping in touch. But maybe that's just me, being cynical.

"Family is very important to me," I state, which is true. Callie means everything. "And I saw, from my mother, the pain of infertility. She had my sister twelve years after me," I explain swiftly. "No one really talks about secondary infertility, but it can be devastating."

Okay, that *may* be stretching the truth just a little. I don't know if my mom suffered from secondary infertility or if Callie was an accident, and, in truth, I can't help but suspect the latter. It's hard not to view my childhood through the lens of my mother's leaving, which made me question everything she did for Callie and me growing up—baking chocolate chip cookies, helping with our homework, tucking us in at night. She was a great mom, or so I thought, until she decided she didn't want to be one anymore. Does that negate all that went before?

Maybe.

"That must have been difficult," Andrea murmurs. She straightens, fixing me with a more direct look. "But being a surrogate is a big commitment—not just nine months of your life, although obviously it is that as well, but an opening of yourself to other people in a way that some might find intrusive or difficult." She cocks her head, her gaze sweeping over me as if trying to test my response to words that feel like a warning.

"Most intended parents want to be intimately involved in the whole process of surrogacy. They want to keep in touch with regular phone calls, texts, that sort of thing. They want to feel like they're going through the pregnancy *with* you."

It sounds kind of creepy to me, but I just murmur something positive.

"You must understand," Andrea continues, as if she can guess the nature of my thoughts, "they have been longing for a baby, usually for quite some time. The fact that they can't have one naturally themselves is often a source of deep pain, even heartbreak. Surrogacy can seem like a dream come true, but it's one that often comes after years of deep disappointment."

"Yes, of course," I murmur.

"So a surrogate needs to be willing and even excited to go on that journey with them, because it *is* a journey." She pauses before continuing carefully, "I know the financial compensation can be a motivating factor in making the decision to become a surrogate, but it can't be the *only* factor. We are looking for women who want to help these families, as well as be a part of their lives, at least for the surrogacy journey." She smiles. "Although some do remain in touch afterwards, I wouldn't necessarily say it's the norm, at least not in the long term."

It sounds like another warning, and one I do not need. I have no intention of hanging around, trying to stay involved with a baby who isn't even biologically mine. My focus is always on Callie.

"I think that sounds great," I tell her, injecting a warmth in my voice that, if I'm honest, I don't really feel. "I mean... I wouldn't want this to be an anonymous, impersonal experience. I think it's important that, whoever I might be matched with... we all trust and respect each other. Like you said, we're on this journey together."

Andrea nods slowly. I've said the right words, I know I have, but I'm not sure she believes me.

To be honest, I don't know if *I* believe me. It all sounds well-meaning enough and my tone is heartfelt, but do I actually *feel* it? Do I care about this blank-faced couple whose baby I might carry? Not really. Not at *all*, if I'm honest. At least, not yet. And I don't particularly want to get emotionally entangled with them. No matter what Andrea said, that sounds messy and exhausting, and maybe even dangerous.

Surrogacy, as a concept, I am coming to realize, is inherently all three. But I still want to do it, because it's the only way I can think of to get fifty thousand dollars in a relatively short amount of time.

As if reading my thoughts yet again, Andrea switches tack. "You know the surrogacy journey is a long one," she tells me—another warning, if given gently. "It can take as long as a year, or even two, for intended parents to find their match and see it all the way through pregnancy and birth."

I swallow. I picked Creating Dreams—I mean, what a *name* —because they promised matches within ninety days. But I don't feel like now is the time to apprise Andrea of that fact. I smile.

"Of course," I say instead. "It's such a big decision. They've got to be absolutely certain."

"And *you* do, as well," she replies. "It's a big decision for you, too, Dani." She speaks like she thinks I don't realize that, and maybe I don't. All I can really think about is that, nine months from now, or maybe in a year, I'll have the money for Callie to have her surgery. I don't have the headspace for anything else, and I think Andrea senses that. "Tell me," she invites in that warm, rich voice of hers. "How does your family feel about your thinking about becoming a surrogate? Your partner, your daughter? There can be a lot of intense and complicated feelings around that decision, I know."

All right, I *might* have told a few bigger white lies. Callie is not my daughter. Ryan might be my boyfriend, but I wouldn't necessarily call him my *life partner*, not yet anyway. And neither of them knows a thing about what I'm doing.

"It's something we've all discussed together," I assure Andrea. "This isn't a journey I'm taking alone. Ryan was a little surprised, I admit, but ultimately he's supportive. And so is Callie." I meet her gaze with a smile that only just stays on my lips. These little lies are starting to feel bigger.

"Well, that's certainly good to hear," Andrea replies after a brief pause. "If we're to continue in this process, we usually like to speak to the potential surrogate's partner, at the very least. Just to get a sense of your support system, make sure you have one in place. That's very important to us, as an agency, and also to any intended parents. And, ultimately, it's for your sake."

My smile slips, just a little. I do not want her to speak to Ryan. I don't even want to *tell* Ryan, but of course I will have to, eventually. He's going to notice if I'm pregnant, after all.

Pregnant.

The word slams into me, shocking me for the first time. Since I've started researching surrogacy all of a few days ago, I've been treating the idea of being pregnant like having a filling or getting a pap smear, or maybe a combination of the two. Something vaguely uncomfortable, even unpleasant, but necessary and soon to be over. It's probably not the healthiest or most realistic way to view it, but I can do it. I know I can.

Because I've done it before.

"Dani?" Andrea's voice interrupts my thoughts, which is just as well, because I really don't want to think about all that. "The next step in this process would be to have another interview, preferably with your partner present, to go over all the logistics and also for you to complete your profile, in terms of what you're looking for in the couple you work with."

I know she's saying that to make me feel supported, but my mind is spinning too much to think about it. "Right. Yes," I say. "That's good to hear." It's an effort to get back in gear, after thinking about pregnancy. *My* pregnancy. "That sounds great," I practically chirp.

Inside, I feel shakier than I want to. This one conversation has brought up all sorts of memories and feelings I simply don't have time for. How much will the whole surrogacy—*pregnancy* —bring up if I go forward with it?

But I already know that I have to. That I will, as long as I'm approved. And I'll do just about anything to make sure I'm approved.

I already have.

"All right, then." Andrea seems ready to draw everything to a close, at least for now. "Dani, do you have any further questions for me at this point?"

"Umm..." I know I should have one. This is like the point in a job interview where your potential employer asks if you have any questions and if you say no, you're basically never going to get hired. "Well, I guess I'm wondering what the next part of the process is, besides what you've just told me? There are some medical tests, as well, I think...?"

Andrea beams, and I feel like I passed some sort of test. "That's a very good question, Dani. I'm going to send you a longer profile to fill out, so we can develop a picture of who you are, and you can also discern whether this really is something you feel called to do. The length of the process helps everyone, because what we really don't want to happen is to get farther down the road and for someone—*anyone*—to have second thoughts or regrets."

"Right," I say, a little woodenly. "Of course."

"Then we'll have another conversation, with you as well as your partner, and after that, assuming everything is going well, we'll set up a medical appointment for you, to complete some basic screening. If that all seems good, *then* we can look at making potential matches."

"That all sounds... good," I say. I don't have the emotional energy to inflect my voice with the necessary enthusiasm. The truth is, twenty minutes in and I'm feeling spent. Going forward, I'm going to need to disassociate from this process more than I have been. I feel way too churned up inside for my own wellbeing.

A few seconds later, the call is over, and I am sitting on the sofa, my head in my hands as a shudder goes through me.

What am I doing?

I can't think like that. I *can't*. For Callie's sake, I have to stay strong and power through this, say or do whatever is necessary to jump these hurdles and get approved. *Have a baby.*

But I still feel uneasy and anxious as I clear my browser of all surrogacy searches—Callie sometimes uses my laptop for her own stuff—and then tidy up the apartment, just for want of something to do.

Ten minutes before Callie is to come home from summer camp, the email comes through from Creating Dreams, with the longer profile to fill out. I download it quickly on my phone, scan through some of the questions.

Why did you decide to become a surrogate? What are your personal values? Can we meet your husband/partner? How do you envision communication before, during, and after pregnancy/labor? Are you open to advice from the intended parents regarding diet, vitamin supplements, exercise and/or lifestyle choices? What is your work and childcare schedule?

My stomach churns. It all feels like too much. Way, way too much. Before I can read anymore, though, my phone rings. It's the summer camp where Callie works.

My churning stomach hollows right out as I take the call.

"Hello?" My voice is hoarse. "Has something happened?"

"Miss Bryson?" It's one of the camp leaders, her voice kindly but concerned. "We're calling about Callie. It's nothing too much to worry about, but I'm afraid Callie had a little bit of an episode at camp just now, as she was about to leave. She's fine now, but she complained of numbness in her feet and then she had a tumble. She's fine, though, absolutely fine..."

I've already disconnected the call. With the questions still there on my phone, I sprint out of the apartment to find my sister.

FIVE

ASHLEY

Two weeks after Mark and I had that brunch, I am sitting at work, trying not to think about just how much has already been put in motion. I love my work. I don't think Mark really understands how much, or even why I do, because, for over fifteen years, despite graduating from UConn with a double major in business administration and history, I am still working as a glorified secretary.

When I graduated sixteen years ago, I had vague and anxious aspirations to do something big—a Master's, maybe work abroad, something that I could really call a *career*. But then I saw how expensive life was, and realized afresh how little safety net I had, and I took the first job I was offered, as an administrative assistant here at Kennett Pharmaceuticals. And even though I *still* don't do anything more taxing or interesting than taking minutes, typing letters, or answering calls, I love it.

I love wearing heels and A-line skirts, silk blouses and smart little blazers. I love putting my travel mug of coffee on my desk with a sense of self-importance. I love when my phone rings and I can answer it crisply, "Ashley Dunning," or, as of the last nine months, "Ashley Weir."

I get that these are small, even insignificant things, like I'm a little girl playing dress-up with her mother's pearls and heels, except my mother never had either. My mother worked two minimum wage jobs to keep us afloat and was always bitter about it. So, yes, I like my job. I like the money that is deposited into my account every two weeks; I like—or liked—the apartment I rented, paid for by that paycheck which I had earned all by myself. It all meant a lot to me, and it still does.

But last night, when Mark and I sat down to look at another surrogacy agency, I had a jarring moment where it seemed like those things didn't matter so much... to my husband.

I'm probably overreacting, because this whole thing has made me so sensitive on so many fronts. Mark and I have spent countless evenings over the last few weeks looking at agencies, researching surrogacy, not just as a concept, but as a reality.

"If we find a match within the next three months," Mark told me last night, his voice buoyant with enthusiasm, "then ideally we could be pregnant by Christmas, our baby brought home by next September. That's a little over a *year*, Ash, and we'd be parents!"

I had to bite my tongue not to correct him that *we* would not be pregnant, some stranger would. And that it wasn't *our* baby, it would be his. Those kinds of thoughts weren't helpful and saying them out loud would just make everything worse. Thinking them was bad enough, especially as I'd been doing my best not to seem reluctant. Not to feel it, either.

But last night, after weeks of passively but positively—I hope—engaging with all the surrogacy stuff, I ventured a question. "If we do bring a baby home next September, what... what's the plan then?"

Mark looked a little blank. "Well, we begin life as a family," he answered in a jovial tone, like it was obvious, which I suppose it was. "The Weirs, family of three!" He practically had stars in his eyes, everything about him glowing just from the thought, and I wanted that for him, simply because he wanted it so much himself.

"Yes, I know," I answered carefully, "and that will be great, of course, but... what about childcare?"

The question seemed to hang in the air, like something that shouldn't have been said. Shouldn't have *had* to be said. We'd talked about sharing parenting responsibilities in general terms, but not in the specifics of who might have to give up their job, and already I knew, based on our paychecks, it would be me.

"Well..." Mark took off his reading glasses and rubbed the bridge of his nose. "I guess I thought—I assumed, admittedly— that you'd take some time off work. Maternity leave is granted for intended parents. You'll have to check your policy at work, but I think you'd get at least three months off paid, and maybe another three, or even six, unpaid. Something like that, anyway... that is, if that was what you wanted?"

I was pretty sure it was what he wanted, and it made sense, so why did I feel resistant? "Right..." I said slowly, less than an enthusiastic response.

Childcare was something we hadn't thought to discuss before, since I'd never even gotten pregnant. Or maybe it was simply because Mark had assumed I would want to stay at home. If I'd been able to get pregnant myself, would I have wanted to? I honestly didn't know the answer to that question, only that since we'd started talking about surrogacy, it had all felt so impossibly distant from me, like I was just a bystander, observing events from afar. I told myself it would feel different later, when the surrogate disappeared into the ether, and I had a baby in my arms. Then it would feel the way it was meant to.

"Is staying at home with the baby not something you want to do?" Mark asked in a careful, non-judgmental tone that still made me tense.

"To tell you the truth, I haven't really thought about it," I replied, trying to keep my tone light. Over the last few weeks,

I've managed to navigate our surrogacy conversations with something approaching enthusiasm, but I felt like we'd run up against a roadblock just then. "I like my job," I stated. I felt compelled to add, slightly stumbling over the words, "I mean, of course I'd want to take time off. *Some* time off. But I don't want to give up my job completely."

"Okay, that's fair." I couldn't tell from his tone if I'd disappointed him or not, and I hated myself for being so lukewarm about it all. Mark deserved better, but he was miles ahead of me in this *journey*—that's what all the agencies always called it— and I was struggling to keep up.

"Anyway, that's something we can talk about later," I told him, trying to smile. "I'm still processing this all. It's going to take some time." I nodded toward the screen of his laptop that he'd put on the coffee table in front of us. "But show me what you've learned about this agency."

It was called Creating Dreams and had a soft-focus, pastel-colored website with lots of images of dandelions and slanting sunbeams. We'd looked at five different agencies so far, all national, all with names like this one's that promise so much and yet say so little.

"Well," Mark said, pulling the laptop a little toward us, "what I like about this agency is that they guarantee a match within ninety days."

That fast, I thought, with a feeling of something close to panic, while I murmured something approving. We really could have a baby—*our* baby—by next September. Why couldn't I actually imagine it happening?

Now, at work, as I fire up my computer and check my in-tray, I'm trying not to think about any of it. I know that's probably not healthy, but I feel like Mark's and my married life has been taken over by discussions about surrogacy. Almost every night we have been looking at websites or researching the process or discussing logistics.

Sometimes, Mark has put away the laptop and chatted, with a dreamy, faraway look in his eyes, more generally about having a baby. Being a *family*. He'd assure me he didn't care if it was a boy or a girl, he'd love either. He promised he'd do his fair share of the work—the night feedings and the diaper changes and the midnight drives around the block to calm a colicky baby. And later on, too—he has talked about scaling back on his hours, being the one to be at home at the end of a school day. He paints such a pretty vision, and when he talks that way I can completely get on board. I can see us, a family of three, a little figure in blue or pink swinging between our hands as we smile at each other over our faceless child's head. I feel a swell of hope, of love, and I know I want that. I really do.

And so I need to put all this pointless, vague unease behind me and embrace what we've decided is the way forward *together*.

"Hey, Ashley."

I turn to see Aimee, a young woman from the sales department, smiling at me. She's one of those ambitious up-and-comers who skipped the whole secretarial thing to go right to being a sales associate. I've done some work for her when her department's been pressed. I didn't realize she knew my name.

"Hi, Aimee." I swivel swiftly in my chair, enjoying the little buzz it gives me. Another little thing, but one I like. "How can I help you?" I cross my legs, looking—or at least feeling—brisk and competent.

"I just wanted to say how much I appreciated you following up those emails for me the other day. My back was really against the wall."

I smile and shrug, all quietly confident modesty. Some people may call me "the Mouse" at work, but I do my job well. I know I do. "It wasn't a problem."

"Well... you work hard, and I appreciate it. I just wanted to let you know that I mentioned your work to Lila."

Lila, the assistant head of sales and Aimee's line manager. I am surprised, and for a second, speechless. In all my years at Kennett Pharmaceuticals, I don't think anyone has ever spoken about me to a higher-up. I've done my job quietly and efficiently, and without much notice. I got one promotion five years ago, mainly because there was no one else, but it was more of a lateral move and didn't even include much of a pay raise.

"Well, thanks," I say finally, trying to mask my surprise. "I appreciate it."

Aimee shrugs and smiles. "We women have to stick together, right? And you really did have my back."

She flutters her fingers in farewell, and I nod, my mind still spinning. In all likelihood, Aimee talking to Lila won't make any difference to me or my job; it's not as if the sales line manager is going to track down a lowly admin assistant and tell me I deserve a promotion, all off the back of one woman's word. But still... the fact that Aimee did it, and then told me, is gratifying. The affirmation is appreciated, even as it splinters my resolve of just a few minutes ago to be more positive about surrogacy and all that it entails.

Because what if it means I have to sacrifice my job?

The question is still bouncing around my head as I leave work, stepping into a sultry August evening, the sky violet with thunderclouds.

I'm meeting my friend Claire for a drink; I haven't seen her in months, and I know we need to catch up. Claire used to work for Kennett Pharmaceuticals; we ate lunch together most days and I really missed her when she moved to a higher-paid job for one of Hartford's many insurance companies a couple of years ago. We still met up after work or on the weekend, but since I married Mark, our regular evenings out have definitely dwindled.

We agreed to meet in Barcelona, a trendy wine bar in West Hartford that I've never been to before. By the time I get there, the sky is heavy and swollen with livid-looking clouds, and it looks like there's going to be a big storm, the kind with vivid, electric forks of lightning and huge crashes of thunder. I text Mark to reassure him that I'll be careful driving home, and then I go inside the bar to meet Claire.

It's low-lit with loud music, full of trendy twentysomethings and middle-aged guys with loud laughs and Rolexes, the kind of guy I often work for. They're not as bad as they look.

I weave my way through the tables to find Claire, her tousled blond bob glinting under the chandelier lighting, sitting on a high bar stool at a table for two; she's already ordered a fish-bowl-size glass of red.

"Hey." I give her a one-arm hug as I drop my bag on the floor and slide onto the stool opposite. "That looks good. What are you drinking?"

"The house Cabernet. I went for cheap and large." She sounds both wry and a little grumpy, her lipsticked mouth twisting sardonically, her blue eyes narrowed as she takes a sip. I raise my eyebrows in query. Claire is usually easygoing, but right now she sounds hassled. It's six o'clock on a Thursday night and we're in a bar, so what's going on?

"Sounds good," I reply lightly, and look around for a staff person.

Claire glugs her wine.

"So what's up?" I ask, nodding meaningfully toward her glass. "Tough day?"

"Tough day?" Claire lets out a hollow laugh as she tucks her hair behind her ears. "Tough year, more like. Tough decade." I stare at her, blankly bemused, and she clarifies impatiently, "Ashley, I turned forty three months ago."

I can't help but wince; I *knew* she'd turned forty, but I'd missed her birthday bash back in May because Mark and I had gone to the Hamptons for the weekend. I'd sent her a hugely apologetic text, along with a generous gift card, but I know it's not the same. It's not the same at all, but at the time I was still in the stage of incredulous, joyous wonder that I could jaunt off to the Hamptons with my *husband* and lie in bed and drink champagne in a swanky hotel overlooking Montauk beach. It had felt like a fairy tale, or a montage moment from a rom-com, and I'd had to keep pinching myself all weekend that it was real.

But now, looking at Claire's glum face, I realize with a jolt that I haven't seen her since before that party. Has it really been over three months since we last got together?

"I'm sorry I didn't come to your birthday party..." I begin, feebly, and Claire waves me away, just as a waitress arrives to take my order. I ask for a smaller glass of Chardonnay—I'm driving, after all—and then turn back to my friend once we're alone again.

"I know forty is just a number," Claire says, her face set in bleak lines. She *looks* older, crows' feet starting at her eyes, lines fanning from nose to mouth. "But it still feels like a milestone, and not in a good way. I mean... you *made* it, Ash. Slid in there three years before you'll be forty, and now you're on the whole husband-and-happy-home train. And meanwhile I'm on the dating apps, trying not to look desperate to all the equally desperate saddos out there..." She trails off, shaking her head miserably, before she takes another generous slug of wine.

I am silent, marshaling my thoughts, trying to figure out how to respond without seeming smug. Because I *have* made it... even if recently I've been tying myself in knots over this whole baby thing. Right now, I am remembering just how lucky I am. Mark is a wonderful, loving, financially stable, *great* guy whom I love very much. Still, I can't exactly say any of that to Claire.

"I know it's hard," I tell her, grateful when I see the waitress bearing down on us with my glass of wine, "but forty is still young, Claire—"

"Oh, really?" Her mouth twists. "Because there are so many forty-something guys out there without crazy exes or three children they see every weekend or who are borderline incel? Right."

"Come on, we're *enlightened* women!" I cajole with a smile, trying for a different tack. "We don't need a man to complete us."

"Says the woman with a man."

"Hey, it's not all it's cracked up to be," I blurt, and then I reach for my wine because I didn't mean to sound so... *sincere*.

Claire stills, her huge wineglass halfway to her lips. "Oh?" she asks, and I can tell she wants me to dish some dirt. Hearing me run down marriage and Mark will make her feel better, I know it, but I really don't want to do that.

"Well..." Mark and I agreed not to talk about the whole surrogacy thing until it was more certain. And yet Claire is one of my best friends. How can I *not* tell her? If we go forward with it, which I'm already pretty sure we will, it's not as if it's something I can hide or brush over. "I found out I can't have children," I say, and Claire's expression softens.

"Oh, Ashley..."

"That's not even the main thing," I tell her, and I realize that this is true. Haltingly, I explain about Mark wanting a baby of his own. His idea to use a surrogate.

"A *surrogate*..." Claire screws up her face, like she's trying to recall everything she's gleaned about surrogacy, most likely from a tabloid magazine involving Ronaldo or the Kardashians.

"It's not just for celebrities," I joke feebly. "We'd use an agency. It would all be reputable and above board." And very, very expensive.

"You don't sound thrilled, though." Claire cocks her head. "Why is that?"

"I don't know." I realize as I say the words that I mean them. I really don't know. "It just feels like it's happening apart from me, somehow. I'm not actually going to be involved, you know?"

"Well, it's understandable to feel that way, because it wouldn't be your baby biologically, and you wouldn't be going through the pregnancy." Claire speaks matter-of-factly, but her words still make me wince. "But that doesn't mean you can't be involved, Ash. You just have to work at it more. And if this is the way for you and Mark to have a family..." She shrugs. "I think it could be really great."

"Yeah." I smile weakly. She makes it sound so simple.

So why does it not feel that way to me?

An hour later, after the two of us dissect Claire's love life, or lack of it, I am heading outside.

The sky has grown even darker, the clouds an angry purple that is nearly black. By the time I reach my car, the first fat rain-drops are hitting my windshield like bullets. It's going to be a doozy of a storm, I can tell, but it's only a ten-minute drive home.

I text Mark and then I start the car, the windshield wipers on full speed as I inch out of the parking lot onto Farmington Avenue.

The next thing I know, there's the blare of a horn, the squeal of tires, a blast of light. The sound of impact, a screech and a thud is the last thing I remember.

SIX

DANI

"What the *hell*?"

Ryan is staring at me, looking torn between disbelief and outrage. I see fury in his eyes but the remnant of a half-smile lurking about his mouth, like he thought I was joking when I said I was thinking of becoming a surrogate and he's still hoping for the punchline. I almost wish there was one.

"Ryan, please keep your voice down," I whisper with an apologetic smile. We're having drinks at the Moonlight Bar on Mission Bay, and right after our gin and tonics were set down, I delivered my bombshell. I know it wasn't really fair, to have this discussion in public, but I couldn't face having a knock-down-drag-out kind of fight about it, which seemed more likely in private.

"Dani..." He shakes his head slowly, his floppy dark hair sliding into his eyes. Ryan is very good-looking. I tease him that he looks like he belongs in a boy band, which annoys him because he's so serious, but most people don't look like he does —sculpted cheekbones, full lips, bright green eyes, and a body to match his face. And he's an *accountant*. "What are you talking about?" he asks, clearly striving to sound reasonable, although his expression is tense, his eyes still sparking. "A surrogate? What does that even mean?"

It's surprising, I've discovered, how many people don't really understand what surrogacy is. They barely get what it entails, beyond that more than the usual two people are involved in the baby-making process. Not that I've told many people what I'm thinking about; in fact, just Ryan, although Anna has sort of guessed. But from what I've read online, the whole process is somewhat shrouded in mystique, as well as controversy.

"It means," I tell him, making sure I sound reasonable, "that I'm going to carry a baby that isn't mine, for a couple who will pay me for the privilege." I make it sound simple when I know it's not. It took me two hours to fill out the profile Andrea sent me. It asked for *everything*. And I still have to have a final interview—with Ryan present—and then a medical check, including the whole gynecological work-up. Nothing about this is going to be easy, and that's without considering the emotional side of things, which right now I am refusing to do.

Ryan is still shaking his head, a slow, determined back and forth. "But Dani... why?"

"Ryan, you *know* why." I can't help but sound a little exasperated. "For Callie. You know she has pediatric spondylosis. I've told you it's getting worse. Last week, she fell over at camp, and I had to go get her." She'd insisted she was fine, but she seemed really shaken, and for the first time, when I mentioned the surgery, she didn't protest. "She needs the spinal fusion surgery," I state, "and for that, I need money."

He looks gobsmacked, like connecting these very obvious dots never even occurred to him. "Dani," he says, leaning forward, "there are better ways to get money—"

I think of Anna joking about OnlyFans. "There really aren't. Not quickly, anyway, unless I want to rob a bank."

Ryan is silent for a long moment, his gaze distant. Then he

rakes his hand through his hair—which flops right back on his forehead—and sits back in his chair. "How much do you need?"

"Fifty thousand," I reply flatly, and his eyes widen. "Even if I change health insurance so I can get the in-network benefit, the surgeon's fees most likely won't be covered by any provider, and they're asking for twenty grand as a deposit, the rest six months later." The hopelessness of it all hits me again. It's just so much *money*.

Ryan frowns. "The insurance really won't cover it at *all*? I mean, that's so crazy, if—"

"Ryan, you *know* what health insurance companies are like." I really don't have the patience for his skepticism right now, not after everything I've been through. "They're looking for ways to *not* cover medical expenses. They hire out their case reviews to a company that *boasts* on how many procedures they deny." It was all exposed last year, just how much insurance companies were getting away with, but nobody seemed to care. "They've told me that the vast majority of pediatric spondylosis cases can be treated with physical therapy and steroid injections, and they do not see any proof that Callie needs surgical intervention at this time. It is *not medically necessary*." I have adopted the voice of just about every insurance representative I've talked to on the phone—sing-songy while resolutely and irritatingly firm.

"Dani..." I can tell by his tone that I'm not going to like whatever he's thinking of saying next. He grimaces in apology—for what? "Have you considered that maybe this surgery might *not* be medically necessary?"

So that's what the grimace of apology is for.

I stare at him for a full ten seconds, until he finally looks away. "Are you *serious*?" I ask quietly. "Do I have to go through all of Callie's symptoms? How things have been getting worse for her just about every day? Did you not just hear that she fell over—"

"I'm just saying, if the insurance and the doctors both—"

"Her doctor has said the surgery could be helpful," I cut across him. "A specialist in this area." Her pediatrician was more on the fence, but she didn't have enough expertise to make the diagnosis. "That's enough for me."

Ryan frowns. "Is it enough for Callie?" he asks quietly.

It's a fair question, especially since Callie has been so reluctant, but it still annoys me. I want Ryan to understand my decision, to be on my side, but I know I'm not making it easy for him. If I was a more patient, empathetic kind of person, I would have involved him earlier. I would have asked his opinion *before* I started filling out forms. I would have understood that *not* telling my boyfriend of two years what I was thinking was a hurtful thing to do. I would have wanted him to be part of this.

The fact that I *didn't* do any of those things says a lot more about me than it does Ryan. I'm just not good at letting people in, not even someone I care about, and I do care about Ryan. A lot. And so I speak reasonably as I explain, "Callie is understandably a little reluctant because the surgery is a big deal." Spinal fusion requires a week in ICU, and then six weeks' recovery at home. She wouldn't be back to full physical activity for nine months, which, at sixteen, I know can seem like forever. Plus, she'll have a foot-long scar along her spine. It's a lot for her, or anyone, to deal with, but the implications of *not* having the surgery are, I know, hard for Callie to grasp. "You know what teenagers are like," I tell Ryan. "They can't always see the bigger picture."

"Callie seems pretty sensible about life, though," he replies, keeping his voice mild—with effort, I expect.

The very air between us feels tense, and neither of us has touched our drinks. Already I wish I'd handled this whole evening differently.

"She is, but this is obviously a very emotional topic for her." I try for a conciliatory smile. "Ryan, I know you mean well, but I don't really want to debate my decision-making here, with regards to Callie. That's... that's not up for discussion." That sounds harsher than I wanted it to, but I know I mean it.

His mouth compresses. "So I'm not allowed to have an opinion?"

"This isn't about *you*," I state as calmly as I can. I reach for my drink, take a needed sip, let the gin flood through me, tangy on my tongue. "Obviously, me choosing to become a surrogate does affect you, which is why I told you. I probably should have told you earlier. I'm sorry that I didn't." If I had, maybe getting his cooperation for the next screening interview wouldn't feel as challenging as it does right now.

Ryan leans back in his chair with a sigh. "I wish you had too, Dani, so I could have talked you out of it."

"Ryan—"

"From here it feels like I'm allowed input on certain, unimportant parts of your life, like what movie we're going to watch, but not on anything important?"

"That's not completely true," I argue. "Ryan, I do value your opinion."

He lets out a huff of disbelieving laughter. "Maybe on your taxes."

I take a deep breath and decide to approach this more reasonably. "What exactly are you upset about here?" I ask. I set my drink down, try to moderate my expression into something more understanding and concerned.

"I'm *upset* that you are making major life decisions without even asking what I think, because what I think is irrelevant to you. Is that clear enough?" His eyes flash, his nostrils flaring, and with a jolt I realize how rarely I've seen Ryan genuinely angry.

I breathe in. Out. I look away as I try to formulate my thoughts. This is too important, I realize, to do what he has accused me of doing—not involve him in my decisions. I need to be honest.

"I'm sorry," I say at last. "I don't mean to treat you that way. It's just... instinct... I guess, to do things on my own."

His voice gentles as he reaches for my hand. "I know."

To my own surprise, I find my eyes filling with tears that I have to blink away. "I don't mean to push you away, honestly." I am, I realize, telling him the truth.

"Just habit, huh?" He squeezes my fingers. "Do you really feel like you need to do this? For Callie?"

"Ryan, Callie is my sister," I say with a throb of emotion in my voice. "I'd do *anything* for her. I've been taking care of her by myself for three years. If... if I'm sensitive about you weighing in on how I do that, well, can't you understand, at least a little?" I add pleadingly. "You're my boyfriend, not my... my *husband*. And Callie is not your daughter."

"She's not yours, either," Ryan says quietly.

"She's as good as," I shoot back without even thinking. When my mother calls—and that is so rarely—she doesn't even ask me about how Callie is managing her condition. I've been her *de facto* parent since she was thirteen, handling her schooling, her medical visits, her moods, her anxieties, everything. Ryan *knows* that.

A sigh escapes him, long and low and weary. "Are you really thinking of becoming a surrogate just for the money?" He still sounds disbelieving, as well as a little sad.

"Yes, basically." I don't think Ryan would buy the line I fed Andrea Dreyfus, about wanting to help a couple on their journey to parenthood. And I'm not about to tell him about my complicated feelings around pregnancy. There are a few things Ryan doesn't know about me, and that is one of them.

"I just think there have to be other ways," he insists. "Work with the insurance company—"

Not this again. "Ryan, trust me, I've tried."

Once again, he stares at me. I stare back, trying not to fidget, although I feel all twitchy inside. Somehow, I have to get Ryan on board enough with this idea to agree to being interviewed.

"Marry me," he says quietly, and my jaw actually drops.

There's a beat of silence.

"Marry me," he says again, before I can form a word, not that I have any idea what it would be. "Then you and Callie can be on my insurance plan, which is a pretty good one. They might cover the surgeon's fees, and even if they don't, we can work on it together. I have savings. Not that much, it's true, but maybe they do a payment plan—"

"Ryan." I have to cut him off before he says anything more that will only hurt us both. "Ryan, I can't marry you for your money."

He sets his jaw, his eyes flashing with little-boy-like hurt. "Is that what it would be for?"

"You just *said*—"

"Marry me because you love me and you want to have a family with me," he cuts me off this time, his voice hardening. "And because we both want what's best for Callie." He takes a breath, then softens his tone. "You don't have to do this alone, Dani, and you definitely don't need to have someone else's baby."

"So, what are you saying? Have yours?" I cringe at the harshness of my own words. "I'm sorry, I didn't mean it like that," I say quickly. "It's just... this is not the solution."

"In time, yes," Ryan replies with dignity, "I'd like to try for a baby. We've been dating for two years. I'm thirty-five, I want a family, I'm ready for that kind of commitment." He shrugs, unapologetic. "I don't think I've made any secret of that."

"I know," I whisper. I am humbled by his proposal, but I am also appalled. I know I'm not ready for this, even if Ryan is one of the best things in my life. The silence stretches on, until finally Ryan breaks it.

"Do you love me?" he asks quietly, an ache in his voice.

"Ryan..."

"Just a yes or no will do."

I've never actually said I loved him. I hardly ever say those words, because both my parents dashed them off plenty of times and, in retrospect, I've had to wonder if either of them meant them. "I don't know," I admit, wishing we didn't have to get into the status of our relationship right now. "I'm not... You know I'm not good with this kind of stuff," I tell him, my voice wobbling. "I care for you, Ryan, a lot. A *lot*, a lot. I really like what we have together. Am I ready for marriage?" Everything in me shrivels up at the thought. Look at my mom—twenty-five years of marriage and she was left with nothing to show for it. I'm only twenty-eight; I need to finish my doctorate, and get a decent job, and figure out how to relax and enjoy life for a change. "I don't think I am," I tell him quietly. "Not yet, but I... I hope to be, one day." I pause, hating how much I'm hurting him. This is not where I'd wanted this conversation to go. "I'm sorry."

"It's okay." He speaks stiffly; I can tell he is hurt, just as I feared. "To be honest, I didn't really expect you to say anything else. It just seemed like an obvious solution."

"Ryan, I wouldn't want to rush into marriage just for Callie's sake. That wouldn't be good for anyone."

"But you'll rush into having someone's baby." He makes it sound sordid, like I'm selling myself on the street, and I can't help but flare up.

"Yes," I tell him, "as part of a legal contract. It's not like I'm... *prostituting* myself. I'm helping an infertile couple to have a child. That's it. It wouldn't even be mine, you know, biologically. They'd use an egg donor. I'd just be... hosting it, I guess."

He frowns, clearly skeptical, but at least willing to let the whole marriage moment pass. "And you don't think you'd get attached to a baby you nurtured inside your body for nine months?"

"No, I don't think so," I tell him. "I really don't."

He shakes his head, seeming almost despairing. "You sound so certain."

"I am." I don't offer any more information.

"It also sounds like you've made up your mind," he continues quietly. I hear a sadness in his voice that makes me ache, and I really wish this didn't have to hurt him. I wish I could be a softer version of myself, and I also wish he could be a little more pragmatic and see my side of things. That's a lot of wishes, and none of them matter.

"I don't want you to feel cut out of this," I offer, and he lets out a huff of tired laughter.

"Are you sure about that?"

I have the grace at least to look down and say nothing, because I know I deserve his skepticism. When I told Ryan about it, I'd already cut him out, and if he'd asked me not to go ahead, I know I would have refused. The least I can do is try to understand where he's coming from.

"What about surrogacy bothers you?" I ask. "Is it me being pregnant? Or..." I can't actually think of another reason.

"It's not even you being a surrogate, Dani," Ryan interrupts me. "*Or* being pregnant. I mean, that's going to be weird, for sure, but it's just how... *independent* you are. How you're only telling me right now because you know you have to."

I sit upright. "Because I have to?" I repeat cautiously. Has he somehow guessed about the interview?

"Well, I mean, in a couple of months I might notice if you were pregnant." He can't keep the bitterness from his voice as he adds spikily, "I might assume it was mine."

I am silent, and Ryan leans forward.

"What?" he demands, frowning. "What did you think I meant?"

I know I can't put this off any longer. "The surrogacy agency," I tell him, like an apology. "They asked to have an interview with you, to check if you're okay with it."

Ryan lets out another huff. "Oh wow," he says, shaking his head. "*Wow.*"

"For Callie's sake, Ryan," I plead in a low voice. "*Please.* Whatever is going on with us, we can figure that out, in time, I promise. I want to figure it out with you. But I can only go forward with this if you're willing to say you're supportive."

"*Say* I'm supportive," Ryan repeats. "But not *be* supportive?"

I feel as if he's trying to trap me with semantics. "Well, obviously I'd like that too, but I understand if you're not there yet."

"Would you want that, Dani?" He shakes his head. "Sometimes I wonder."

For a second, fury spikes through me. All right, maybe I could have handled all this better, but his self-righteousness is starting to wear more than a little thin. "You know, I get that you're hurt I thought about this without running it by you first," I tell him, my voice vibrating with anger, as well as a hurt of my own. "And that maybe I could have been a little more sensitive about it all. I know I could have. But have you taken one second to consider what it's like to be in my shoes? Every day I see Callie struggling. Last week, she fell over. Yesterday, it was numbness in her arm. The other night, she woke me up at two a.m. because she was in pain and couldn't find any ibuprofen. This surgery will change all that, Ryan." My voice breaks, but I force myself to go on. "I have spent *hundreds* of hours—and that is no exaggeration—trying to convince my insurance provider to cover the surgery. I've researched the surgery, the costs, the aftereffects, *everything*, so I could practically do the damn thing myself. I wish I could!" I dash at my eyes, annoyed at myself for getting so emotional. "Surrogacy feels like the last option. And I *know* you said I could marry you. But that wasn't on the table until tonight, and it's hardly something to rush into. This is nine months of my life, Ryan. Of *our* life together. That's it."

He is silent for a long moment, his downcast gaze on the table. I can't tell anything from his expression; I realize I have no idea what he's thinking. For the two years we've been dating, Ryan has been easygoing, affable, with a surprisingly sharp sense of humor. We both like running, Mexican food, experimental jazz, noir thrillers. We've had *fun* together, but none of it has felt like the basis for marriage, and while I've enjoyed being with him, I have never let myself think further than that. And that's on me, I know, not him, but I really need him to cooperate now.

Ryan lifts his head. His expression is full of regret as he reaches over and takes my hand. "Dani, I'm sorry. I'm being a jerk. It just surprised me so much... but I do get where you're coming from. And if you feel you need to do this, then yes, okay, I support you." He squeezes my hand. "But let me be a part of it, okay? Don't shut me out anymore, please."

I manage a wavery smile. I know I shut people out without even meaning to; it's something of a default, a form of self-defense since my dad died and my mom left, and it's so ingrained now I don't think I even know how to stop. "I won't," I say, but what I really mean is, *I'll try.*

At least I hope I will.

SEVEN

ASHLEY

I open my eyes to bright white light. For a few seconds, I feel like I'm floating, hovering alone in the ether. Am I *dead*? Surely if I was, I wouldn't be asking that question. Then I start to sense the world around me—scratchy white sheets, the persistent beep of a monitor, sunlight streaming in from the window. I'm not dead, I'm in a hospital.

"*Ashley.*" Mark's voice is full of both anguish and relief.

I turn my head, and I see him sitting by my bedside, unshaven, his eyes bloodshot, his skin with a sickly, grayish cast.

"I hope," I manage, my voice sounding as scratchy as the sheets, "that I don't look as bad as you do."

He lets out a choked sound that is meant to be a laugh but sounds more like a sob.

Heaven help me, I think. *How hurt am I?*

"Do you remember what happened?" Mark asks, like something out of a movie—the man by the bedside, the woman coming out of a coma. But surely I haven't been in a *coma*. I don't feel that bad, just a little fuzzy-headed.

"Yes..." I reply slowly. I remember having a drink with Claire, leaving the bar, the rain coming down in sheets, the sky forked by lightning. I pulled out of the parking lot, and sensed something hurtling toward me—another car, presumably, that must have hit me side-on. "Who hit me?" I croak. "Are they okay?"

"Oh, Ash." Mark wipes tears from his eyes, which scares me. Am I going to get some really bad news? "They're fine," he assures me as he draws a ragged breath. "But it's so like you to think of them first."

I try to move my feet, and my toes skim the top sheet, which fills me with relief. I'm not paralyzed, at least.

His voice is so full of love and sorrow that fear grips me again, a painful vise. "Mark..." I lick my lips, which are dry and cracked. "How hurt am I?"

He reaches for my hand, holding it carefully like I'm made of glass. "You have three cracked ribs, a broken wrist, and a concussion. They checked for internal injuries, but they don't think there are any. But you've been pretty much unconscious for twenty-four hours. I've been out of my mind with worry. *Ash...*" He sounds like he wants to say something else, but then he stops.

I am silent, trying to absorb what he's told me. Cracked ribs and a concussion, not so bad. A broken wrist? I might not be able to do my job for a while, a thought that fills me with something like panic, but none of it is life-threatening or even, hopefully, life-changing.

"It could have been so much worse," Mark tells me as he gently—very gently—squeezes my hand. "You were hit side-on by a Suburban. Of course the guy in that behemoth was fine. But he could have... You could have..."

"Mark." I try to smile at him. "I'm fine." At least, I'm mostly fine.

Now that I've been lying here awake for a few minutes, various aches and pains are becoming apparent. My chest hurts every time I breathe. A headache is starting to throb at my temples, and my brain feels like it's sloshing around in my head. My right wrist is encased in a plaster cast that stretches from my elbow to my knuckles. I breathe out slowly, trying to absorb it all, figure out what it's going to mean for my future, but already I feel myself sinking back into sleep. I wonder if they gave me some seriously strong painkillers, because it's like a tide washing over me, pulling me under, and I am relieved to surrender to it.

"Ashley..." Mark says.

But I'm already gone.

I stay in the hospital for two days, mainly for observation—and because Mark has great health insurance, it's all covered. I insist Mark return to work, and so I spend hours sitting in bed, staring out at the blue summer sky, thinking about my life.

It didn't flash before my eyes in the moment when I was hit, the way you hear about in movies and books, but it is moving in slow motion, reel by reel, now. My childhood with my mom, after my dad left when I was just a baby—a grimy montage of cheap apartments, my mother working two jobs to keep us afloat, nights spent alone, watching bad TV until she came home, exhausted and resentful. I don't resent my mom for being resentful; she had a hard life, and I was part of that. But sometimes it was challenging to live with.

I think of high school, when I worked as hard as I could, because I knew I didn't want a life like my mother's. No time for a social life; I kept my head down and got straight As, and a full ride to UConn, Hartford campus.

I think of my career—if I can even call it that—enjoying my work but accepting that I was far from changing the world. But not everyone has to be a mover and shaker, I tell myself, as I acknowledge that wearing heels and typing one hundred words a minute isn't exactly the pinnacle of achievement, even if it's been enough for me.

Finally, I think of Mark. Of how he catapulted into my life through a dating app, with me doing my best to keep my expectations low, and then filled it with hope and happiness, laughter and love—yes, it sounds like a Hallmark card, but it's been real and wonderful, and I've loved it.

Then I think of the baby he wants to have. Of the baby *I* want to have, because something that has become clear to me as I lie in this bed and consider how close I came to losing it all, is that I do want a family. The ambivalence, and even reluctance, I felt before has melted away in the clarity of my current reality. I almost missed out on being a mother. And even if parenthood as a concept still fills me with some trepidation, especially when it's happening apart from me—I don't want to back away from it, especially when I consider how much Mark wants it, too.

And so, when he picks me up to go home, and walks me slowly into our townhouse like I'm eighty years old, I decide to tell him just that.

"Oh, Mark." The house is full of my favorite flowers—at least six bouquets of purple irises and bright yellow sunflowers, punctuating the endless, sleek gray of our décor with bright splashes of color.

He smiles sheepishly. "I just wanted you to have a nice welcome."

"You're amazing." I stand on my tiptoes to kiss his cheek; Mark is only five nine, but I barely brush five feet. "Thank you."

"I'm just so thankful for you, Ash," Mark says. "When I thought I might have lost you..."

"But you didn't." I walk gingerly into the living room; my cracked ribs make it hard to move and just leaving the hospital has exhausted me. "I'm okay." I raise my wrist, smiling wryly. "At least I'm going to be okay." I'm signed off work for the rest of the week, but I am determined to go in on Monday, and do my job as best as I can, even with a broken wrist.

"I know." He sits down next to me, his expression somber. "Ashley..." he begins, just as I say, "Mark."

We both laugh self-consciously.

"You go first," he tells me.

"Okay." I take a deep breath. "I had a lot of time to think in the hospital, and I realized that this whole surrogacy thing..." I pause as his expression tenses, the look in his deep brown eyes decidedly wary.

"Yes..." he prompts, sounding cautious.

"I've been reluctant about it because it felt so strange. And also like I wasn't part of it, which was not your fault. It was mine, not because of my infertility necessarily, but because I wasn't trying as hard as I should have, to embrace the whole thing. I'm sorry."

"Ash—"

I shake my head, knowing he'll want to rush in with his own apologies and assurances, but I need to say this. "No, let me finish. Getting in that accident has brought me some perspective. I don't want to go through life without at least trying for a family, Mark. This isn't the ideal, we both know that, but it could work, and I want to go ahead with it. Full speed, whatever that looks like." A tremor runs through me at my own words; I believe what I say, but I'm still scared. Still uncertain how it's going to work, and, more importantly, how it's going to feel, even if I've determined to try.

Mark's eyes have taken on a glossy sheen as he blinks rapidly, a rueful smile twisting his lips. "And I was about to tell you that if you wanted, I was willing to scrap the whole thing."

I can't help but gape. "*What?*"

"I didn't want you to feel pressured. I could tell you weren't as excited as I was, and I've never wanted to drag you along on this, Ash. It has to be both of us wanting it. I know I get carried away, but I really do mean that."

"I know you do."

We are both silent, absorbing what the other has said. I am trying both to figure out how I feel and not think about it at the same time, because what Mark just said has already sent a little sliver of doubt needling through me.

"But you do really want this?" he asks, and I hear eagerness in his voice. Hope.

I look around at all the flowers he's bought me, then at the tenderness in his face, the joy in his eyes, and I smile.

"Yes," I tell him firmly, truly meaning it for the very first time. "I do."

Mark takes the next day off work, the pretext being that he isn't ready for me to be home alone yet with my concussion and cracked ribs, but really so we can do a comprehensive deep dive back into surrogacy, pick an agency, and maybe even a surrogate. Now that I'm firmly on board, we are full steam ahead, just as I knew we would be, and I am determined to be positive about everything.

"I've been looking at Creating Dreams a little more closely," he tells me as he opens his laptop and starts clicking. We are curled up together on the sofa, cups of herbal tea to hand. Outside, the August humidity has once more given over to rain, and so even though it's ninety degrees out, inside I feel tucked up and cozy, a fleece blanket draped over my lap to combat the chill of the AC.

"And what have you discovered?" I ask as I carefully reach for my tea with my left hand, wincing slightly at the pain in my ribs.

"I think they're a really solid agency. They're national, with the head office in Los Angeles."

"Los Angeles." I can't help but frown. "That's kind of far away."

He shrugs, his gaze on the computer screen. "Yes, well,

California has the most liberal surrogacy laws, so it makes sense for an agency to be based out of there."

"The most liberal?" I ask. I haven't really thought too much about the legal aspect of this whole process, although obviously that's going to be important.

"Surrogacy is illegal in some states," Mark informs me as he taps away. "Louisiana, Nebraska, and Michigan. And other states are considered unfriendly to it. Even New York."

Illegal? This shocks me, makes me feel like we're doing something illicit. "Why?"

"Well..." He shrugs, seeming a little uncomfortable, his gaze still on the screen. "You know, the ethics around a woman getting paid to be pregnant. Probably feels a little *Handmaid's Tale* to some. And, of course, enforcing parental rights can be difficult... I mean, there are a lot of different people involved, and they'll all have feelings, as well as rights to consider."

"The intended parents, the surrogate, and the egg donor." Four people who can claim some kind of emotional or maybe even legal right over this unborn child. Already it's starting to feel overwhelming. Again.

I swallow hard, trying to push away the doubts that have started crowding in.

"Yes, well... about that." Mark pauses, and then lowers the lid of his laptop as he turns to look at me, his expression both anxious and somber, lines bracketing his mouth.

"About what?" I ask warily. I feel like he's about to spring something on me, and I have no idea what it could be. What more is there? I meet his anxious gaze, willing him to explain. I so want to be on board with this, but already I'm feeling nervous. "Mark?" I prompt, because he still hasn't spoken, which is making me even more nervous.

"I've been thinking," he begins slowly, his gaze moving to his hands loosely clasped in front of him. "About the practicalities. Having a separate egg donor, having the surrogate have to do IVF, maybe even multiple times, with multiple embryos... it means introducing so many more variables, it will take a lot more time, *and* it's a lot more expensive."

He stops, waiting for my response, but I don't know what to say. Even though I've been trying to keep up with all the facts and figures he's thrown at me over the last few weeks, I'm struggling to remember all the ins and outs of surrogacy, how the whole process actually works.

"What's the alternative, though?" I finally ask. "I mean... there isn't one, is there? If we're going to go with surrogacy?" We haven't talked about anything other than finding an egg donor, a surrogate, and going from there.

"Well... " Mark pauses. "You know how there's two kinds of surrogacy? Traditional and gestational?"

"Umm... yes." Vaguely. I thought we'd dismissed traditional back at the beginning, hadn't even looked into it, because it's so rarely done.

"Traditional is cheaper," he explains. "It's a lot simpler. And further down the road, it might be better for our child, as well."

Our child. The words send a frisson of wary pleasure through me. "Okay, but... what *is* traditional surrogacy?" I ask.

"It's where the surrogate is also the biological mother," he explains, his voice quiet and sounding so very reasonable. "She uses her own egg, which means not having to pay for an egg donor, and having the conception occur through IUI rather than IVF, which is a simpler procedure and has a higher success rate. Everything could be simpler and go a lot faster, if we took this route."

It takes me a second to realize what he's saying. One woman will do it all... all the things *I* should have been doing. Experiencing. Instead of having a stranger's baby, the surrogate will have her own.

I absorb all that, seeing the positives, but *feeling* the negatives. Intensely. "But then..." I say slowly, "if the egg is the surrogate's and she's the one who is pregnant..." The conclusion is glaringly obvious, at least to me. "She might feel like this baby is hers." This baby *will* be hers. Hers and my husband's. The thought is like a punch to the gut; I recoil instinctively, spilling my tea, and Mark reaches out and takes my mug.

"There can be complicating emotional factors," he agrees, "which is why it isn't as common. And why some states prohibit it entirely. And there's also the legal factor—we can't have a pre-birth parental order the way we could with gestational. We'd have to... to adopt the baby after he or she was born."

So it comes back to adoption, albeit in a way I never considered. And while Mark was against adoption, he's obviously not against *this*. "So can the surrogate... change her mind?" I ask.

Mark nods soberly. "Potentially, yes. She is considered the biological mother, obviously, with parental rights, until after the birth."

And he *wants* this? I am stunned, as well as deeply apprehensive, but then I remind myself that Mark would have parental rights too. *I* would be the only one who wouldn't. I tell myself there is no reason to feel more left out than if we used an egg donor; it's pretty much the same process, just fewer people involved, which *could* be beneficial. Couldn't it? And yet... it sounds like an absolute minefield, and one that most people very sensibly avoid.

"But you want to do this?" I clarify uncertainly. "It sounds so risky." And so emotionally fraught.

"I'm just putting it out there," Mark says, but I can already tell by the set of his jaw that his mind is made up, even if mine isn't. "You were worried about the costs—"

"How much would it save?"

"Around fifty thousand."

I take a deep breath, then let it out slowly. That's far from an insignificant amount of money.

"And it would potentially happen faster," he continues. "IVF can take years. And there is something, I think, to putting a face to the... the egg donor."

Was he about to say *mother*, I wonder numbly, or am I being too sensitive?

"And what about the surrogate?" I make myself ask. "Do you think she'd be okay with using her own egg? It's one thing to give away a baby that's not biologically yours—"

"Well, obviously we'd have to clear it with her beforehand." He tries for a jovial tone, but as far as I'm concerned, it falls completely flat. "We need to select someone who *is* okay with that," he says more somberly. "That would be critical, obviously, and only if you're comfortable with it, Ashley. That's really important to me. But if a potential surrogate is okay with it... in the long run, I think it will be easier. For us, and for the baby."

I shake my head slowly. My mind is still whirling. Moments ago, I felt so certain, so hopeful, and now...? Now I really don't know how I feel, and I don't want to figure it out. "For the *baby*?" I ask. "How?"

"Well..." Mark hesitates. "It's just there would be fewer people involved, wouldn't there? I mean, if some anonymous donor gives the egg, another woman gives birth, and you raise this child... it could potentially be very confusing. When he or she got older, the baby might wonder where they came from, the way I did."

"But if the surrogate uses her own egg... it would be even more like adoption," I point out. "Like she gave away her own child, which is *precisely* what you wanted to avoid." I can't keep a slight edge from entering my voice.

"But different," Mark counters with swift certainty, "because she wasn't backed into a corner, the pregnancy wasn't a surprise, she didn't *not* want the baby, if that makes sense. It was all planned and can be explained that way, which will be easier in the long run."

"We'd better hope she doesn't want it," I retort before I can temper my reply, and Mark presses his lips together to keep from issuing a similar retort back. We're not exactly arguing, but it feels close, and I hate that. We never argue. At least we didn't, before we started talking about surrogacy.

"Can't you see the difference?" he finally asks, and now there is a sorrowful note in his voice that gives me a pang of guilt, because I can tell he's not thinking of our as-yet-unconceived baby, but his own childhood. The mother whose name he'll never know, who gave him away for a reason he'll never understand.

"I suppose I can," I say slowly. "Sort of." I reach for my tea and take a sip, mainly to stall for time. I can't rush into as monumental a decision as this. "I need to think about this," I say finally. "There's a lot to absorb."

He nods, seeming relieved. "Ashley, of course. Of *course*. That's totally understandable." He glances at the closed laptop, and I'm afraid he's thinking, *But don't take too long.*

And does it even matter anyway? Whether this baby's biological mother is an anonymous egg donor or the surrogate we haven't yet chosen, one thing is certain: his or her biological mother can never be me. It will be Mark's—and this unknown woman's. *Theirs.*

EIGHT

DANI

I set up a Zoom call for Ryan and I to talk with Andrea for an afternoon when Callie is at school—I still haven't told her what I'm thinking about, but I know if this goes ahead, I'll need to—and he comes to my apartment straight from work, still in his suit and tie. I've forgone the silk blouse for a more "me" outfit—a plain white fitted T-shirt and beige cargo pants.

To my surprise, Ryan pulls me in for a quick kiss before we start the call.

"I know I was shocked at first," he tells me, "but I'm actually proud of you, Dani," he says, which leaves me speechless for a few seconds. The last few weeks have felt full of unspoken tension, but I'm very glad we might be moving past that. "You're doing this for your sister. I respect that."

This feels like the best, and maybe the only time, to tell him something I know I should have told him before. "Ryan... on the call... Andrea might think Callie is my daughter."

He stares at me, the look of confusion in his eyes slowly morphing into one of shrewd understanding. "And why would she think that?"

"Because I told her," I admit, trying for an abashed smile. "I know, I know, I shouldn't have, but it just made things easier. They like surrogates to seem maternal—"

"And you couldn't have just explained how you've been taking care of her?" His voice rises just a little; Ryan is a stickler for honesty, something I usually admire. "That's pretty maternal."

"Like I said, it was easier," I repeat, my tone apologetic. Now is not the time to explain that surrogates have to have given birth before. That is a whole other conversation I know we need to have... but not now. "It doesn't make a difference to anyone," I add, and Ryan sighs.

"Maybe not, but why lie?"

"I just need this to work," I tell him, my tone turning pleading. "For Callie."

Ryan stares at me for a moment and then he puts his arms around me and pulls me close for a hug. I wrap my arms around him, craving his solid warmth. "Okay," he says, his lips brushing my hair. "I don't like this, Dani, but I do understand. At least, I'm trying to."

"Thank you." My voice is a whisper. I really am so grateful that Ryan is being supportive. I couldn't do this without him— not logistically, and not emotionally. As strong as I try to be, I need him... more than I want to, even.

He kisses me before letting me go, and then we sit down on the sofa, thighs brushing, the laptop in front of us. I join the Zoom call, surprised at how *not* nervous I feel. I'm going to be more myself today, instead of trying to pretend I'm some trad-wife who loves being pregnant, the way some surrogates seem to present themselves. If Ryan can respect that, then surely Andrea can too.

"Dani." Andrea's voice is as warm and rich as I remember, and she smiles at both of us from her desk, the ocean print behind her. "So nice to see you again. And this must be Ryan."

"Yes." Ryan clears his throat and then smiles. "Hi."

"So wonderful to meet you."

A suspended silence tautens between the three of us as we all gaze expectantly at one another.

"First of all," Andrea finally says, "I just want to thank you, Dani, for filling out the extended profile. I know it can seem like a daunting document, but I appreciated your thoughtful answers."

"No problem," I say, and then wonder if that sounds too offhand.

"It sounds like you've really thought this through."

"I think I have."

Andrea nods slowly before swiveling her gaze to Ryan. "And what about you, Ryan? How do you feel about it?"

"I want to support Dani," Ryan says. He sounds a little wooden, but I know he means it. "I'll admit, we had some things to work through when she first floated the idea, but I am definitely one hundred percent on board." His voice is firm, and my stomach flutters with both nerves and relief.

Thank you, Ryan.

"And what about your daughter?" Andrea asks him, before her gaze flicks back to me. I feel Ryan tense next to me, but he doesn't say anything, and I'm grateful that he's willing to go along with my lie, simply by being silent. "We don't usually interview a surrogate's children," she continues, directing this at Ryan, "because it can be a bit invasive and unsettling for them. But we like to make sure they're on board, too." She smiles, her gaze flicking to me and then back to Ryan as a faint confusion comes into her eyes, because we're both staying silent.

I realize, way too late, that Andrea has assumed Callie is Ryan's daughter.

"Callie is totally on board," I assure her hurriedly. "I mean, like Ryan, she was surprised, but she can understand how, um, I want to bless another couple the way, uh, I've—we've—been blessed." I feel my cheeks heat. I am making a mess of this. "Just to be clear," I continue, because I can tell Andrea senses something is not quite right, "Callie isn't Ryan's daughter." Which is *not* a lie, but from the corner of my eye, I see how frozen Ryan's expression has become and inwardly I cringe. I have not made this easy for him.

"Right." Andrea nods slowly, her gaze moving slowly between us. "Thank you for clarifying that, and I'm sorry for the assumption I made. So, how does Callie feel about it all?"

Callie still doesn't know. "Like I said," I tell Andrea, "she was surprised and uncertain at first, but she's come around." My tone is repressive even though I'm trying to sound upbeat. I should have been more prepared for the subject of Callie to come up.

"Okay. And she is..." Andrea glances at her computer screen, where she must have my profile up.

"Twelve?"

"Yes." Ryan breathes out, shifting where he sits. He is not comfortable being complicit in my lie, I know. "Twelve last April," I add.

"All right." Andrea hesitates before continuing, "The next step in this process is a medical screening for you, Dani. Even though you've had a child before, and, as you know, Creating Dreams only takes surrogates who have given birth before, we need to make sure everything is in good running order." She makes a wry little face, and I manage a hollow laugh.

"Right. Yes. Of course."

Ryan's neutral silence has taken a tense turn. Maybe I should have told him that surrogates have to have given birth before, but I didn't want to open that complicated can of worms just yet. It looks like I'll have to as soon as this conversation is over.

"After that," Andrea continues, "we can put your profile up on our website. Our intended parents have access to all profiles on the site, with no last names or locations, other than the state

provided, in order to protect your privacy. If a couple is interested in your profile, they'll let me know and then I'll give you
access to their profile. If you like what you see, then we can
arrange an initial supervised Zoom meeting, for you to get to
know one another."

"Great." I glance at Ryan, knowing I need to defuse the
tension, as well as draw him back into the conversation. "Do
you have any questions about the process, Ryan?"

Thankfully, he manages to relax his expression at least a
little. "No, I don't think so," he tells Andrea tonelessly. "It all
seems pretty clear."

We exchange a few more pleasantries and then the call
finally, thankfully, ends.

"What the *hell*, Dani?" The words burst out of Ryan the
second the screen goes blank. "Surrogates have to have given
birth before? You neglected to mention that fact. I thought you
lied about Callie just for convenience, but it was a lot more than
that, wasn't it?"

"Ryan—"

He's too wound up to listen to me, not that I even know
what to say, or how to say it. "Dani, you're messing with these
couples who might believe you're a sure bet. You don't even
know if you can get pregnant, or carry to term, or whatever." He
shrugs angrily as he spreads his hands wide, so scathingly
incredulous about all my devious deceptions. Maybe I should
feel guilty for all he thinks I've done, but right now I only feel
weary.

"I didn't lie," I say quietly. I rise from the sofa and collect
my half-drunk cup of coffee I had earlier, taking it to the sink.

"Just because Callie feels like your daughter doesn't mean
she is," he says in a low voice. "When are you going to accept
that?"

There are two arguments here, running side by side, but I

know which of them is the most important. "Ryan," I tell him tiredly, "this is not me feeling like Callie is my daughter."

He lets out a disbelieving huff. "What is it, then?"

"I used Callie's name," I continue, my back to him as I wash the cups, "because it seemed simpler, like I told you. But that was all."

"Dani." Ryan sounds exasperated now, along with everything else. "I have no idea what you're talking about."

I turn around slowly, because this is too important a conversation to have with my back to him, as tempting as it is. I fold my arms and meet his gaze levelly as I explain, "I have been pregnant before. I had a baby when I was sixteen, that I gave up for adoption." I say this tonelessly, without any emotion, because, the truth is, I have so completely shut down that episode in my life that it almost feels like it happened to someone else. Basically, it did.

For a few loaded seconds, Ryan only stares. Then: "You never thought to tell me this before?"

"It wasn't relevant," I reply shortly. "It happened twelve years ago, Ryan, way before I met you. And I chose to have a completely closed adoption, with no further contact with the adoptive parents or the baby. So…" I realize my lips are trembling and so I press them together, hard. Maybe I'm not quite as emotionless as I wanted to be.

"Dani…" Ryan sinks back onto the sofa as he rakes his hand through his hair. He looks completely gobsmacked. "That's…" He shakes his head slowly. "I'm not angry, but… this is a big deal. A big part of who you are. I wish I'd known before. Why didn't you tell me? I mean… is it a secret? Does Callie know?"

"Callie doesn't know," I say quickly. "No one knows, except my mother, and you know how much I talk to her."

Ryan's expression softens with sympathy. "Dani…"

Sometimes I wish my boyfriend were a *little* less of an emotionally intelligent, sensitive twenty-first-century kind of guy. Right now I want him to shrug, say, "Fair" and then ask me what we're having for dinner.

"It's not something I consider at all relevant to my life today," I explain stiffly, and Ryan gives me a who-are-you-kidding kind of look. "I'm serious," I insist. "I put it behind me for good a long time ago. It's ancient history, Ryan."

At least I want it to be. And it *was*, absolutely, until this whole surrogacy thing brought it back into the light. But I can shove it back into the dark again, once Ryan and I get past it. I know I can.

He sits there for a moment, lost in thought, while I will him to move on. "And what about the father?" he finally asks.

I let out a huff of humorless laughter, because that is someone I try never to think about. "What about him?"

He shrugs, seeming at a loss, but also a little defiant. Is he angry that I didn't tell him about this? Does he have a right to be? "I don't know," Ryan says. "Was he your boyfriend? Did you tell him about the baby? How did he react? Or your parents, for that matter? Does Callie not remember—"

"Callie was only four years old at the time. She doesn't remember." Ryan looks like he wants to object, and I continue shortly, "And there was never any *need* to tell her, because by the time she would have been old enough to have that discussion, it really was ancient history in every way that matters."

"And the father?" he presses.

Clearly Ryan is feeling some kind of sympathy for the faceless father, maybe because he feels somewhat in the same position... even though this baby won't be his, or even mine.

"The father wasn't interested," I say. To put it mildly.

"Did you ever tell him?" Ryan asks, a harder note coming into his voice.

"No, but he found out, anyway, because we were in high school together and I couldn't hide it forever, and when he did, he texted me a massive screed threatening me if I told anyone he was involved, and that he would deny everything. Does that answer your question sufficiently?" My voice is vibrating with remembered pain, my hands clenched at my sides. I really do not need all this being raked up right now.

"Oh, Dani..." Ryan's expression softens as he holds his arms out as if inviting me to walk into them. "How can you say this is ancient history? It sounds like it was very traumatic."

You think? A laugh escapes me, high and wild. "Well, yes, as a matter of fact, it was," I reply, my voice wobbling, "which is why I've consigned it to ancient history. I'm not that girl anymore, Ryan." I take a deep breath in an attempt to get my emotions under control. "I don't *want* to be, so unless you feel the need to keep combing through all these details, can we please leave it?" Infuriatingly, at the end of this heartfelt speech, my voice catches on something like a sob and I have to turn away to hide the fact that I am alarmingly close to tears—not that I've fooled Ryan at all.

"Dani..." His voice is full of tenderness that makes me both prickle and yearn to be held. I hear him walk into the kitchen and then his hands are on my shoulders, warm and comforting as they draw me back toward him, except part of me resists going.

I've always been stronger on my own. It's one of the reasons I've kept Ryan at a distance, why I know I'm not ready for marriage. Why I'm certain I won't have any trouble giving this baby away. I've done it before, after all, haven't I? And that baby was mine biologically. This one won't be.

"Don't," I say, sniffing as I pull away. "Please."

He lets his arms fall to his sides as I turn to face him.

"I'm sorry," I tell him, meaning it. "I'm not trying to be difficult, honestly. I'm just not... This isn't..." I can't finish.

"Okay." Ryan nods somberly. "I get it."

"Good." I'm not sure he does, but I want to leave this conversation far, far behind us. "Thank you for not saying anything negative on the call with Andrea. I really do appreciate it."

"You're welcome."

We're both silent, and it feels both like there is nothing more to say and yet far too much.

"Callie will be home soon," I tell him, even though she won't be for half an hour. "And you probably need to get back to work."

Ryan's mouth twists. "Yeah, okay," he says, and I know he's hurt by my obvious attempt to create some distance between us. But the truth is, this afternoon has been exhausting, I'm behind on my work, and I need some time to regroup emotionally.

He steps forward and kisses my cheek, the gesture tender despite the tension between us, and in response I hug him briefly, grateful for his presence, his steadiness which feels so different to my own chaotic emotions.

"I'll see you tomorrow?" he asks.

"Yeah, tomorrow."

And then he's gone, and a sigh of relief, as well as sadness, escapes me in a big whoosh as I walk over to the sofa and practically collapse on it. I still feel far too fragile.

I know I should be working—either on my thesis or on the papers I have to grade—but I can't summon the will, never mind the desire. Instead, I find myself doing something I hardly ever do—I call my mom.

"Dani?" As she answers, she sounds wary. "What's wrong?"

It's a fair question, because I call my mother so rarely, and when I do, it's usually because something is wrong—Callie's had another symptom, or we've run out of money.

"Nothing's wrong," I tell her. Not exactly, anyway. "I just thought I'd call."

"Okay," she says cautiously.

"How are you?"

"I'm fine, Dani." A pause and then my mom asks, "How are *you?*"

I close my eyes. "I was just thinking about..." My throat tightens and I can barely make myself say it. "The... baby."

My mother is completely silent, and even through the phone I can sense her shock. I have never, in twelve years, talked about the *baby*.

"How come?" she finally asks, her voice soft.

I didn't want to tell my mom about my plans before I told Callie, but I can't keep myself from it, and maybe I shouldn't. I need someone to talk to, someone who isn't as emotionally invested, and that just happens to be my mother. "I'm thinking of becoming a surrogate."

"A *surrogate*—"

"To pay for Callie's surgery."

A sigh escapes my mother, a soft, sad breath of sound. "I wish I could help with that," she says. "Financially, I mean."

My hand tightens on the phone as I feel a familiar frustration steal through me. After my dad died, leaving us with his gambling debts and not much else, my mother joined a pseudo-convent outside Casa Grande called Sisters of Mercy. She's not quite a nun; she works part-time at a craft store and can visit us for holidays, wear her own clothes, that sort of thing. But it felt like she retreated not just from life but from *us*, in a way that didn't seem fair. Admittedly, she sends small amounts of money when she can; she visits at least once or twice a year, and she calls Callie regularly, but she's our *mother*. And while I'm an adult, Callie isn't. Three years on, I'm still so angry she chose to walk away... and my mother has always known it.

"I assume you've thought this through?" she says. "And have decided it's the best way forward."

"Yes, I have." It's both annoying and gratifying that she respects my decision more than Ryan has, at least initially.

"And I suppose thinking about being pregnant again has brought it all back?"

I find I have to swallow hard. "Yes."

A silence settles on us, as soft as that sigh was, that makes me close my eyes. "I'm sorry, Dani. For back then."

It's the first time she's said anything like that.

"You don't need to be sorry," I whisper.

"I worry I pressured you to give the baby up for adoption. You just had so much life ahead of you, and I didn't want you to be held back from that."

"It was the right thing to do." I believe that, but it hurts in a way I haven't let it in twelve years.

I never think about that baby—I don't even know whether it was a boy or girl; I asked them not to tell me. I never even looked at him or her, never mind held them. There's nothing to remember but the pain of labor and the relief when I felt my sagging, empty middle as they took the baby away. The only thing I remember is the thin, trembling sound of its cry, although I've done my best to block that out. That baby has been like a ghost in my mind... but it never haunted me, until now.

"Are you sure you want to do this?" my mom asks, and for the first time since I started on this journey, I'm *not* sure.

But then I think of Callie, and I remember I have no choice.

"Yes," I tell my mother. "I'm sure."

I *have* to be.

I say goodbye a few minutes later, and I sit on the sofa, the phone held to my chest, my eyes closed, as memories assail me. The labor—a blur of pain and fear, because I refused any anesthesia, I'm not even sure why. Maybe I felt like I had to punish myself. I was so stupid, to fall for a guy who had zero interest in me. And my dad... my dad was so disappointed in me. I still remember the look on his face when I was forced to tell him I was pregnant, like he'd been sucker-punched. He turned gray. I disappointed him, I know, way before he disappointed me.

I remember the emptiness afterward, when the baby was whisked away and I stared out at the bright blue sky and told myself my life was beginning again. I was back home within twenty-four hours, training for spring track just a week later, even though I still needed to use maternity pads. I didn't care. I was determined to move on and make everyone move on with me.

I recall the months after, when I rejoined my class and refused to talk about it at all. I closed off the whole experience like sewing up a surgical wound, the stitches nice and tight, everything tidied away.

Until now.

It isn't until I hear a drawn breath that I realize Callie has come home.

"Dani," she asks, sounding alarmed. "Why are you crying?"

NINE

ASHLEY

After our discussion, Mark more or less tiptoes around me, giving me the time and space to think about traditional surrogacy. We intentionally *don't* talk about it, but it's always between us, the air heavy laden with expectation. I know what Mark wants me to decide.

What he doesn't know is just how much I *am* thinking about it. And not just thinking about it but doing my own research as well. Two days after I get home from the hospital, I insist I'm well enough for Mark to go to work, and I spend the day on the sofa, surfing the internet.

I read surrogate message boards and glom all the information on various surrogacy websites. There are so many agencies —most of them with names like Creating Dreams—Giving Tree, Brightest Star, the Kindest Gift, Another Way. Some intended parents, I learn, go "indie"—that is, they find their own surrogate, often a family member or a friend. For a second, I think of Claire, but of course she couldn't, even if she wanted to. Surrogates have had to have been "gestational carriers" at least once before in order to qualify.

I can't read any profiles online, since they're only accessible once you've signed with an agency, but then, three days after Mark goes back to work, I discover he's already made an account with Creating Dreams, because when *I* try to make one, it says the email address—a joint one we share—is already in use. It doesn't take me long to reset the password and go online to see what he's filled in.

He's completed the whole application, including a heartfelt paragraph on why we want to choose surrogacy.

It felt like the best way to have our own family, after we decided, that due to our own experience, adoption wasn't for us. We can't wait to welcome this baby into our lives.

I should be annoyed by his use of "we" as I had *nothing* to do with this, but I only feel sad and a little wistful. If I'd been able to give a baby to Mark... but there is no point thinking that way. I have to look ahead, to how we can have that family he so desperately wants, and that I now want, too.

I start reading the surrogate profiles, their last names and specific locations hidden for privacy, and see what kind of woman might be the biological mother of my child.

It's heady stuff, frightening and fascinating and completely overwhelming all at once, and I spend hours going through the profiles of the two dozen or so women on the agency's books. I'm grateful that Creating Dreams lets me view them, because something I learned from my deep dive into this whole world is that many agencies don't. They select intended parent profiles to show surrogates, and then the surrogate chooses you, rather than the other way round.

It's a way to protect the surrogate and give her more agency in the situation, since she is potentially the one who will feel the most vulnerable. But *I* feel vulnerable, because in this scenario I'm the only one who isn't bringing something to the table. Already, from what I've seen on the internet, I sense that the women in the intended parent couples—the would-be mothers—are both vulnerable and desperate, at the mercy of biology, as well as the woman they've picked, treading so carefully so they won't seem as if they're pressuring her in any way, yet always longing to have more control.

Is that me? I don't think it is, as I've come at this much more cautiously... but it might be Mark, I realize.

The profiles I view are incredibly detailed—a photo, height, weight, their general health, the state they live in, where they've traveled. I read about their interests, their work experience, their personality and parenting style, and then all the questions that I suppose could be deal-breakers for some—whether they're willing to reduce a triplet pregnancy to a twin, or a twin to a singleton, or abort a baby with severe physical or mental abnormalities. They also list what kind of relationship they want with the intended parents, the two words abbreviated throughout to IPs. Whether they'd be willing to pump and freeze their breast milk. Whether the IPs can be in the delivery room. And even whether they're willing to have the child contact them at a later date.

And then, finally, a few sentences in their own words—almost all of these are bubbly assurances about what an honor and privilege it is to help a family, anodyne sentiments that convey enthusiasm without any real sense of the person.

After reading all two dozen profiles, my head is swimming, and I almost wish I hadn't read any. It's *too much*—too much information, too much emotion, too much of being involved in a stranger's life, and them in yours. I'm amazed that several of the surrogates have done this before—two, three, even four times. How do they keep themselves separate from the IPs, the baby they carry, over and over again? It helps, I suppose, that they're not biologically related to the children they've carried. Whether they'd be open to traditional surrogacy isn't even a question on the profile. Will we even find a surrogate who is willing to go down this route?

I pull the laptop back toward me to go through the profiles again, to see if I can glean any clue about whether traditional surrogacy might be an option for one of the surrogates.

My gaze skims down the names. Bethan, from Indiana. Lynne, from Texas. Nadine, from Washington. These are real women with real families who are, according to their profiles, ready and willing to carry a baby for a stranger—and, of course, around fifty or sixty thousand dollars. It's no small amount of money, especially as some of these women look as though it would mean a lot to them. Still, it's mind-boggling. Carrying a baby for someone… it's such a big ask. And yet we're planning to ask someone.

I keep reading through them, the names and faces becoming familiar. Julie, from Arkansas. Laura, from Wisconsin. Then my gaze stops on a woman I recognize from my last trawl through, although I can't recall her details. Dani, from California.

She's tall and blond and blue-eyed, with a direct stare for the camera that feels like a challenge. Her mouth has the barest beginning of the curve of a smile, but the photograph seems as if it was taken a second too soon, and so her expression borders on severe, yet something about it is compelling. Maybe it's the blueness of her eyes, or the way it feels as if she's staring at me. I find I can't look away.

I click on her profile and start to read. I recall some of the details from my previous reading—PhD student in microbiology, twelve-year-old daughter Callie, with a supportive partner. Others I had forgotten and have to read afresh. She has never smoked, drinks occasionally, and has no diagnosed mental health problems. Her interests include hiking, watching black and white movies, and jazz. Her favorite food is Japanese; she's traveled to Colombia for a semester during college. She can speak decent, if not quite fluent, Spanish. Her family and friends are "100% supportive." In answer to the question "what reassurance can you give that you will not change your mind about relinquishing the child," she has written, rather starkly, *I would not be filling out this profile if I thought that would ever be a possibility.*

There's something bare bones and no-nonsense about her which I like. When asked what qualities of the intended parents are important to her she simply wrote "loving." It feels almost as if she considered the profile a waste of time, and in some ways I can respect that. Do I need to know that she likes jazz music? No, not really. I certainly don't need to care about it.

I scroll down the page and keep reading. She is willing to abort a triplet or a twin or for mental or physical deformities, something which gives me slight pause, because written on the page like that it sounds so cold. Could intended parents really demand that a surrogate abort a baby? Apparently.

She is comfortable with the IPs being in the delivery room but is not willing to pump or freeze breast milk, which I find interesting; it feels like one line she has drawn in the sand, for whatever reason. In the space where she is meant to write something warmly enthusiastic, she has simply written, *Thank you for considering me for this opportunity.*

Like it's a job application.

I sit back, my gaze distant as I sift through all the facts I've just learned. Dani from California, a microbiology PhD student. Surely that's enough to find out who she really is?

The internet is a tempting, treacherous place, with so much tantalizing information at your fingertips. It only takes me a few minutes to find Dani Bryson of the University of San Diego; she's teaching an introductory course in microbiology for the fall semester. I try to find her social media accounts, but there aren't any.

The closest I get is a photo on USD's microbiology department's Facebook page, of a bunch of faculty and PhD students going on some fundraising hike in the Cuyamaca Mountains. She's standing slightly apart from the others, her arms folded, her expression similar to the one in her profile photo—like the photo was taken before she thought to smile. She's tall, rangy, clearly athletic. In fact, she looks nothing like me, which, weirdly, I decide I also like. I will not be futilely looking for echoes of myself in a baby that is biologically this woman's—I am petite, curvy, dark-haired, pale-skinned. The exact opposite of Dani Bryson.

I search fruitlessly for more information about her online, but there is very little. I learn that her PhD is in molecular determinants of bacterial pathogenesis, whatever that means. She is in her fourth year of study. She's written an article for the *Journal of Clinical Microbiology*; I can access the first page of it, but it's so technical it might as well be gibberish.

Still, I am impressed. Dani from California seems like a smart, focused, ambitious young woman. Why, I can't help but wonder, does she want to be a surrogate? She doesn't seem like the other ones—homemakers with small children who revel in the whole maternity thing. At least, that's how they're presenting themselves.

But Dani from California seems to be going to lengths *not* to appear that way. Or am I wildly projecting my own feelings onto her? Because even though I've given Mark the green light, there's a part of me that's still not sure about all this, as much as I want to be.

A week later, my mom comes to visit me. Mark had called her when I'd first had the accident, and she'd asked to be updated, but she didn't rush to my bedside—not that I was expecting that. My mother is not one for dramatic gestures, or any gestures at all, really. She is dependable, in a stolid, no-nonsense kind of way, but when it comes to anything innately thoughtful, never mind over-the-top... well, you're going to be disappointed. The constant refrain of my childhood was a weary entreaty not to make a fuss—which was kind of ironic, because I never did.

She comes for brunch on Saturday, and Mark does all the food—eggs Florentine, wholegrain toast, freshly squeezed orange juice, and fruit salad, the perfectly ripe, organic strawberries glinting like rubies. He greets her effusively, with kisses on both cheeks; he's always been incredibly warm to her, maybe because she's the only parent figure in his life—not that she acts like one. She smiles stiffly and steps away from his embrace as she nods to me.

You look as though you're getting back on your feet," she says matter-of-factly.

"Yes, I think so." I step toward her and then I awkwardly hug her with one arm, which she returns without actually seeming to touch me. My mother is not the most affectionate woman on the planet, but I've learned to live with it. She tries, I think, in her own way. At least that's what I keep telling myself.

"Ruth, what can I get you?" Mark asks as we move toward the kitchen. "Orange juice, coffee, or something stronger? We've got the makings of mimosas..." He waggles his eyebrows expectantly, smiling, bottle of champagne at the ready.

"Just coffee, please." My mother stands in the doorway of the kitchen, holding her pocketbook to her chest like she's scared we might steal it. She's never been comfortable in Mark's house, with all its sleek, modern décor. I doubt that will ever change.

We exchange somewhat stilted pleasantries while Mark makes the drinks, and then my mother and I retire to the living room while he finishes making our brunch. She perches on the edge of the sofa, holding her cup of black coffee, her pocketbook next to her, her expression tense.

I feel a sudden sweep of sadness, the kind I usually try to keep myself from. Because I wish my mother *wanted* to be here;

I wish she was the kind of mother who I couldn't wait to call with my news, ask her opinion, listen to her advice.

But I could be that kind of mother.

The words slip slyly into my mind, startling me. It's the first time I've ever thought like that.

"So what's new with you?" my mother asks in her stiff way. "Besides the accident, of course. I was very sorry to hear about that." A pause. "I would have visited you, but I couldn't take time off work."

"I understand." My mother works all the hours given to her, and then some.

After we married, Mark and I offered my mother some financial help, which she refused with great dignity. I felt guilty for offering it in the first place, and yet when I consider how hard she works, and for how little, how could I not have? Every so often, we've thrown out hints that we are willing to pay for things—dinner at a nice restaurant, or help with her health insurance or rent. Mark even floated the idea of buying her an apartment closer to us. But she's refused it all.

"I haven't been up to too much," I tell her. "I'm back at work, at least—although with limited duties." I hold up my cast. "Kind of hard to type with this, but not impossible."

She nods without saying anything; my mother has never worked an office job, having scraped by with a high-school diploma and never even considering college. My secretarial work, such as it is, is completely beyond her scope of imagination.

"Actually," I find myself saying, to my own surprise, "Mark and I are considering something kind of big."

My mother raises her thin eyebrows, her lips pursed. "Oh?"

"I found out back in July that I'm in early menopause." Something it hadn't even occurred to me to share with her, which makes me feel both guilty and sad. Again. "But Mark and

I really want to start a family, so we're actually considering surrogacy."

My mother doesn't offer any commiserations about my infertility; maybe she'd see it as a blessing herself, as I know how hard it was for her, raising me single-handed while working two jobs. The mention of surrogacy, however, has her raising her eyebrows even higher.

"Surrogacy?" she repeats cautiously. "You mean you're going to hire a woman to carry a baby? Isn't that what that is?"

"Yes, it is. It will be Mark's baby biologically, but not mine." I do my best to sound upbeat about this, no big deal, I'm totally okay with it, but saying it aloud hurts. "But the important thing," I continue determinedly, "is it means we can have our own family."

My mother frowns. "And who will be the mother, then?"

"*I* will," I tell her, trying to pitch my tone both gentle and firm. "But if you mean biologically, then it would be the surrogate."

"So, like giving a baby up for adoption, but planned?"

This is more or less what I said to Mark, but for some reason it sounds worse when my mother says it. She never did sugar-coat anything.

"In a way," I demur. "But also different." Although right now, I have to admit I'm not really sure how.

My mother shakes her head slowly. "The things people do these days," she says.

It's the end of the discussion. I wonder why I told her at all.

The rest of brunch passes with lurching attempts at conversation, as it always does, although my mother perks up when Mark finally persuades her to try a mimosa.

He's so patient with her, coaxing her with his smiles and jokes, never taking her stiff tone to heart. *He'd make a great dad,*

I think with a pang. And then I remind myself that he *will* be a dad, one day. We're going to make this happen.

By the time my mom leaves later that afternoon, I am wilting with exhaustion from the effort, and even Mark is starting to flag a little.

As the door closes behind her, I turn to him. "I guess it just goes to show that being blood related doesn't always seem to count for that much," I tell him wryly, and his expression freezes.

"Ashley, I know you might not think it's important—"

"For *me*, Mark," I cut across him, because I can tell to where his mind immediately jumped. "Not for you. I know it's important to you, but..." I feel like I have to say it, the elephant in the room neither of us has seemed to want to acknowledge. "You do realize *I* won't be biologically related to this baby, right?" I ask, halfway between a criticism and a joke.

"I..." He falters, looking abashed. "Yes, I have realized that," he admits. "And I know I should have addressed it before, but..." He stops, clearly at a loss.

I fill in flatly, "But since there's no way I can have a biological child of my own, it was off the table anyway?"

"I wouldn't have said it like that," Mark replies quietly. His forehead is furrowed, his eyes dark with misery, and I feel a flicker of guilt for pushing the point, even as part of me acknowledges that surely I'm the one who has a right to be upset in this situation.

"How would you have said it?" I ask, half out of curiosity, half out of pique.

Mark is silent for a moment.

"Is this going to be a problem for you?" he finally asks, without any rancor, like he genuinely wants to know the answer. "Either with a traditional surrogate or an egg donor? I mean, you not being biologically related while I am. Because I understand if it would. Obviously I do, since I'm the one harping on about it." He tries to smile, but he still looks worried.

And how am I meant to answer? My impulse, as ever, is not to make a fuss. To reassure him, tell him I was having a moment of feeling sorry for myself, but it'll all be okay.

And while the words are right there, hovering on my lips, I find I can't say them.

"I don't know," I admit quietly, and then, because old habits die hard, "I'm sorry."

"You don't need to be sorry," Mark replies. He sounds sad, and I know I've disappointed him.

The funny thing is, I was on the cusp of telling him that I'd made my decision about traditional surrogacy. I was even considering showing him Dani's profile; I practically have it memorized by now. I don't know how I can be so sure about her, but I am. If we're going to do this, she is the one. She won't get involved, she won't be a threat. I've convinced myself of that; I feel absolutely certain, even if I don't sound it right now, to Mark. Even if I just told him I wasn't sure about the whole thing.

"I'm sorry if I haven't taken your feelings into account enough," he says after a moment, his voice soft and sad. "I really am. The only way we can get through this is with honest communication, and if I've failed in that, then please—"

"Well, I've just told you how I feel," I remind him, and now I sound querulous. I take a deep breath and reel my emotions back in. Mark is not responsible for my own complicated ambivalence. "But you're right," I tell him. "I'm not trying to be argumentative. In fact, I wanted to tell you, these last few weeks I've thought about it all, and... I'm willing to move ahead with traditional surrogacy."

Mark's face suffuses first with surprise, and then with gratitude and warmth, and he starts toward me. "Oh, *Ashley*..."

"And," I continue, edging away slightly because I'm not ready for a hug, "I think I've found our surrogate."

TEN

DANI

When, in early September, Andrea calls me to tell me I've been approved to be a surrogate, subject to the necessary health checks, I practically wilt with relief. I was worried that Ryan's reluctance might have messed up the whole thing, but, amazingly, it seems it hasn't.

There is, of course, the little matter of my white lie, how I wrote on my profile that Callie was my daughter. But I've already learned from my research into surrogacy that giving up a baby for adoption can be seen as problematic—why, I don't know, since that's what they're basically asking you to do again. But from what I understand, most IPs and agencies want surrogates to be *maternal*. And you can't be maternal, I guess, if you haven't been a proper mother—taking care of a baby, raising a child.

I justified the lie because I *have* been maternal... toward Callie. I walked her through her first period, I sat in the ER with her overnight, eyes gritty with fatigue and stomach churning with fear, when she was first diagnosed. I've tested her on her chemistry, I've taught her how to drive, I've listened to her rants and her snark and her gushing over a boy who later broke her heart by never even noticing her. I have *been* her mom, over and over again, in so many ways.

And anyway, the main thing is that I've given birth, I can do it, even if the memory of it is a blur. All my lady parts work like they need to; I fell pregnant all too easily before, and I didn't even realize I was pregnant until I was nearly five months along, which was all part of the problem. To the anxious intended parents, I'm surely a match made in heaven.

At least that's what I kept telling myself, but now that my profile is online—I passed the medical screening, with its accompanying, invasive gynecological element—fine, I feel nervous. I'm waiting for some IPs to look at my unsmiling photo —I just couldn't summon the cheery expression so many other profiles have—and say: *Yes. She's the one.*

It seems unlikely, which depresses and relieves me in turn.

It also feels weirdly vulnerable and exposing, to have all my personal details up there, for these perusing parents to see, assess, and ultimately judge. Even with the so-called privacy of last name and town withheld, I'm pretty sure someone could find me online if they wanted to. They could find me in real life, and for a moment I let myself imagine some eager IPs tracking me down to my apartment.

As the days pass, though, and no IPs come forward to register their interest, I feel the sting of potential rejection.

It's worse than Tinder, I want to joke with somebody, but there's nobody to tell. I haven't explained the whole surrogate thing to Callie yet; when she came home and saw me crying, she was seriously alarmed, and I knew I needed to handle anything emotive carefully. I fobbed her off with an explanation that Ryan and I had argued, which was pretty much the truth.

Ryan and I have reached an understanding now, but we agreed not to discuss the surrogacy until it's happening, which works better for both of us. We've gone back to the safe and steady routine we had—dinner or drinks on the weekend, a check-in midweek, sometimes a morning run together. It's enough for me, even if sometimes I think about the kind of what-ifs I never used to—a life with Ryan, contemplating *our* baby rather than one belonging to strangers.

I can't joke about this with Anna, either, since she's been treating the idea as akin to getting an OnlyFans account. My colleagues in the department or acquaintances or neighbors are hardly the people to confide in. I'm not lonely, I never have been, but I still feel the lack.

I briefly consider calling my mom to update her, but then I don't. While she was more understanding and accepting of the whole idea than I expected, I'm not about to invite her into my life any more than she already is, which is not very much at all.

Then, a week after my approval, when the fall semester is in full swing, Callie is back in school—and insisting she's fine, when I know and see better, I catch the times she stumbles, the way the ibuprofen in the medicine cabinet steadily dwindles—I get the call from Andrea.

"Hi, Dani, how are you?" she asks warmly, and I reply a little flatly because I want her to get to the chase, and fortunately so does she. "There's a couple who has indicated interest in your profile. I'll forward their profile to you, but first I wanted to flag up a request they have, which, I have to say, is fairly unusual these days, so it definitely bears some serious thought."

That sounds like a warning and a half, and so I immediately tense. What kind of weird request do they have? My mind darts in all directions, from the innocent to the kinky.

"What kind of request?" I ask warily.

"Almost all surrogacies now are gestational," she begins. "Traditional surrogacies which were once the norm did not involve a separate egg donor, since that wasn't medically possible." Then she launches into a history of surrogacy I really don't need to hear, and the innovations that have occurred with egg donation and IVF in the last few decades. "Technology has allowed us to explore new ways of optimizing fertility," she concludes, but my brain is buzzing because all I heard in that long-winded speech was that traditional surrogacy means *I* would be the biological mother, and that's what this couple wants.

"Why?" I ask numbly. "I mean, since it isn't the usual...?"

"There are a few reasons—it's simpler, cheaper, and quicker, usually. But obviously there could be emotional complications for you, which would create emotional complications for them." She pauses. "Under California law, this baby would be yours by right, as well as the husband's, until you signed an adoption order after he or she is born, just like with a regular adoption. Obviously, that could feel like a very different scenario to what you were anticipating."

My heart is thudding, and my hand is slippery, clenching my phone. I really wasn't expecting this. I need to be honest with Andrea.

"It is different," I tell her, "Very. But... it's one I'm familiar with."

Now *she's* the one sounding wary. "Oh?" she says.

Haltingly, I force myself to explain. "I wasn't... completely honest with you, about my... child," I explain. I can *feel* Andrea's tension through the phone, and I really hope I'm not ruining everything. "Callie is my sister, not my daughter, but I've been raising her by myself for the last three years. I did have a baby... but I gave it up for adoption when I was sixteen. I was afraid to say that before, because it seemed like, from some of the stuff I read online, IPs might look down on surrogates who gave up their children for adoption. I'm... I'm sorry. I should have been upfront with you from the beginning."

Andrea is silent for a long moment.

I close my eyes, cursing myself for telling the truth. "All this is to say," I finish painfully, "that I think... I think I could be a traditional surrogate without any problem, since I've basically done it before." Which makes me sound ice-cold, but at this point I can't let myself care. Isn't that what the IPs *want*, really? Someone who's willing to walk away?

"Thank you for telling me," Andrea finally says after a tense pause. "I appreciate your honesty."

Too little, too late? I wonder. I can't tell from her tone.

"Normally," Andrea continues after another laden pause, "we prefer our surrogates to have had some parenting experience. It reassures intended parents, and it gives the surrogates empathy for what they might be experiencing."

I stay silent, because I am really hoping for a "but."

"However," Andrea adds, and already I am filled with relief, "considering the nature of this request, your experience might be relevant and helpful to this couple. If you're willing to go ahead, I suggest you amend your profile to reflect your lived experience accurately, and when you have, I'll forward it to them to see what they think."

I take the gentle, but pointed, rebuke humbly. "I'll do that," I promise. "Today."

"This is something you should consider carefully," Andrea tells me, rather sternly. "It's not something to be undertaken lightly, Dani, even if you've done it before."

"I know," I assure her. "Trust me, I will think about it carefully."

I think about it for fifteen minutes. After I get off the phone with Andrea, I consider just how different this might make me feel, and I realize the answer is, not that much. This whole thing has just been a way to fund Callie's surgery. The parameters or particulars don't change that.

Still, I wait an hour before I amend my profile to show Andrea that I *have* thought about it, at least a little. I email it to her with some trepidation; will this change the IPs' view of me? Why *did* they pick my profile? I click on it and start reading, trying to view it from these strangers' perspective. What about my unsmiling photograph appealed to them? My answers to most questions are short, even terse. Did they like how to-the-point I was, compared to some of the other, more flowery profiles? If so, why?

I have no answers, because I know nothing about these people. I can only wait until they read my updated profile and hopefully accept it, so Andrea can send me theirs.

Fortunately, that only takes another hour. I'm shocked when, on clicking to refresh my inbox, I see the email from her, with the profile attached. *Couple are happy to proceed*, she writes. *Let me know what you think.*

With equal parts trepidation and burning curiosity, I click on the profile to download and read it.

Compared to my checklist of medical questions, the IP profile is surprisingly short and chatty. There's a photo of A and M from Connecticut—they're on a beach, their arms around one another, her dark hair blowing in the breeze.

He looks friendly and open—a round face, warm brown eyes with glasses, balding, with a fringe of dark, curly hair. I turn my attention to A, the wife, the potential mother to my baby, although I know I shouldn't be thinking like that, because this baby *won't* be mine. She is smiling, but I see a sadness in her eyes, or maybe a reserve. Or maybe I'm just being fanciful because I can relate to that feeling, but there's something contained about her, I think, something withheld. She's pretty, in a petite and curvy way, her dark eyes huge in her pale, heart-shaped face.

A and M from Connecticut. I let the words roll around in my mind, reverberate. Then I turn to the text of the profile.

> *Hello, We are so excited and grateful to begin this journey. A works for a large pharmaceutical firm and M is an attorney. More importantly, we long to have a family life together. We value honesty, compassion, tenderness, and caring. In our free*

time, we love to cook, go to restaurants, hike, and simply spend time together. As M is adopted himself, he is eager to start his own family, a lifelong dream of his. A is very supportive of this and is also excited to welcome a baby into their lives. Thank you so much for considering us for this very special and important step.

It reads like an extended Hallmark card, but I'm guessing all the profiles do. What's interesting is the way it is phrased—I'm pretty sure the whole thing was written by M, and that he's the driver when it comes to pursuing surrogacy... which makes me curious about A. She's supportive, but is that in the way Ryan is supportive? Would she rather not be doing this? I feel a weird empathy for her, because I really do understand having an ambivalence toward motherhood, but I'm also concerned. This is my biological child we're talking about. I want to make sure he or she is in a loving family with two parents who want a baby equally.

Really? Because you've already got one out there and you have no idea what kind of family they were put into.

I push that thought away as I read through the profile again, trying to discover more clues. Their hobbies are cooking, going to restaurants, and hiking? Aren't everybody's? And are they even ready for the way a child implodes your ordered life, the ease of everything? And who doesn't value honesty and compassion, tenderness and caring?

"What are you looking at?"

I nearly jump out of my skin as Callie appears behind me, bending over the sofa to peer at the screen of my laptop. I was so engrossed in the profile that I didn't even hear her come in.

"Nothing," I say far too quickly, and slam the lid of the laptop down. Not the most subtle of responses.

Callie raises her eyebrows. "*Okaay...*" She plants her hands on her hips. "What's the big secret?"

"Nothing..." I am such a bad liar when it comes to my sister. She can read me like a book.

"Wait. It said..." She screws up her face. "Intended *parents*? What does that even *mean*?"

I did not want to force this conversation, but I know Callie has seen too much for me not to. "Intended parents for a baby," I tell her as I rise from the sofa. "For surrogacy."

"Surrogacy... isn't that, like, when a woman has a baby for someone else?"

"Pretty much." I bustle around, mindlessly tidying up as my stomach churns. I have an instinctive feeling that Callie is not going to be thrilled by my news. In fact, I think I can predict she's going to be horrified, especially when she learns the reason *why* I'm doing it.

"Why are you looking at that?" she asks, sounding more bemused than alarmed. "It's not for your research or something, is it?"

As if. My doctoral thesis is on molecular determinants of bacterial pathogenesis, which is about the genetic code of virulence that enable bacteria to invade a host. If there's a parallel to getting pregnant for strangers, I don't want to imagine it.

"No, not research." I take a deep breath and turn around to face my sister. "I'm looking into it for me, Callie. I'm thinking about becoming a surrogate."

She goggles for a second, her blue eyes wide, her lips parted in soundless shock. "What? *Why*?" she finally manages.

"For the money," I admit. I pause and then add staunchly, knowing she'll figure it out anyway, "For your surgery."

Callie's expression immediately darkens, her blond brows knit together. "Are you kidding me?" she demands, sounding angry. "You'd do *that*... Dani, I'm not sure I even *want* the surgery—"

"But if you decide you do," I cut across her swiftly, "or it becomes medically necessary, I want to be able to pay for it."

She shakes her head slowly. "So you're going to have a baby? For *who*?"

"Maybe the couple you saw on the screen." I try for a lighter tone. "They're interested in my profile."

"Your *profile*?" She sounds scathingly incredulous. "What is this, Hinge?"

Hinge, the gen Z answer to the millennial's Tinder.

"Kind of," I tell her, smiling. "But for babies."

Callie is scowling as she shakes her head hard, blond hair flying. "I didn't ask you to do this."

"Cal, I know you didn't." I gentle my voice. "This is my choice, one hundred percent. And I want to do it, trust me."

"And if I don't want the surgery?" she demands, her chin thrust out.

I take a deep breath as I try to sound as reasonable as possible. "Callie, the doctor we saw advised you to have the surgery—"

"She said she could see the *case* for it," Callie flashes back. "Come on. That's totally different, Dani."

"It's not that different," I argue, my voice rising with the strength of my feelings. "And that was three months ago. You have another checkup in a couple of months—what if she makes a stronger case then?"

Callie shrugs, all determined defiance. "And what if she doesn't?"

I am silent for a second, weighing my options.

"Callie, did you fall over today?" I ask quietly. "Did you have tingling in your legs or arms? Did your feet go numb? Did you—"

"*Shut up*," she cries, surprising us both with her ferocity, the words a ragged roar.

I fall silent, chastened. My sister never shouts.

"Please, Dani, don't," she says more quietly. Her lips tremble and she presses them together. "I know what my symptoms are. I'm the one who has them, not you." Her voice rises as she continues, "I'm the one who decides whether I have surgery, not *you*."

Again, I am silent. I don't want to antagonize her, but why can't she see how important this is?

"You know," I finally say, "that once you start with these symptoms, they are only likely to get worse."

"They can stabilize," she snaps back. "The doctor said that, too. And sometimes they even get better. At least, you can manage them better."

The doctor did say that, but it felt like futile reassurance. Spinal problems don't just *get better*, and from what I've read online, they often do get worse, especially with age. But, of course, every case is different, and neither Callie nor I can know what the future will look like for her back. "But," I am compelled to point out gently, "they're *not* stabilizing—"

"Thanks for reminding me!" Now she sounds near tears— and also like she's furious with me. I'm making this worse, I know I am, but I don't know how to get through to her. She *needs* this surgery. I really do believe that.

"Callie, I know the surgery is scary," I say, in the tone of trying to calm someone down, which seems only to infuriate her more. "It's a big deal. A very big deal. I'll be the first to admit that. But I'll be with you every step of the way, I promise—"

"You're not the one who will be in ICU for over a week," she flings at me. "Or will lose all flexibility in your lower back. Forget touching my toes ever again, never mind doing track. You know I won't be able to fulfill your track dreams, right?"

I flinch, because that is a low blow. I had to quit track junior year when I became pregnant, not that Callie knows that part of it. She just knows I had to quit, but I am *not* living some long-forgotten sports dreams through her. I know I'm not. "This is not about me," I tell her. "And loss of flexibility is not guaranteed—" I begin, because limitations to flexibility are definitely varied.

"Or has to be on bedrest for over a month," she steamrolls over me. "Or has a huge scar down my *entire* back."

I take a steadying breath. "Like I said, I know it's hard—"

"But you don't," she exclaims brokenly. "Because you've never had the symptoms, you've never had the surgery, and you never will."

There's not much I can say to that. I end up simply holding my hands out in mute appeal. "Callie," I insist finally, my voice breaking, "I love you. I only want to help you—"

"Then here's an idea," she rages at me. "*Back off!*" And then she storms into our shared bedroom, separated only by a flimsy divider, slamming the door behind her.

Slowly, I lower my arms. We've never fought like that before, and it's shaken me to my core. I don't want to fight with Callie, but she still needs this surgery.

And I am going to say yes to a discussion with A and M from Connecticut, because right now they feel like my—and Callie's—only hope.

ELEVEN

ASHLEY

"Is the sound on?"

My voice comes out high and squeaky with nerves as I tuck my hair behind my ears for the third time. Next to me, Mark smooths a hand over the top of his head, frowning at the laptop screen in front of us.

"I think it's connecting..." He sounds nervous, too.

It's been over a week since I spoke to him about Dani from California. I think he was surprised I was a step ahead of him on this *journey*, but he got on board quickly enough. We looked at Dani's profile together, poring over every detail.

"She doesn't offer that much information," Mark ventured cautiously.

"Short and to the point. That's why I like her."

"I can see that," he replied slowly. He took off his glasses and rubbed the bridge of his nose. "But we want to have a *relationship* with her, Ash. I want her to be friendly with us. Warm."

I had thought about this whole relationship aspect quite a lot over the last few weeks. "We do," I told him, "but only to a point. I mean..." I hesitated, because, the truth was, we hadn't talked about the "after" all that much, beyond us heading off into the sunset with a little blanket-wrapped bundle. "Not after, right? After the birth. I don't really want the surrogate being part of our lives then." It sounded so cold when I said it like that, but I meant it. I was already feeling enough self-doubt about not being able to carry a child. I didn't need the woman who had popping up in our lives every so often, reminding me of my own deficiencies.

Mark was silent for a long moment. I was pretty sure I knew what he was thinking—that he'd wanted to have some relationship with his biological parents and had never had the opportunity, and he wouldn't want the same for our child. It was part of the reason why he hadn't wanted to go the anonymous egg donor route, although I was coming to realize—too late—that I would have preferred that. It's easier to compete with some faceless entity rather than the strong, beautiful woman staring at us so directly from the computer screen. But this wasn't, of course, meant to be about competition.

"Okay," Mark said at last, like a concession. "I can see that. But she's not just a... a vessel, Ashley. She's a person who is doing us a huge service—"

"Which we'll be paying her for handsomely," I replied, a little too sharply.

"Okay," Mark finally said, relenting. "I get where you're coming from. I just want to make sure this works for everyone— you, me, *and* the surrogate... whoever she is."

So Andrea had sent our profile to Dani, and then come back with the surprising news that she'd already given up a child for adoption, when she was only sixteen years old. We'd read her own words, how she'd been so young at the time and was now caring for her younger sister. It made me like her more—if like is even the right word—but Mark was silent, absorbing this new information. I know he struggles with the whole concept of adoption, a mother who chooses to give up her child the way his had. But, in the end, although still a little reluctant, he saw it as I did, that this could be a good thing, because it meant we were less likely to have the emotional complications that traditional surrogacy could entail.

And so now we are here, about to connect with Dani and Heather, our intermediary who is meant to introduce us and smooth the whole process. The screen flickers and then Heather's kindly face comes on the screen—round, smiling, framed by a gray bob.

"Ashley, Mark," she greets us. "So good to see you. I just wanted to spend a few moments with you before I introduce Dani, to make sure you're both aware of what to expect."

"I think we are," Mark replies in a jovial tone. He's been ready to take the next step in this so-called journey for a while. "This is just an introductory get-to-know-you chat, right?"

"Right." Heather's smile is meant to be reassuring, but I'm already feeling way too nervous, my stomach writhing, my heart racing. I clasp my hands tightly together in my lap, fix my smile on Heather. "Right now, you just want to get to know one another. It should be comfortable, relaxed. There's no need to talk about finances or terms, as those things will come up in the contract negotiations, between your legal representatives."

It's hard to be relaxed, I reflect, when you know the next step involves lawyers.

"Of course, Dani might have some questions for you," Heather continues, and Mark nods while I tense up even more. "She's given you a lot of information about her preferences, but obviously she doesn't know yours yet, in terms of contact during the pregnancy, embryo transfers, and so forth. I advise you to be as upfront and honest as you can be about what you envision, but also be willing to be flexible. Ultimately, we want this to work out for everyone involved."

Heather gives us a smile which feels both reassuring and perfunctory, but maybe that's just because I'm starting to freak out. So much is riding on this one conversation, and I still don't know how I feel about it. My emotions have been flip-flopping like a dying fish, from hope and excitement to trepidation and even dread.

"Are we all ready?" Heather chirps, and Mark nods, while I murmur something incoherent.

A second later, Dani is on the screen. She looks just like her photo—blond and blue-eyed, strong-boned, unsmiling, although when she sees us, she manages a little wave, the corners of her mouth flicking upward for a millisecond.

"Hi..." She trails off, and I realize she doesn't know our names, because in our profiles we were just A and M.

"Hi, Dani," Mark says before I can think to speak. "I'm Mark, and this is my wife Ashley. We're so pleased to meet you." He gives her a warm smile, seeming relaxed, while my shoulders are steadily inching further toward my ears.

"Hi, Dani," I manage in little more than a whisper. I need to get a grip, but everything about this situation is overwhelming me. To be fair, Dani looks a little overwhelmed too. Her gaze flicks between Mark and me as she tries again for a smile.

"So, how are you?" she asks uncertainly, and then lets out a little, apologetic laugh. "Sorry, I don't really know what the protocol is here. Are we just supposed to get to know one another?"

"That's exactly right, Dani," Heather interjects. "And I'm here to help in any way, or just be quiet if that works better." She lets out a light laugh, but I can't help but feel that she's policing us. Making sure neither Mark and me nor Dani do something that upsets the delicate, tenuous balance we're all trying to maintain.

"Okay... well..." Dani's eyes widen as she glimpses my cast. "Oh, Ashley, what happened to your arm?" she exclaims.

"I was in a car accident. Not my fault," I add quickly, in case she's worried I am a dangerous driver. "I was sideswiped while coming out of a bar." Belatedly, I realize that that sounds even worse. "It was evening," I explain hurriedly. "I was meeting a friend..." I sense Mark's tension, and I know I'm blowing it. "Sorry," I tell Dani with a shamefaced smile. "I'm so nervous that I'm babbling."

"It's okay," Dani says, smiling genuinely for the first time since we got on this call. "I'm nervous, too."

"Maybe, Dani," Heather interjects once more, "you could tell Ashley and Mark about what motivated your decision to become a surrogate?"

This suggestion has the effect of pouring cold water all over us. I know she means well, but I wish Heather would just fade into the background and let us stumble through this in a way that feels more natural. Dani is looking ill at ease again, and I have the urge to comfort her, but I'm not sure how.

"Whatever you feel comfortable sharing," I blurt, and Dani gives me what I hope is a grateful look.

"Well, I suppose there are two reasons," she says slowly, choosing her words with care, her gaze fixed somewhere between Mark and me, so she isn't meeting either of our eyes. "I'll be honest with you, the first consideration was financial. As you probably read in my profile, I have a younger sister I take care of, and she needs a spinal surgery that isn't covered by my health insurance. So finding the means to finance that is very important to me." She meets our gazes directly, first mine, then Mark's, as if to challenge us.

"I'm sorry to hear about your sister," Mark murmurs. "And of course we understand the financial considerations." He pauses. "I hope, should we all be able to go forward, that she's able to have a successful surgery."

"Yes, I do, too." Dani takes a little breath before resuming. "The second reason was more personal and emotional. As you read on my updated profile, I gave a baby up for adoption twelve years ago. I was sixteen." She pauses and we both wait for her to continue; I have no idea how to respond, how she *wants* us to respond. "Anyway," she adds, "that experience was very... challenging. I pretty much disassociated myself from it all during the pregnancy and birth, and even for a long time after. And I realized that I wanted to do things differently, redeem that situation, in a way, if that makes sense." She gives an apologetic grimace, her gaze sliding away.

A silence falls as both Mark and I struggle to respond in a way that will be helpful for Dani. I feel desperately sorry for her, but I also can't suppress a treacherous little flicker of concern, because don't we want her to *dissociate* from this pregnancy too, at least in a way? And what does she mean, *redeem*?

"It might be helpful to remember," Heather says into the silence, "that intended parents and surrogates are required to go through several sessions of counseling during the process."

Dani looks startled, and then slightly annoyed, and I can't blame her. Heather has an unfortunate way of seriously killing the mood.

"I'm sorry to hear about that experience," Mark finally tells her, his tone somber. "As you read on our profile, I'm adopted myself, so we're coming from the other side of the equation, as it were, but no matter what, there is a brokenness at the heart of adoption that can't be fixed." He pauses while Dani regards him warily, no doubt wondering where he's going with this. I am, too. "But I think broken situations, like you said, can be redeemed. They might still have the cracks, but like *kintsugi*—if you know it—the brokenness can become beautiful."

It's a heartfelt sentiment, and not the first time he's mentioned *kintsugi* to me, the Japanese pottery that fills the cracks of broken bowls with powdered gold. I find myself thinking of my own brokenness—my relationship with my mother is fractured and always has been. If that can't be fixed, can it become beautiful? I struggle to see how.

"I hope you're right," Dani says after a moment. "I want this pregnancy—should we all go forward—to be a positive experience for everyone."

"Maybe this is a good time for you each to talk about your expectations," Heather suggests. Although no one responds, it feels like we all inwardly groan. This conversation really would go better, I think, without her well-meaning prompts.

"Okay," Dani says finally. "Ashley, Mark… what are your expectations? How involved do you want to be in terms of the pregnancy?"

For a second, we are silent, because we haven't discussed this very much. Our conversations around surrogacy have been so tense that we've never attempted to tackle the nitty-gritty details, but obviously we should have, and before this conversation.

"I think," Mark finally answers, glancing at me for confirmation that I can't give because I have no idea what he's going to say, "we'd like to be as involved as we can be and that you're comfortable with, whatever that looks like."

Which is kind of a non-answer, but Dani nods and smiles, so I guess it was the right one. "So, what would that look like for you?" she asks, batting it right back at him.

"Well, regular updates on your health and how the baby is doing," Mark muses cheerfully. "And also updates after hospital appointments, obviously… We'd love to see the scans of the ultrasounds, and I think we both are hoping to find out if the baby is a boy or a girl."

Are we? It's something we haven't yet discussed. I stay silent, even as I am conscious that I should be the one saying these things. *I*, as the mother, should be the one saying how involved we want to be, talking about catching up with Dani about her morning sickness or her swollen ankles, or whatever it is pregnant women suffer from, because, the truth is, I don't even know, and I never will.

I rise suddenly from the sofa, surprising everyone, including me. "Sorry," I murmur. "I just need a drink of water."

I leave the room quickly, knowing it's a terrible thing to do, but unable to keep myself from it. My stomach and mind are both churning, and I feel sick. I don't even know why.

I go to the kitchen and get a glass of water from the sink and force myself to take several sips. I stare out at our little scrap of manicured lawn, the one maple tree's leaves just starting to turn scarlet. It's nearing the end of September, and Mark wanted to be in the pregnant part of this journey by Christmas. Looks like we just might make that timeline, after all.

"Ash?"

I turn to see him standing in the doorway. "Is the call over?" I ask in surprise.

"No... Dani and Heather are both waiting. I was just worried about you, the way you left so suddenly."

"I'm fine." I'm irritated that he made it more of a big deal than it needed to be. "I just wanted some water."

"Is this hard for you?" he asks quietly and, to my annoyance, tears prick my eyes.

I blink them back quickly. "Let's get back to Dani," I say before I finish my water and then brush past him. "We can talk later."

I take my seat on the sofa and force myself to meet Dani's concerned gaze as I try to smile.

"Sorry about that," I tell her, doing my best to ignore Heather's presence. "Sometimes the emotional aspect of this springs up on me and takes me by surprise. I only found out I'm not able to become pregnant three months ago."

"I'm sorry." Dani's words sound heartfelt, and I think she appreciated my candor.

I nod, and then, as Mark takes his seat next to me, Heather intervenes once more.

"So, in terms of expectations..." she resumes, clearly intent on moving the conversation forward. "It sounds like everyone is flexible and on the same page? What about the delivery room? Mark? Ashley? Do you have strong feelings about whether you want to be in the room or not?"

This time, I'm the one who jumps in first, before Mark can tell us what he's been thinking. "I think that's really up to Dani," I say firmly. "As it's obviously a vulnerable experience for you. I think you're the only one who can make that call."

I glance at Mark and see what I fear is an uncharacteristic flash of irritation in his eyes. I suspect he's probably hoping to be in there for the whole thing, with a video camera and a pair of scissors to cut the cord himself, and why shouldn't he? This will be the once-in-a-lifetime experience he's been desperately hoping for. "Absolutely," he murmurs after a brief pause. "Dani, what are your thoughts?"

"I... I don't know," she admits. "I appreciate you letting me decide. Can we maybe table that one for later?"

"Of course," I say, as at the same time, Heather says warningly, "Yes, but that is something that should be decided sooner rather than later. Some couples don't like to go ahead if they can't be in the room."

Well, then, I think, *they sound like spoiled children.*

"We don't think like that," I tell her, an edge to my voice. "Just like marriage isn't only the wedding, having a child isn't only the delivery. Mark and I can miss it if needed, if that's what makes Dani the most comfortable."

She smiles at me, a grateful look of solidarity that is aimed solely at me. I smile back; I feel like I've made a friend.

We chat a little while longer about lighter things; Dani tells us about her doctorate in microbiology, with ninety-five percent of it going over our heads. Mark mentions his love of cooking; I say how much I like my job. When we finally end the call, with us all promising to be in touch soon, I realize I am utterly emotionally spent.

"I think that went okay," I venture after Mark has closed the laptop. I feel like we managed to recover the conversation after my abrupt departure. I'm still feeling fragile, but it's manageable. I realize I like Dani, and I'm glad that I do. I turn to smile at Mark, but he is staring into space, a slight frown marring his friendly features.

"Yes..." he agrees after a moment, sounding somewhat unconvinced.

"Do you have any concerns?" I ask.

"I don't know. She seemed a little... *distant*, maybe? A little cold?"

She did, but I didn't mind that.

"I think she was just nervous," I say.

He glances at me, almost in apology. "I was hoping to be in the delivery room. I don't want to shut that down completely."

"I didn't shut it down," I reply quickly. "But I do think it should be Dani's decision."

"I know." He stands up, moving restlessly around the room, like he can't sit still. I've never seen him this unsettled.

"Mark, what's going on?" I ask after a moment. "You don't seem happy." And I have come to rely, I realize, on his unflappable happiness. His calmness and steadiness root me, but right now he is neither, and it's making me feel even more anxious than I did before, when I left the call.

"I'm just realizing afresh how complicated this all is," he admits as he turns around to face me. "I think, until we spoke to her, Dani wasn't a real person to me. She was just... a concept." He grimaces, abashed. "I know that sounds pretty heartless. I talked the talk, I thought I was considering her as a person... but until I saw her on the screen..." He shakes his head, his gaze open and vulnerable. "She wasn't real to me. Not the way she should have been."

I stay silent, because I'm not sure how *real* I want Dani to be to me, never mind Mark.

"But you were thinking about her, Ash," Mark continues. "I could tell you were concerned for her feelings, for how this whole situation affected her. And it really humbled me."

I am both bemused and pleased, because, yes, I suppose I was thinking of Dani that way... and yet my feelings for her remain so ambivalent. Is it possible to be considerate and thoughtless at the same time?

"And then hearing about her first pregnancy, and her sister..." Mark sighs. "Well, it made me realize there are a lot of unforeseen elements and emotions, for everyone involved. Things will happen that we won't be able to predict. I don't want anyone to get hurt... least of all you."

It's been something I've been worried about all along—not that I want to say that now. "Do you want to reconsider gestational surrogacy?" I ask tentatively. I'm not sure how I want him to answer; I've settled on Dani, but if Mark said he did want to reconsider, I don't think I'd be disappointed. Would I?

"I don't know." He pauses, frowning. "No," he amends after a moment, and I feel a slight sinking inside that I know *is* disappointment, if only a treacherous little flicker. "It would take so long, otherwise. Years, sometimes. And intrauterine insemination has a higher success rate, and we wouldn't have to deal with the whole complication of extra embryos, the possibility of twins or triplets..." He nods, decided. "This is as close to the real thing as we can get. I think we should go forward."

I flinch, because I know he didn't say it to hurt me, but it still did. *The real thing*, except I am not involved, not in any way that really matters. But then I tell myself, the way I *can* be involved is as a support to Dani, the way Mark just said I was. I can be her advocate and cheerleader, a role I never expected to take but which I felt instinctively on that call, despite my own ambivalence. If Mark struggles to think of Dani as more than a concept, I want to be different. I want to think of her as a friend.

Even if it ends up causing more emotional complications than we ever expected.

TWELVE

DANI

I lie flat on my back, trying not to flinch at the feel of the cold speculum, icy against my inner thigh. I stare at the ceiling so hard, my eyes start to water as Dr. Freedman, the fertility specialist, murmurs, "This might be a little uncomfortable."

You think?

I don't answer, just brace myself for what's ahead—the insertion of a catheter replete with Mark Weir's sperm, which is frankly a pretty uncomfortable thought.

It's been two months since I had that surreal, awkward, and strangely encouraging conversation with the Weirs. Two days later, they told Creating Dreams that they would like to proceed, and I responded in kind.

I didn't even think about it, which, in retrospect, I think I probably should have, but at the time I felt as if I were on autopilot, numbly moving forward without question because Callie had woken up crying with pain the last two nights, and I just didn't feel like I had any other choice. I still don't, and I am coming to terms with that. I might feel like I was out of options, but as I told Ryan, this is still my choice... whether he likes it or not. And although he doesn't say as much, I'm pretty sure he doesn't.

"Dani? How are you feeling?" Dr. Freedman asks, her voice a soothing murmur.

"Okay." My voice is a breathless squeak, and I force myself to take a slow, careful breath.

"Just let me know if, at any time, you feel uncomfortable."

"Okay," I say again, my voice dropping an octave as I close my eyes. I don't want to be here, don't want to be tensing my whole body as I try to relax and keep staring at the ceiling.

Yesterday, Mark Weir flew into San Diego to give his sperm toward this endeavor—a process I really do not want to dwell on. It was either that or have me go to Connecticut for the procedure, and I told them flat out that with Callie to take care of, I couldn't consider leaving San Diego. To their credit, they were very understanding, as they have been all along.

In fact, Mark asked if we could meet while he's here, but I demurred. I just wasn't ready, no matter what I might have said on our call, and I really wasn't comfortable meeting him on his own; Ashley didn't accompany him, apparently because she had to work, and it felt too weird to meet the father of this child—*not* my child, I'm trying not to think like that—without his wife.

In the two months since we agreed to go forward, Ashley has been sending me texts every so often. She asked if she could first, sounding so hesitant and hopeful that I said yes, and since then she's sent them two or three times a week, nothing too pushy or personal, just "thinking of you" or "hope you have a good day," as well as the occasional inspirational meme or funny GIF, a method of communication she seems particularly fond of. They're kindly meant, I know they are, and if they put me on edge a little that's totally my own fault. She seems like a genuinely nice woman, and I think she's concerned for me, which I truly do appreciate. It's just... the situation is so *weird*.

In any case, I've told myself that there's no point creating some sort of bond until there is something to bond over—that is, a baby. And even then, I'm not sure how much of a bond I want to make, with either Ashley or Mark, but I keep those thoughts to myself.

"Okay, this might feel like a pinch," Dr. Freedman warns, and I suck in another breath, because *pinch* is a little bit of an understatement. I keep my eyes closed as she talks me through the procedure. I've been tracking my cycle for the last four weeks, and today is the optimum time for fertility. In ten days, I will be back here for a blood test to find out if I'm pregnant.

It wasn't until after I agreed that I learned that IUI— intrauterine insemination—has only a ten percent success rate. How many times am I going to have to do this? Initially, according to the contract we all signed three weeks ago, it will be three. The lawyer representing me and assigned by the agency hammered out all the details with Mark and Ashley's lawyer—the number of transfers, their involvement in the potential pregnancy, and most importantly, the compensation. Sixty-five thousand dollars, plus all medical and accompanying expenses—I received five thousand dollars upon signing the contract and another five thousand today. After that, I'll be paid a little over six thousand dollars monthly, plus expenses.

This really *is* worth it, I tell myself.

"All right, Dani," Dr Freedman says as she steps away from the examination table. "We're all done."

It took maybe three minutes, and yet has the potential to completely transform my life—as well as Mark and Ashley's.

"You'll need to lie flat for about thirty minutes," she tells me. "Just to make sure everything stays where's it's meant to. I hope that's okay. I'll dim the lights and put some music on, so you can just try to relax."

As if.

I nod jerkily, wishing I didn't feel so emotional about this. I've been numb, more or less, since this whole process began, but every once in a while the enormity of what I'm doing comes up and grabs me by the throat. This is one of those times.

Dr. Freedman dims the lights and steps out of the room just as some soothing music—a pan flute, it sounds like—floats through the speakers. I close my eyes. Breathe. Try not to think, because what I've come to realize is the way to get through this is not to probe too deeply into what's going on in my subconscious, how the thought of being pregnant again is churning up all sorts of memories and feelings. Last week, Andrea reminded me that I have to have counseling at some point, but right now I feel like putting that off for as long as possible.

Since Ashley and Mark and I all agreed to go ahead, I haven't really talked about this whole thing with anyone. Ryan agreed to my suggestion not to discuss it until it was a reality— after all, I'd argued, I didn't even know if I'd be able to become pregnant, and there was no point borrowing trouble, or really, anxiety, especially when we'd finally reached a thankfully even keel in our relationship. It wasn't as much of a battle as I had expected; I think he wanted a break from the stress of it all, too.

As for Callie... she refuses to talk about it because she thinks it's "totally gross," and I'm worried she's still angry with me for proceeding with it all, on her behalf, especially when she didn't ask me to.

Anna is completely mystified by my decision, half-jokingly insisting that OnlyFans would have been a better bet, and, according to her, a lot more enjoyable.

My mother texted me to say she was offering her support, whatever that meant. Not much, judging by the lack of contact we've had since then, although that might be as much my fault as hers. She's texted me and I didn't reply.

But, right now, I don't know what to think about anyone's response, or the fact that I'm even here in the first place. I don't want to think at all. And so I keep my eyes closed and breathe in and out, and, amazingly, maybe because I'm so strung out and exhausted, I fall asleep.

When Dr. Freedman comes in, I am startled awake, and she laughs softly, almost in approval.

"Glad you were able to relax," she tells me. "You're free to go now, unless you have any questions?"

I shake my head, and she smiles.

"Great, then we'll see you back here in ten days for a pregnancy test."

She leaves again to let me change out of my hospital gown—does anything make you feel as vulnerable and exposed as that flimsy garment?

I get up slowly, moving around gingerly, like I'm afraid something will fall out of me. When I looked online, I saw that it only takes a few hours for the sperm and egg to meet, and a few days for the fertilized egg to implant in the uterus. It all seems so miraculous and strange, and it might be happening right now, inside *my* body, which frankly makes me feel queasy rather than amazed.

Once I'm dressed, I do my best to get back into real-life mode—I'm teaching a class later this afternoon, and meeting with my supervisor afterwards. I don't have time to dwell on the pregnancy possibilities, the surrogacy what-ifs. I have a life to live—and with ten grand in my bank account, I can call the orthopedic surgeon to discuss scheduling Callie's surgery. Open enrollment for changing my health insurance starts this month, and I've already made enquiries.

I am striding out of the waiting room, oblivious to anyone in there, when, to my surprise, I hear a hesitant voice call my name.

"Dani...?"

I stop, turn, and then stare in complete shock at the man rising rather sheepishly from an armchair, dressed in khakis and a navy polo shirt. It's Mark Weir.

"What..." I shake my head, unable to grasp the fact that he's here, right in front of me. I knew he was in San Diego, of course, but I never expected him to find me. Hunt me down, because right now that's what it feels like, although I'm pretty sure he didn't mean it that way.

He's about an inch shorter than me, balding, round-cheeked, shoulders slightly slumped, smiling in a way like he definitely knows he's in the wrong. In any other context, I think I would like him, assume he's a friendly, non-assuming kind of person, but right now I feel only shock—as well as a growing anger.

"I'm sorry. I really didn't mean to ambush you like this," he says, which is laughable because that is exactly what he has done. He knew the time of the appointment, as he and Ashley are privy to all my medical details that pertain to surrogacy, but I *told* him I didn't want to meet.

I don't respond, because I don't trust myself to say something civil. I also don't want to damage our relationship before it's even begun, but *seriously*? Is this the kind of thing I will have to expect if it turns out I am carrying his baby—ambushes in medical clinics, invading my personal space, my privacy, my *life*?

"I really am sorry," he says quietly, his soft brown eyes tracking my expression as he gauges my mood. Is he wondering if he's violating some clause of our contract? Maybe he has, but it's not like I could back out at this point, even if I wanted to. "I can see this was a bad idea," he continues. "A really bad idea." He tries for a laugh and doesn't quite manage it. "I didn't mean to alarm you or invade your... your privacy. I just... I just wanted to be a part of today."

"You have been a part of it," I manage to say stiffly, hating that I have to point it out. "Obviously."

He blushes, which perversely makes me soften. "I meant personally," he says. He looks so dejected, that against my will, as well as my better judgment, I feel a small stirring of pity. He shakes his head, seeming to come out of his sorrowful stupor. "I'm sorry. This was such a mistake. I'll go." He half-turns, then stops. "Unless you need a ride somewhere...?" He looks so hopeful now that I almost laugh.

"Thanks," I tell him shortly, "but I brought my car."

"Okay." He nods, clearly struggling not to look glum. "Well, then... I guess... we'll... we'll talk to you soon." He waves uncertainly and then walks out of the doctor's office, taking care to hold the door open for me after him.

I murmur my thanks, feeling like this whole episode has been utterly surreal. Mark is heading toward his car, which is just a few away from mine. He came all the way to California from Connecticut for a very quick trip, I remind myself, already starting to feel guilty. The least I can do is be a little bit nice.

"Look," I call over to him, trying to keep from sounding too reluctant. "I'm sorry. You took me by surprise. But... if you wanted to get a coffee or something..." I peter out because I'm not sure how much I actually mean it.

Mark is already turning around, his face alight as he grins at me. "That would be wonderful," he replies, "but only if you're sure...?"

I'm *not* sure, but I nod anyway. "Yeah, there's a place near here I know, down in the Village. You can follow me in your car."

I drive slowly to La Jolla's downtown, known as the Village. A former artists' colony right on the beach, it's a cute place with stunning scenery and exorbitant real estate prices. Lilli's is an Italian bakery and coffee shop right in its heart. The pastries are usually too expensive for me to afford, but I figure Mark is paying this time.

Sure enough, as we enter the espresso-scented café, he nods toward the glass display case filled with delectable-looking pastries. "What can I get you, Dani?"

I peruse the offerings before selecting a slice of sbrisolona, or crumble cake, and a cappuccino, and then tell him I'll find a table.

I pick one in the back, grateful to sink down into my seat and have a few minutes of solitude to gather my thoughts—and my composure. Having Mark here has made everything a lot more *real*. In ten days' time, he and Ashley might very well become a huge part of my life. I wish, when we were first talking, I'd considered what that might mean, but I hadn't wanted to jeopardize anything. Now I'm not so sure.

"Here we are," Mark says cheerfully as he sets a tray down on the table. "Cappuccino and cake for you, espresso for me." He smiles at me, looking so lighthearted, and yet I see an anxiety in his eyes. This has to be just as stressful, if not more so, for him than it is for me. I feel another flicker of sympathy, but not much more than that.

"How did today go?" he asks as he sits down, and I can't help but flinch.

I do not want to get into that with him, or anyone, just yet. "Fine," I say briefly, and stab my cake with my fork.

"Sorry. I don't mean to be..." He laughs, shakes his head, and starts again. "This feels like a minefield. I don't know what to say, or really, how to act. I hope you know that Ashley and I just want to support you in whatever way we can."

"Yes, I know," I reply as graciously as I can. "Thank you. This is bound to be difficult for all of us. The agency warns you about it, but it's different when you're actually going through it."

"Yes..." He takes a sip of his espresso before putting the little cup down. "But we can make this work, can't we, Dani?"

The way he says my name, so deliberately, puts my teeth on edge, although I tell myself it shouldn't. I'm being way too sensitive. He's trying to be nice.

"I think so," I reply as I take a sip of coffee. "I suppose the important thing is that we just need to be honest with one another."

"Yes, absolutely." He nods his head several times before lapsing into a silence.

I feel like he has something more he would like to say, and so I wait, trying not to tense as I imagine what it might be.

"Ashley and I were wondering, were things to be... successful... this time," he says finally, "if we might come out for a visit. We'd love to spend some time with you, as well as Callie, and just... be part of this experience in whatever way you felt comfortable with. In time, obviously, when the pregnancy is established..." He trails off, waiting hopefully for my response.

I let out a shaky laugh, trying to lighten the mood, because I am blindsided by his request, even though I know I shouldn't be. "I don't even know if I'm pregnant yet. The procedure only has a ten percent success rate, you know."

He gives a small smile of acknowledgment. "Yes, I know." I have the sense that he has researched everything about it, probably way more than I have. "I just meant if and when, you know, *hopefully*. That's something we'd like to do."

"Of course." I take a sip of coffee to stall for time, because my visceral reaction is absolutely not. Meet *Callie*? No way. And yet... I'd intimated that I was willing to have as much contact as they wanted, pretty much, in my profile. It's not fair for me to go back on it now, and I don't want to jeopardize anything, although maybe it's already too late for that. It's too late for a lot of things.

And, if I'm honest, the very fact that Mark is here, looking so eager but also with a steely determination in his gaze, is more than a little worrisome. What am I letting myself in for, if I agree?

"I can see how a visit might work," I say carefully. "But I think it would be wise for all of us to take it one step at a time."

After the tiniest hesitation, Mark nods. "Of course. I understand completely. I just wanted to float the idea, so you have time to think about it."

"Thank you."

An uneasy silence falls upon us, and I have no appetite for my sbrisolona, delicious as it is.

"I imagine this brings up a lot of feelings for you," Mark remarks after a moment. "As it has for me." I can't think how to reply, and he continues stiltedly, "I don't know anything about my biological parents, and I have no way to find out. It's different these days, usually, with adoptions much more open. But I didn't have that choice."

I feel my face flush, because he almost sounds as if he knows that my baby's adoption was just as closed as his sounds like it was. Maybe he'll judge me for it.

"I can't help but wonder," he continues, "what they might have been like. Did my mother wish she could keep me? Did she try to? I have no idea."

I swallow dryly. "What were your adoptive parents like?" I ask.

"They were loving," Mark says after a moment. "Kind. A little anxious, like they didn't quite trust the whole process, almost as if they were always afraid something would go wrong. And, to be fair, I did go through a period of rebellion in my teenaged years—the usual stuff, nothing too serious, but I was angry at them. It's fairly natural, I think, for adopted kids to go through something like that, especially in adolescence."

Is that what my child is doing, or will do when they become a teenager in just a year's time? I don't even like to think of him or her as my child, because they *aren't*. And why is Mark telling me this? Is he trying to make me feel guilty? I have enough to deal with, without adding yet more guilt to the potent mix.

"Anyway," he finishes, "I thought maybe you were having similar thoughts, from the other angle."

"Well, naturally it brings up some memories," I say after a pause, hoping we can leave it at that.

"In our conversation on Zoom, you mentioned that this baby—the surrogacy, I mean—might redeem your previous pregnancy. The adoption." He leans forward, his gaze intent. "What did you mean by that?"

Clearly he doesn't shy away from asking the emotional questions or waiting intently for the answers. I can't prevaricate, as much as I want to. "Just... just that the last time, it was... traumatic," I say. I swallow, feel the thickening in my throat, and realize, alarmingly, how close I am to tears. "I was sixteen," I force out. "The... father—if I can even call him that—wasn't even my boyfriend. I'd never had a boyfriend. He was a guy I met at a party, I'd drunk a little too much..." I have to close my eyes as the memories assail me—the sugary taste of too many rum and cokes, the scratchy nub of the rec room carpet on my back. My head spinning and spinning.

"Dani, that sounds like a very difficult and coercive situation. I'm so sorry." Mark touches my hand very gently. My eyes fly open.

"No, it wasn't like that," I protest, more out of instinct. "I mean... I remember everything that happened. And I consented to it all." I was ridiculously pleased that one of the cool guys liked me. "But consent doesn't take into account just being young and naïve and stupid," I finish as I manage a wobbly smile. "We met up a few times after that, secretly. I thought it was romantic, but it was actually because he didn't want anyone knowing we were doing anything. I was kind of a geek in high school, at least to that kind of guy. Brainy and on the track team, but socially sort of awkward."

I shake my head, wanting to stem this flood of bitter memories. Why did I blurt this all out to Mark? And yet he is looking at me with so much sympathy, almost like a dad might... except, of course, my dad *didn't*. My dad was horrified, deeply disappointed, and scathing all at once. I'd been a daddy's girl, until I very suddenly and comprehensively wasn't, ever again.

"I'm so sorry," he murmurs, and I feel like I need to explain more.

"What I meant about redeeming that experience was," I tell him, "that I didn't even realize I was pregnant until I was nearly five months. I basically acted like it was happening to someone else, and I... I don't want to be like that this time around." How I want to be, I can't say. All I know is that some part of me believes in the impossible mathematical equation that one plus one can equal zero. If I give this baby away, deliberately and for Callie's sake, it makes up for last time. It cancels it out. I know it doesn't, but somehow, in my head, in my heart, it *does*. And now I find I can't say anything more, because I'm too close to tears.

Mark seems to understand, though, because he just squeezes my hand as I sniff. He reaches into his pocket with his other hand and pulls out a starched handkerchief, which he hands to me.

"Thanks," I mumble as I wipe my eyes and Mark murmurs something soothing. I look up, the handkerchief scrunched in my hand, to give Mark a watery smile, only to freeze when I see who is coming through the front door, his shocked gaze trained right on me.

Ryan.

THIRTEEN

ASHLEY

I'm having dinner with Claire in Blue Back Square in West Hartford when Mark's text comes through, with an accompanying selfie. For a second, the image doesn't compute. It's Mark, grinning from ear to ear, his arm around a tall, blond woman next to him whose wide smile still doesn't quite reach her eyes.

Dani.

Shock trickles through me, icy and unpleasant. My husband has his arm around the mother of his potential child, and he didn't even tell me it was happening. They weren't supposed to meet. They weren't supposed even to *see* each other. Why are they pal-ing around together, clowning for the camera, the ocean glinting in the background? My stomach churns and, for a second, I think I might be sick.

"Anything interesting?" Claire asks as I slide my phone into my purse, my fingers trembling as they let go of it.

"Just a text from Mark." Amazingly, my voice sounds calm, even dismissive, although inwardly I feel completely wrecked. "He flies home tomorrow." I've kept Claire informed of this whole surrogacy process; she's my best friend, after all, and also she asked. I'm not sure if I would have told her much other-

wise; as it is, I tend not to go into details, and I don't want
to now.

"So it all worked?" she asks as she takes a sip of her gin and
tonic.

I shrug as I reach for my own drink, needing the hit. "Well,
we won't know if it *worked* for ten days, when she has the blood
test."

"The long wait," Claire states dramatically, rolling her eyes
so I can't tell if she thinks it's over-the-top or she can empathize.
"Or so I've heard."

"Yes." I've read about the "TWW" on the surrogacy boards
—the two-week wait, with the extra four days just to be sure.
I've cringed a little at some of the posts: *Help!! How can I get
through the next two weeks without eating my body weight in
sugar?! Am so stressed & anxious... any tips SO appreciated...*

But, actually, I'm content to wait. I know if Dani is pregnant
we will be flung headlong into this *journey* that I still feel
ambivalent about, if I'm honest. I try not to feel that way, and
I've been as enthusiastic and supportive as I know how to be—to
Mark as well as to Dani, always willing to sit down in front of
the laptop for yet more research or send her an inspirational
meme, which feels like a lazy form of communication, but at
least it lets her know I'm thinking about her, which I am. I think
more about Dani, weirdly, than I do about this potential baby.

But when I picture that selfie of Mark and Dani, I can't help
wonder what the hell any of us is doing. Why did he meet her
without telling me? Did it even cross his mind how much of a
betrayal that would feel like?

"Hmm," Claire muses after a moment as she narrows her
eyes. "I'll be honest, Ash, you don't really sound all that
enthused." She cocks her head. "Is it the whole biological thing
still?"

The whole *biological* thing.

"Kind of." I haven't told Claire that Dani will be this baby's biological mother, rather than a comfortingly anonymous egg donor. I haven't told her, or anyone, just how vulnerable that makes me feel.

"Is it something else?" she presses, and, deciding I need to level with my best friend, I slide my phone out of my purse, swipe to show the selfie, and then wordlessly hand it to her.

She glances down at the photo, her eyes widening. "*That's your surrogate?*"

"Yes."

Claire shakes her head slowly. "I've got to say it, she's... kind of a bombshell."

"I know," I agree, trying to sound matter-of-fact but coming across as miserable instead. Seeing them there together like that... it rocked me in a way I really didn't expect—or like. "Her looks didn't bother me," I tell Claire, "until Mark just texted now to say he went and *met* with her without even telling me." I practically spit the words, the hurt and anger and fear all reverberating through me, even stronger than before.

"He looks a little more into the meeting than she does," Claire remarks with a wry frown, and I shake my head, doing my best to swallow down my churning emotions.

"You know what?" I tell her. "That doesn't make me feel better."

Claire hands back the phone. "You don't need to feel threatened, though," she insists. "Mark adores you, Ashley. And I know it's his baby biologically—or will be if it happens—but it's not like they're having a kid *together*."

"Actually, they are." Claire's eyes widen and I clarify hastily, "I mean, not... you know, not in the natural way, obviously. But Dani will be the biological mother. We went for traditional surrogacy, where the surrogate uses her own egg."

Claire goggles at me for a second and I reach for my drink, take a long, burning swallow. "*Why?*" she asks, sounding genuinely and understandably flummoxed, and so I explain, wearily, about all the sensible reasons why—cheaper, easier, better success rate, simpler overall...

Why do all these reasons sound so hollow right now? So... *absurd*? And why was my husband's arm around Dani's shoulder?

"And did you know this when he chose her?" Claire asks. She still sounds mystified.

"Yes, and actually *I* chose her. I mean, I found her profile first." I sound defiant, almost proud, and Claire notices.

"*You* chose her? Why? I mean... what stood out to you?" She sounds like she doesn't understand why I wouldn't choose a dumpy-looking surrogate who would never be a threat to my self-confidence or my marriage, and in this moment, I don't understand it, either.

"I actually liked that she looked nothing like me," I try to explain. "I didn't want to... to deceive myself, I guess, in thinking that this baby is going to look anything like me. And I liked—well, *like*—a lot of things about Dani." My voice rises as I try to make Claire understand, as well as myself. "I mean, besides her being beautiful. She's forthright, smart, dedicated to her sister, she seemed to get the need for a little distance..." Or so I thought. But what was she doing, meeting Mark? "There's a lot to like," I finish a little lamely. *Just not her cozying up to my husband,* I can't help but think. To be fair, I have a feeling that might have more to do with Mark than Dani... but where does that leave me?

Claire is silent for a moment.

"I'm going to be honest with you, Ash," she says finally, and I stiffen, my glass halfway to my lips, because her tone is so serious. "This kind of sounds like self-sabotage."

"*What*—"

"Choosing a knockout woman who looks nothing like you —not that you aren't beautiful, because you *are*," she continues quickly, "but you don't look like you could grace the cover of

Sports Illustrated Swimsuit Edition, if you know what I mean?" She gives a grimace of apology as I try not to feel stung.

"Yes," I concede. "I know." Dani could be on that kind of cover, easily.

Claire leans forward, her eyes alight with conviction. "Ash... it's just, you've seemed like you're not sure about any of this from the beginning. And agreeing to the traditional surrogacy with *that* woman"—she points to my phone—"it's like you're making it harder for yourself. Almost like you're setting yourself up to... not *fail*, that's not what this is about, but... to be hurt. Almost like you want to be, like that's the only acceptable outcome."

"I'm not some kind of masochist," I reply, trying to laugh, but I can't quite manage it, because although Claire is a little too earnest in her psychoanalysis, I'm afraid it does hold a grain of truth, if I can bear to sift through it all. Right now, I'm not sure I can.

"Mark wasn't supposed to meet up with her?" she asks.

"I think he might have wanted to, but we agreed we would wait until we could meet her together, once she was actually pregnant." I'd been the one to suggest that we wait, after I'd told Mark I couldn't take four days off work to sit in a hotel room while he went to the clinic to jerk off into a vial.

Mark had suggested, timidly, that I was allowed to be in the room with him, a prospect that filled me with something close to revulsion, although I did my best to hide it.

"I'm not sure that's a good idea," I told him as diplomatically as I could. "It would just feel kind of... weird."

He grimaced in understanding apology as he tried to explain, "I know it sounds strange, but... I just meant, I want you to be a part of this, Ash—"

But I'm not. I kept myself from saying it out loud that time, but I told him I couldn't take the time off, and he'd have to manage without me, which he apparently did, with flying colors.

"So what did that text say?" Claire asks. "Did he explain why he saw her?"

"It just said, 'Look who I ran into,'" I reply, the words like ashes in my mouth.

Claire tuts. "*Ran into*? Really?"

"I know." He must have found her at the clinic. Dani was getting the procedure done this afternoon; did Mark skulk around, waiting for her outside? How did she feel about that? Not so bad, it seemed, that she wasn't willing to pose for a selfie.

Honestly, I don't know how *I* feel about any of this anymore. Part of me, whether I'm willing to admit it to anyone or not, hopes that Dani *isn't* pregnant. That we can move on from this... except, of course, I realize with a hollow feeling, we won't, because we'll try again next month, and then the month after that, and subject to further contract negotiations, the month after that, and that, and *that*, with Dani receiving five grand from us for every try.

It feels like it will never end, and maybe it won't, because the hope is that we'll ultimately have a baby, and parenthood *never* ends.

"I can understand why you feel a little threatened," Claire tells me, "but I wouldn't worry, honestly, Ash. Like I said, Mark adores you. And if he's seeming a little over-the-top about it all, well, it's just because he wants a baby so much, which, frankly, is pretty cute and endearing."

Yes, he does want a baby so much, I think but don't say. *Maybe even more than he wants me.*

Claire kindly changes the subject then, and we talk about work and her latest blind date and what we're doing for the holidays—Thanksgiving is next week, and my mother is joining us with her usual seeming reluctance. By eight o'clock, Claire and I are both ready to call it a night as we have work tomorrow.

I'm walking back to my car, through downtown Hartford, trying not to give in to the pull of anxiety I feel about everything, when I see it—a baby boutique, with tiny pink and blue hangers suspended from gold wire in the window, each holding the *sweetest* little outfit. My steps slow, almost of their own accord. I'm generally not one to coo over baby onesies or booties or what have you, but in this second, I am transfixed by the sight of a pink floral smocked romper suit. It's *tiny*, and it makes something in me ache, because instead of thinking about the logistics, I can just think about the possibility. A baby. A son or a daughter. *My* son or daughter.

I stare at the romper suit for a long moment, willing myself to see a lovely little baby girl wearing it—with Mark's dark hair and round cheeks, his soft brown eyes... Of course, this mythical little girl might look like Dani. She might be tall and blonde, and I'll have a lifetime of "she doesn't look anything like you" remarks to field—why didn't I think of that? Maybe I did, but in this moment none of it matters.

I press my hand against the glass, as if I could reach through it into some alternative universe where I had my own bump, my own dream of a baby that was really mine... except I'm not sure this is even about biology anymore. It's about something deeper, as well as darker, something that seethes within me but which I don't understand. Which I don't *want* to understand.

I let my hand fall away from the cold glass. Maybe I'll come back to this boutique when it's open, browse through the rails with all their tiny outfits and let myself get excited, just a little bit.

I recall Mark with his arm around Dani, and I think that, then again, maybe I won't.

But during my lunch hour the next day, sure enough, I find myself back at the boutique, drawn there reluctantly and yet with determination. Last night, Mark called me to check in, but I didn't answer the call, choosing to text him instead that I was already in bed, and that I'd talk to him in the morning. He texted me this morning to say he was getting on his flight, so the reality is we haven't spoken since he saw Dani, or since either of them went through their procedures. I tell myself it will be better anyway if we speak in person.

But now I'm walking into a boutique of baby clothes.

The store is empty, save for a smiling sales assistant who starts forward the minute I cross the threshold.

"May I help?" she asks. "Or are you just looking?"

"Just looking," I murmur. For one wild second, I consider telling her I'm pregnant, but I know how pathetic that will make me feel, and I'll end up slinking out of the store, shamed by my deception. I brush my fingers against a cream-colored dress, so tiny, with an intricate smocking of broderie anglaise on the front.

"Are you looking for a boy or a girl," the sales assistant asks, "or either?"

"Either," I tell her and then, almost defiantly confess, "We don't know what we're having yet."

"Oh, congrat—"

"We're using a surrogate."

"Oh." For a second, she looks startled, maybe even disapproving; with all the research I've done, I've come to realize there is something of a stigma surrounding surrogacy, maybe because of all the high-profile celebrity cases, or maybe just because people don't really understand it. Then the woman rearranges her expression into something more affirming. "That's wonderful. When is the baby due?"

There might be no baby. "In about six months," I reply blithely. I might not want to pretend I'm pregnant, but I'm willing to lie about this.

"So, a spring baby! We just got some of our new spring

collection in. There are some absolutely *darling* pieces..." She
ushers me toward the side of the store, where some springtime
dresses and romper suits in a variety of floral patterns and
pastels hang on tiny, satin-swathed hangers.

"Oh..." Despite myself, I am entranced. I want to buy just
one tiny, perfect dress. Or not even a dress, but a onesie. A little
pink onesie with a yellow tulip on the front.

"That's so sweet, isn't it?" she murmurs as I take the onesie
on its hanger from the rack, drape it over my arm.

"It really is," I say. "I know it's early, and we don't even
know if we're having a girl..."

"Oh, it's never too early," the woman assures me cheerfully.
"And if she's three months along, she's just finished the first
trimester, which is the riskiest time. Have you seen an ultrasound yet?"

I swallow. I'm being crazy. Dani probably isn't pregnant,
simply based on the success rates of the procedure. "Not yet," I
tell the sales assistant. "But soon."

She nods, and I glance down at the onesie. I still want to
buy it. I want to have some ownership in this whole experience,
that doesn't involve me just cheering Mark and Dani on,
watching them together from afar. Buying a onesie isn't much,
but it's *something*.

The sales assistant shifts from foot to foot, clearly waiting
for me to make a decision.

"I'll take it," I say, and she smiles.

"Wonderful. It really is so cute. And that's a newborn size,
which should be perfect."

I nod woodenly and follow her to the cash register set
behind a white lacquered counter in the middle of the boutique.
This isn't a big deal, I tell myself. It's just something I'm doing
for *me*, because I've felt so helpless and distant from it all. I
won't even show it to Mark; I'm not sure if he'd be touched or

think it was weird, but in any case I already know I'm going to keep it a secret. My secret.

"I can put the receipt in the bag...?" the sales assistant asks as she holds out her hand for the onesie that is still draped over my arm.

"Oh, sure..." I glance down at the onesie, blink it into focus, and then a sudden twist of horrified revulsion clenches my stomach, visceral and intense. I practically fling the garment onto the counter as I take a step away. I can't even look at the sales assistant; her sharply indrawn breath is bad enough.

"Miss...?" she queries, her voice caught between concern and suspicion. "Are you all right?"

"I'm sorry," I gasp, and then I run out of the store and keep running until I'm halfway down the block.

I wipe my face as I take several deep breaths to restore my sense of calm. I'm not crying, but almost. *What just happened to me?* That sense of... of *disgust* was so sudden and overwhelming; disgust not just for myself, but for this whole process. I can't even begin to explain it to myself, and clearly I can never go into that boutique ever again.

I shake my head, doing my best to push the whole episode to the far reaches of my mind. I want to try to forget it completely, act like it never happened. At the same time, I need to figure out what's going on with my emotions, which are clearly all over the place, and in ways I really don't understand. Maybe I should book that counseling sooner rather than later—a prospect which causes me even more anxiety.

I return to work without having even eaten lunch; my stomach is churning too much to manage anything. To my surprise, there's a Post-it on my computer screen from the assistant head of sales, Lila, asking to see me. Nerves flutter through me; is something wrong? I know I've been a little distracted lately, but I still think I do my job well, and in any case, I don't report directly to her. I take off the Post-it note and throw it into the trash, and then I go to the bathroom to comb my hair and splash water on my face, which is still looking flushed.

I study my reflection in the bathroom mirror as critically as I can—yes, I'm short and curvy, and I could certainly afford to lose ten pounds, but my skin is clear and without wrinkles, even though I'm staring down forty pretty soon. My hair is dark and lustrous, too, without a single streak of gray. I'm no stunning blonde Amazonian warrior like Dani, but I still look good... for my age, anyway. I'll take my wins where I can.

I straighten my pink silk blouse and gray A-line skirt, take a deep breath, and turn smartly on my heels.

"Ashley." Lila's voice is full of warmth as I step into her corner office after having tapped on the door, so I'm pretty sure I'm not in trouble. She's a single woman in her late forties, with close-cropped gray hair and sharp cheekbones; she dresses in well-tailored trouser suits and has amazing nails, in a different color every week. I've always admired her look, as well as been just a little intimidated by her self-assured personality.

"Come, sit." She motions to the chair in front of her desk, and I inch forward nervously. I've only been summoned to her office once before, when I did some work for the sales department, and she supervised me for a few weeks. "How are you?" she asks as she perches one hip on the edge of her desk, her arms folded, every inch the powerful businesswoman.

"Fine. Good, I mean." I smile and smooth my skirt over my thighs. "Very good," I say firmly, because, for a few moments, I want to seem like Lila, someone who knows where they are going in life, not a madwoman who runs out of baby boutiques like her hair is on fire and is anxious about just about everything.

"Good, because I've been noticing your work, Ashley." She pauses to let this sink in. "And so have other people."

I think of Aimee, who said she was going to mention my

work back in July. Has it finally paid off? What does that even mean?

"That's... good to hear, I think," I reply with a light laugh. "At least I hope so."

"It is," she says firmly. "I had a look at your resumé, as well. You've been with us for fifteen years, and you've pretty much stayed as a secretary, but you've got a BA in business administration. Why is that, do you think?" I stare at her a bit blankly and she clarifies, "Why have you stayed as a secretary all this time?"

"I suppose..." I swallow, not wanting to say the wrong thing, but I'm not sure what the right answer might be. "I suppose because of the job security," I finally admit. "I grew up without that, and it means a lot to me."

Lila nods slowly, respectfully, like I've stated some great truth, and maybe I have.

"That's certainly important, isn't it," she agrees somberly. "And women often place security over ambition—we feel like we can't be the risktakers in life, because we're usually the ones not rocking the boat. We're the ones working hard to keep it stable."

I think of Mark, being far more willing than I am to take the risk of surrogacy, and I simply nod, because I am certainly not about to go into all that right now.

"But the two don't have to be mutually exclusive, Ashley," Lila continues. She pauses, straightening and looking at me in a way that makes me feel like she's about to say something important. And then she does. "Ashley, how would you feel about a promotion?"

"A promotion?" Is this another horizontal move for convenience's sake, or something bigger? I'm scared to hope, to think what this could mean.

"Yes." Lila nods, leaning forward to convey her enthusiasm and excitement, both of which I feel, like a flame running through me. A *promotion*. "How would you like to become a sales representative, Ashley?" she asks. "Admittedly, it would be more intense, longer hours, bigger commissions. Some travel too, maybe a trip somewhere in the country once or twice a month. I'm not saying you'll see the world," she warns me with a light laugh. "Mainly the conference rooms of a lot of bland hotels, but it still can be interesting, and you'll be on the cutting edge of the pharmaceutical industry, bringing our newest and best products to hospitals and suppliers." She fires all this at me like I'll leap at the chance, and how can I not? I realize I've been waiting for something like this for years; I just never thought it would happen... a chance to prove myself, to show I have more to offer than typing letters or answering the phone. "Obviously, we can sit down and go through all the details, and Aimee has said she can act as your mentor for the first few weeks, show you the ropes and get you going, but I'm confident you'll get the hang of it super quickly."

She claps her hands together lightly as she smiles at me, full of energy and enthusiasm.

"Well, Ashley? Are you up for the challenge?"

FOURTEEN

DANI

The air practically crackles with tension as Ryan strides toward us. I lurch up from the table, while Mark frowns, perplexed. Then he sees Ryan bearing down on us, and he quickly jumps up as well, his welcoming smile starting to morph into a frown.

"Hello," he says, still half-smiling. "You are…?"

"Ryan. Dani's boyfriend." Ryan gives me a coolly challenging look, his eyebrows raised, his lips twisted into something like a sneer. "Right?"

"Right," I reply, unable to keep from feeling annoyed that he's forcing some kind of confrontation. Now really is not the moment. Mark is looking confused, because I haven't mentioned Ryan to either him or Ashley, whereas I think Ryan has figured out exactly who Mark is. "Ryan, this is Mark," I say, and then leave it there.

An uneasy tension pulses between us. I can tell Mark is confused as to why I haven't explained who he is, and judging by the fury sparking in his eyes, Ryan definitely has already guessed.

I turn to Mark. "I'm afraid I need to get going," I say firmly. The stuff I shared just a few minutes ago about my pregnancy feels like a big mistake now. It was nice to have someone listen, and Mark seems like a genuinely kind person, but I know I need to keep a certain distance between us if I'm going to get through this, for my sake as well as Ryan's. It's all just too complicated, too emotionally fraught, and it exhausts me.

"Oh, right, of course..." Mark looks a bit taken aback, as well as disappointed to be brushed off so quickly, but, to his credit, he rallies. "Well, it was great meeting you in person, Dani. So great. And I really appreciate you being willing to come out for coffee." He glances uncertainly at Ryan. "I know you're probably in a rush, but do you... do you mind if we take a photo, maybe with the ocean in the background? Just so I can send it to Ashley?"

I wonder what Ashley will think of that, and then decide it's not my problem.

"Yeah, sure, fine." I just want him to go, and I feel like he will sooner if I agree. Mark beams as he gets out his phone.

Ryan does not offer to take the photo, staying in the bakery as we head outside and then shuffle awkwardly together, Mark putting his arm around me rather gingerly as he holds up the phone and we squint into the sunlight. As soon as he takes the photo, his arm drops, and I step away.

"I'm sorry about in there," Mark remarks with a decisive nod to the bakery. "It seemed like there was some tension. Is Ryan not supportive of your surrogacy journey?"

If I have to hear the word *journey* one more time, I might throw up. Right now, this isn't feeling like a journey but an endurance test, and it hasn't even begun, not properly.

"He's coming to terms with it," I tell Mark shortly.

"Okay." Mark seems reluctant to let the matter drop, but at least he is willing. "Do let us know if there's anything we can do to help with that..."

"I will," I promise, knowing I don't mean it, and then we say goodbye, agreeing to be in touch soon, before I head back into

the café to deal with the other unhappy person in this triangle...
Ryan. I know I should have told him what was happening, but it
just would have caused more drama, and for what? I might not
even be pregnant, and I'm still not entirely sure if I want to be.

As I step into the café, I see he's got a coffee and is sitting at
a table in the back, looking morose. I feel a flicker of pity as well
as guilt; I know I am a very bad girlfriend. Sometimes I wonder
why Ryan stays with me, but at the same time I know I absolutely depend on him sticking with me, even when I'm being
difficult. I can't imagine him not being there, and I wonder if
that has made me seem complacent when I know inside I feel
anything but.

"Hey," I greet him quietly as I sit opposite. "Sorry about all
that."

Ryan's gaze stays on his coffee cup. "So, he's the dad?" he
asks.

I nod. "Yes, Mark and Ashley. They're the couple I've
contracted with." All Ryan knows so far is that I met online
with a couple from Connecticut and then signed a contract.
Telling him that much felt fraught, and so we've skirted the
issue since, with me promising I'd keep him informed of
anything important. I guess today didn't feel important
enough... To me, anyway.

"I thought they lived far away?" Ryan asks. "What was he
doing here?"

I hesitate, then admit, "He came to San Diego to... to donate
his sperm. I... I had the intrauterine transfer today."

Ryan's head jerks up, his eyes widening, pupils flaring.
"What? *Today*?"

Okay, clearly he thought that qualified as important.

"A couple of hours ago," I admit. "I was going to tell you
when I saw you tomorrow. I'm sorry, Ryan. Maybe I should
have told you it was happening before it did."

"Maybe?" he repeats disbelievingly. "*Maybe*?"

"This is my body," I remind him as I fold my arms across my chest and stare him down. "My choice."

Ryan shakes his head in disgust. "Come on, don't politicize this, Dani, please. This isn't about me telling you what you can or can't do with your body. It's about you having the decency to be upfront and honest with me as your boyfriend, or to consider my feelings for one millisecond, which it never seems to *occur* to you to do."

Abruptly, he lurches up from his chair and strides toward the door of the bakery. For a moment, I consider not following him. I don't want an argument, and neither do I want to be manipulated or guilted into trying to appease him, apologize for not keeping him informed every step of *my* so-called journey.

Then I take a few breaths and calm down enough to remind myself that he has a very good point, and we are in what is meant to be a serious relationship, and that requires a certain level of communication, as well as trust, which so far I have not been giving. And so, reluctant but resolute, I follow him outside. He's standing by the door, his head tilted to the bright blue sky, like he's contemplating the mysteries of the universe or maybe was just waiting for me. Without a word, he starts walking down Pearl Street toward the waterfront, and I fall in step with him, even though I really don't have time for a stroll. I'm teaching an Intro to Microbiology class in less than an hour.

"Why didn't you tell me it was happening today?" Ryan asks after we've walked in silence for a few minutes. He holds up his hand to keep me from replying. "It's a genuine question, because sometimes I really can't understand what goes through your head, Dani. Why didn't you tell me, why didn't you *want* to tell me? It's kind of a big deal."

"Because I didn't *want* it to be a big deal," I reply after a moment. "I've got enough going on in my life, and whenever I tell you anything surrogacy-related, it causes all this tension. We've both been avoiding talking about any of it, Ryan, and today didn't seem worth it, especially as I'm probably not even pregnant." I wince inwardly because that all sounded less harsh in my head. "It wasn't really personal," I add, and then wince again, because that sounds even worse.

"Right." Ryan nods mechanically, his jaw bunched as he stares straight ahead. "Right. Not *personal*."

"All I'm saying is, I might not even be pregnant, Ryan," I tell him, a sop to my conscience. "The procedure has only a ten percent success rate. I'm probably not, so it would have been a drama over nothing—you getting anxious or upset or whatever..." I trail off because I realize I am not painting a very flattering picture of him in this scenario, or even of me, for not considering his feelings, whatever they might be. I should have handled this so differently, and I didn't even realize until this moment.

"That's not even the point, though, is it?" he replies, in a tone that suggests I should know what the point is.

"Okay, I'll bite," I tell him wearily. "What *is* the point?"

He doesn't answer until we've reached Marine Street Beach, a thin sliver of white sand with the ocean stretching endlessly blue to the horizon. It has a few walkers along it, but it's pretty empty on a Wednesday afternoon in mid-November, and for a second I let myself enjoy the open space, the fresh, brine-scented breeze. I'll never get tired of living near the ocean, the way it lets me breathe... even as the stress of the current situation settles onto me, a heavy weight. This conversation feels far from over.

We head down onto the beach as I discreetly check my watch. I know this is important, but I can't be late for my class—not that I'm about to tell Ryan that.

"You know, when we first met," Ryan begins, and inwardly I groan because I really do not need a complete recap of our relationship right now, "I thought you were so cool. So *confident*." He glances at me with the ghost of a smile. "Do you remember, it was at that open mic night at USD? I went with Jack, he was doing his MBA..."

"Yeah, I remember." I'd noticed Ryan almost immediately, because he was crazily good-looking, without seeming to be aware of it. I'd had a couple of drinks, and it had emboldened me to go up to him and flirt, albeit clumsily because it's not my MO. He was the kind of guy you just couldn't *help* but flirt with. I think every woman in the bar would have tried it on with him, just because.

"It was one of the things that drew me to you," he continues. "I just thought you seemed like someone who had everything together, who knew where she was going, who was focused and intent and just, I don't know, totally present in the moment."

Or had just been a little too drunk, I think, but I know what he means. Back then, I *was* focused and confident—at least I felt like I could be. Before Callie's injury, before her condition seemed to take over our lives, casting everything else into shadow... my life felt brighter. Simpler, too. "Thanks..." I reply with an uncertain laugh, because I sense a big "but" coming and I know I need to brace myself for it.

"And then I got to know you, and I realized you *weren't* all those things, at least not as much as I'd thought you were," Ryan explains. "Oh, you could put it on, and most people bought it, because you're smart and beautiful, but I started to see underneath, to basically what a *mess* you actually were."

Ouch. I have no response, and so I stay silent.

"But you know what, Dani?" Ryan turns to me, and to my shame and horror, I see tears glinting in his eyes. He's baring his soul, being so emotional, and right now I can only feel numb.

"What?" I prompt when it seems like he's waiting for me to say something.

"All that just made me like you more," he tells me, and it comes out sounding dispirited, like he wished it hadn't. "Because you *aren't* strong, but you are trying so hard to be for your sister. And life's given you some seriously hard knocks, first with your dad and then your mom and Callie's condition, and that's not even taking into consideration giving up a baby for adoption when you were sixteen... but even with all that, you keep getting up and going on even when you don't feel like you can." He draws a shaky breath as he stops walking to stare out at the ocean.

"And I've always admired that," he continues after a moment, "but I guess I thought, since we were dating, that I was becoming part of it. That you'd let me be a part of it, you know, once you trusted me and *loved* me. You'd let me be the one to help you up, and we'd be strong together." He stops, draws another breath, and then lets it out slowly before stating flatly, "But you have *never*, not once, invited me into any part of your life that mattered. I mean, fine, let's just keep cooking Korean food and listening to jazz and going to another arthouse movie. *Cool*." He sounds almost sneering as he shakes his head slowly.

"No matter how patient I've been, or how hard I've tried, you just keep shutting me out. First, with Callie. No, I don't need to hear about her doctor visits. Your mom visits? I'm not there. I'm not *asked* to be there. Even your stress about your doctorate, it's all, 'no, Ryan, let's talk about something else.' And you didn't mention the fact that you gave a baby up for adoption until you absolutely had to."

He shakes his head again, his expression more resigned than angry. "And I've been okay with all that for a while," he continues, "because I could tell you had a hard time trusting people, and I got it. Your dad let you down, with all his debts, and then your mom did by checking out the way she did. I was willing to be patient, Dani. I tried everything to get you to trust me. I've been kind, I've been encouraging, I've been annoyed, I've been hurt. Nothing works."

I jerk back a little at that. "Don't try to manipulate me into feeling something I—"

"*You're* the one manipulating me," he fires back, and for the first time he sounds angry. "*Managing* me, like I'm some inconvenience, just another person to be dealt with rather than a... a life partner." I don't answer and he finishes quietly, "Because I've never been that, have I? I'm just someone to hang out with, have sex with, and keep at a distance."

I flinch at that. "Ryan... You make me sound so cold."

"No, I don't think you are that," he replies after a pause, his gaze still steady on the ocean. "But I'm not sure you know how to be anything else than what you are, or even if you *want* to be anything else. And I'm tired of trying. So." He turns to face me, a resolute look on his face, and with a terrible jolt, I realize what's happening.

"You're breaking up with me?" I ask, sounding incredulous.

Ryan lets out a huff of laughter. "You thought I never would, didn't you? You thought I'd just take it and take it, whatever you dished out? Sorry." He shakes his head. "I'm thirty-five, I want a wife, a family. You don't seem to want to be on that track, at least, not with me."

I feel a sudden terror grip me, far stronger and more overwhelming than anything I might have expected to feel in this moment. "*Ryan—*"

"This isn't some trick to get you to commit, Dani," he tells me quietly. "I've done some stupid stuff out of desperation, I admit, like asking you to marry me when you first mentioned the whole surrogacy idea, but this is *not* that." He squares his shoulders, his jaw, as he gives me a bleak look full of resolution. "This is me saying enough. I'm *done.*"

The utter certainty in his voice floors me. Maybe I should have seen this coming, but I really didn't, and I am dumbfounded, reeling from what I know should have been obvious.

And yet, a treacherous little voice whispers inside me, *weren't you waiting for this all along? Weren't you trying to make it happen?* I've been pushing people away for most of my adult life, so they couldn't push me away first—the way my dad did, when I was pregnant, and my mom, when he died. And Ryan, all along. Why shouldn't he be the first to walk away?

"Ryan..." I falter, reeling. I have no idea what to say to him.

"Isn't this what you've wanted?" he asks me in weary challenge. "All along? It took me a while to figure that out, but I think I get it now." He pauses before finishing sadly, "Well, at least one of us got what they wanted."

And then he's walking away from me while I simply stare, still too shocked to say a word, even as I realize that Ryan knew me better than I knew myself...

And now he's gone.

FIFTEEN

ASHLEY

I practically float through the rest of the afternoon. Lila is as good as her word as she sends me an initial contract before the end of the day, and I skim through it, my eyes widening at the salary figure. It's twice as much as I make now. I feel like I've entered some alternate reality, one where I am no longer "the Mouse" but "the Lion." To match my mood, I blast Katy Perry all the way home.

I am grinning as I unlock the door and step inside.

Mark greets me in the hallway. "You don't know how good it is to be home," he says and envelops me in a hug. He's just had a shower; his skin is still lightly damp, and he smells of soap.

I put my arms around him automatically, my purse sliding off my shoulder, but inside I am mentally having to do a screeching reversal of thought, from promotion and career woman to surrogacy and motherhood. Not to mention the whole him-meeting-Dani thing, which is a confrontation I do not want to force, but at the same time know we need to have.

"Hey," I say, a little feebly, and then slip out of his arms and head for the kitchen.

"Everything okay?" Mark asks, sounding both light and a

little troubled, and I wonder when we started tiptoeing around each other. The answer is swift and obvious: when we started talking about surrogacy.

"Yeah, everything's great. Really great, actually." I take a can of seltzer out of the fridge and then turn to face him, resolute but also not quite meeting his eyes. "I was offered a promotion today."

"Ash, that's wonderful!" His voice is so warm and enthusiastic that I feel a buzz of pride, as well as a rush of relief. Of course Mark would be glad for me, I scold myself. Did I think he wouldn't, just because we're trying to have a baby? What decade do we live in? "Tell me about it," he invites as he comes into the kitchen. "While I start dinner."

"Okay." I lean against the counter as he gets out pots and pans. "It really came out of left field," I admit as I crack open my can of seltzer. "A woman in the sales department whom I did some work for said she was going to mention how impressed she was with me, and I guess she did, because Lila, the assistant head of sales, asked me to be a sales associate. Like, not just an administrative assistant anymore, but, you know, a position with some serious responsibility." I hear the pride in my voice as I take a sip of my seltzer.

"Whoa." Mark is mincing a bulb of garlic, his forehead furrowed. "That's crazy. Crazy great, I mean." He flashes me a quick smile. "What does it mean in terms of your work schedule?"

"Well, it will be a little more intense, and there will be some travel, to visit clients." I picture myself walking smartly through an airport, my briefcase swinging by my side. "Once a month, maybe." *Or twice*, I think, but don't say.

"Wow." Mark is silent for a moment, focusing on the garlic, which is minced to practically a pulp.

A flash of irritation slices through me. "Aren't you pleased?"

I ask, but I realize the question sounds petulant rather than reasonable.

"Yes," he says quickly—maybe too quickly. "I mean, of course I'm pleased for you, Ash. You deserve this. You absolutely do." He gives me another swift smile, but I know my husband and I can see the concern in his eyes, maybe even something bordering on alarm. "But yes, I am wondering what it will mean," he continues, clearly reading my thoughts. "In terms of when and how we go ahead with the surrogacy. If Dani's pregnant—"

"She's probably not," I return quickly. "Ten percent success rate, after all, isn't very high—"

Mark frowns, like he's not happy with this response, and I realize I sounded a little too hopeful.

"Okay, but when she is, you know, *hopefully*," he resumes as he swirls olive oil in the bottom of a pan, "you're going to want to take some time off like we talked about... right?"

"Right," I reply, wishing I meant it more. "But that could be a year from now, Mark, or even more. Meanwhile, I can learn the ropes with this new position, so when I *do* take some parental leave, I've already got some experience under my belt, you know? There are no downsides to this."

"Yeah, that makes sense." He nods slowly and then scrapes the garlic from the cutting board into the pan.

The sound of it sizzling keeps us from talking for a few seconds, which is probably a good thing. I feel like I'm on the verge of feeling furious, and I don't *do* anger. If given a choice, I'll apologize rather than accuse, but right now I am working myself up into a towering rage and I'm not even sure why. Everything Mark has said is completely reasonable. Everything he's reminded me of is something I've already agreed to.

So why do I feel like I've been boxed into a corner *again*?

"You don't... have a problem with that, do you? Me taking this promotion?" I ask carefully.

"A *problem*?" Mark sounds disbelieving. "No, of course not, Ash, I know how important your job is to you. I just want to make sure we're on the same page about everything, going forward. Communication, right?" He flashes me a brief smile, but I don't think it reaches his eyes.

"Speaking of being on the same page..." I pause, because this kind of confrontation really isn't like me, and yet somehow right now I can't keep myself from it. Maybe getting this promotion has already emboldened me. I'm a mouse no more, not in my work, and not in marriage. "That selfie you took out in California... I thought we were going to meet Dani together?"

Mark grimaces and hunches his shoulders in a little, playful sort of apology that doesn't appease me in the least. "I know we did, and I'm sorry for going ahead like that, without telling you. I was just so excited, Ash. I mean... finally, it felt like we were *doing* something, you know. And I was so close, I just... I just wanted to put a face to... to..."

"The mother of your baby?" I fill in coldly, surprising us both.

A silence descends on us like concrete, rendering us speech-less and immobile.

"Ashley, *you* are the mother of my baby," Mark finally replies. He speaks firmly, like he's talking to an unruly child. "You always will be."

Immediately, I am filled with remorse. Claire was right; I don't feel threatened by Mark seeing Dani, not in that way. Any sense of insecurity I have comes from me, not my husband. "I'm sorry," I say, blinking rapidly. "It just took me by surprise, that's all, seeing you together, without any warning."

"I'm sorry," Mark returns quickly. He steps away from the stove to put his arms around me. "I should have asked you first. I know I should have. And I probably shouldn't have gone at all. Dani wasn't thrilled, let me tell you."

I rest my cheek on his shoulder as I let him hold me and my waves of fury and hurt slowly begin to recede.

"So, what was she like?" I ask after a moment.

"A little guarded," Mark admits. "I took her by surprise, and not in a good way, but she got over it eventually. Still, it wasn't a great move on my part." He sighs as he strokes my hair. "She has a boyfriend, Ryan... we ran into him in this coffee shop. He didn't seem very supportive. And she didn't even tell us about him."

"Maybe it's not serious enough?" I suggest. I got that same sense of guardedness from both Dani's profile and our Zoom call, but I liked it. I *wanted* someone who was willing to keep a little distance, who wasn't going to steamroll over our lives, wrecking everything.

"I don't know," Mark muses, his arms still around me as he strokes my hair. "He really didn't expect to see me, and there was some serious tension around it all. I just don't want this to be... complicated."

"It's already complicated," I reply and then I sniff and step out of his arms. "That's the nature of this thing, Mark, and it always will be." Too many people involved in the making and raising of a baby. Of course it's going to be complicated.

"Complicated doesn't have to mean hard or bad," Mark returns, before he sighs and shakes his head, his eyes drooping with sadness. "I just really want this to work, you know?"

"Yes," I reply after a moment as I slip off my heels to head upstairs. "I know."

I sign the contract on Monday, right before I take off for Thanksgiving.

Lila makes a big deal of it, introducing me to the rest of the team in the conference room, saying "a few words" and then having everyone clap. I am both mortified and thrilled; it's hard to let go of my instinct to keep under the radar when everyone is congratulating me and telling me how great it is that I'm joining their team. For the first time since I started at Kennett Pharmaceuticals fifteen years ago, I feel like someone else there thinks I'm important. It's not just about my smart suit or my swivel chair, it's who I am and what I can bring to the team. I feel as if I am glowing.

When I come home, Mark has bought champagne and flowers and has set the table with our best dishes.

"I knew you were signing the contract today," he says as he takes me into his arms. "I wanted to celebrate."

I wrap my arms around him as I rest my cheek against his chest. Just when I feel like things have been tense between us, he does something like this, reminding me of all the reasons why I love him... and why I need to make this work.

"Only five more days," I tell him, and his arms tighten around me.

"Are you counting down to the pregnancy test, too?" he asks in a voice of surprised pleasure.

"Of course." Although maybe not with the same kind of excitement he is, but I am trying. "Do you think Dani will call us either way?"

I feel rather than see Mark's worried frown. "I certainly hope so. We made that clear—"

"I'm sure she will." I slip out of his arms. "It is just a couple days after Thanksgiving, though. She might be busy."

"It's the Monday after," Mark replies. "I think the holiday is pretty firmly over by then."

I shrug, deciding this is not a point we need to debate. I was just trying to show him I'm on board with it all, because I *am*.

"Speaking of Thanksgiving," I say instead, "are you ready for my mom?"

"I love your mom," Mark replies loyally. "She's had a hard life, and I like being able to treat her a little."

Mark is going to cook Thanksgiving dinner with all the trimmings—turkey, homemade cranberry sauce and stuffing, two kinds of potatoes, at least three different pies. I'll be the sous-chef, but he's the mastermind, and I know he'll ply my mother with drinks and nibbles, insist she puts her feet up while he gets to work. I really do appreciate all the effort he's going to for her sake.

"You're so kind with her," I say on something of a sigh. "I wish..." I don't even know how to finish that sentence. It's not something I voice very often, if at all.

Mark turns to me, champagne bottle in hand, his eyebrows raised. "You wish your mom was different?" he fills in gently, and I nod.

"Just... more of a *mom*, I guess."

"She took care of you," he reminds me, his voice still soft. "She put food on the table. She held down two jobs to keep a roof over your head."

"I know." It's what I've reminded myself every time I've wished she could be a little... *cuddlier*. "Trust me, Mark, I've given her a lot of leeway because of all that."

"I know you have." He pops the cork on the champagne with a flourish, interrupting our conversation, which might be just as well, considering how on edge I am starting to feel, but then he goes on. "I think," he continues as he pours us both glasses, "I was saying that more for my sake than for yours. I know you know all that, Ash. Really."

I take the glass of champagne, trying to wrap my head around that statement. "*Yours...*"

"Dani told me about her first pregnancy," he says in a low voice, and I am jolted, because I really did not think we were talking about Dani right now. "How difficult it was. She was only sixteen, Ash, and the guy... well, he sounded like a total jerk. I mean, she said it definitely wasn't rape, but..."

"Dani told you all this?" This is even more to wrap my head

around, especially when I thought we were talking about *my* mother, *my* life, not Dani. Again. When I saw that selfie, I hadn't realized they'd been having such an intimate heart-to-heart. "And *rape*?"

"Not rape," he says quickly. "I mean, she said it wasn't. But she was young, and he sounded pretty awful about it, so..."

I take a sip of champagne, but it tastes bitter on my tongue. "Why are you telling me this exactly?" I ask in what I hope is a neutral voice.

He sighs and puts down his glass without having taken a single sip of champagne. "Because it just shed some light for me on being a parent," he explains. "Or *not* being a parent, I suppose, as the case may be. I mean, I always wondered why my biological mother gave me away. There could have been a million reasons, and I feel like I've thought of them all, but they never really made sense, you know? They were never enough, because I felt like I could always figure a way around them, so it could have worked. She... she could have kept me."

For a second, he sounds like a lost little boy, and my edginess softens into sorrow as my heart aches for him.

"But then, hearing Dani..." he continues, and my heart immediately hardens right up, "I understood it. It wasn't about the practical reasons—the lack of money or support or whatever —but the *emotional* ones." Mark has the evangelistic light of a zealot in his eyes, like he's cracked some kind of code, and he's got to make me understand it. "Dani completely shut down during her pregnancy," he explains, "because she was so traumatized by what had happened. And I wondered if my mother was like that. If she couldn't keep me, because she wasn't in that place *mentally*, rather than physically, to be a loving mother." He pauses. "And I've wondered if maybe *your* mother was like that, too, because of the way your father left, without giving her any support. She was so *young*, Ash, barely more than twenty."

So now we're talking about my mother again? My head is spinning from all this.

"Wow," I say, and then take a large sip of champagne, needing the hit of alcohol to blunt whatever it is I'm feeling, and, in truth, I can't name it. "That's a lot." I don't quite trust myself to say anything more. I need to process everything he's told me, everything he's implied. Clearly he and Dani had quite the serious chat.

"Yeah," Mark says seriously, and now he's reaching for his champagne as an uneasy silence settles over us. "It is."

The next few days pass in a pleasant haze—a crisp, autumn walk in Westmoor Park as the last of the maple leaves fluttered down and a rainy afternoon browsing art galleries in Hartford, dinner out at Salute, one of our favorite restaurants, and a cozy evening in, watching Netflix and drinking wine.

It's as if Mark knew we needed these reminders of why we were together, how good it was between us, when it was *just* us. And I needed the assurance that I was enough for him... even if deep down I knew I'm not. At least we didn't talk about surrogacy or babies for three whole days.

When my mom arrives on Thursday afternoon for Thanksgiving dinner, Mark is, as usual, a host extraordinaire. He ushers her in, hands her a glass of sherry, puts a bowl of gourmet potato chips on the table in front of her. He even plumps the pillow behind her back, insisting she needs to put her feet up and "have a good rest." I flutter around, wishing I'd thought of all these things. Usually, my mother resists or even refuses them; today, however, she accepts them with barely a murmur.

Outside, a gray, drizzly rain is trickling down the windows and Mark has turned the gas fire on, its silent, elegant flames providing a comforting warmth, if not the coziness of an actual log fire.

"How are you, Mom?" I ask as Mark returns to the kitchen to continue his meal preparations.

"Oh..." My mother sounds more tired than usual. "I've been better," she says, and she takes a sip of her sherry.

Whenever I ask, my mother says she's fine.

I sit down on the chair opposite her. "Has work been hard this week?" I ask. She works ten-hour days as a housecleaner, so I imagine every week is pretty hard, not that my mother complains.

My mother frowns. "I guess I'm feeling my age," she says at last.

I nod, not sure what to say. We both know retirement isn't an option for her, and now that we're sinking all our savings into surrogacy, we can't even offer her the sort of financial help we once might have.

"How are *you*?" she asks, which also surprises me. She doesn't often ask.

"I'm good," I reply, and then haltingly I tell her about my promotion, unable to keep the pride from my voice, even though I'm pretty sure she'll act unimpressed, or maybe just indifferent, the way she so often does.

Instead, her face creases into an unexpected smile; I so rarely see her smile that for a second the sight of her mouth turned upwards, the laugh lines deepening from nose to mouth, shocks me. She almost looks like a different person. "That's really good news, Ashley," she says, sounding like she means it, and for the third time in the space of a few minutes I am jolted. Actually, I am floored; my mother hardly ever says stuff like this, and I've wanted her to for so long.

"It is good news," I agree shyly. "If I'd been bolder, I think maybe I could have gone for it earlier, but I'm glad it's finally happened."

"It can be hard to put yourself out there," she replies. "But you did, and I'm proud of you."

Proud? Where is this coming from? It's as if she eaves-
dropped on Mark's and my conversation from a few days ago,
how I said I wished she could be more of a mom. The funny
thing is, I'm not even sure how to respond to it.

"Thanks," I finally say, and my mother's smile suddenly
drops.

"Maybe I should have said that before," she admits, and
now I feel like we are entering surreal territory.

"Mom..." I really don't know what to say.

"How are things going with the... the surrogacy?" She stumbles slightly over the word. "I think I'd like to be a grandmother
one day, if I could."

What? She's never said anything like this before; her atti-
tude of weary indifference has become so ingrained, I barely
know how to respond to her seemingly heartfelt words.

"We're actually waiting to hear," I tell her slowly, still reeling. "We'll know Monday whether it worked this time."

"Well, keep me posted," she says, with another smile, but
this one slides off her face and for a bewildering second, she
looks almost near tears.

I lurch forward. "Mom... is something wrong?"

"Well, I suppose you could say that," she replies after a
moment. She takes a sip of her sherry and then puts the glass
down. "I had some upsetting news this week."

I have a feeling I'm about to find out why she's been acting
so differently, and I'm not sure I want to hear it.

"Ashley..." she says, her voice wobbling. "I have cancer."

SIXTEEN

DANI

On Thanksgiving, Callie and I have a quiet day, just the two us. I haven't told her that Ryan and I have broken up, so I just tell her he's spending it with his family, who live in Orange County.

Last year, we drove out to Arizona to help my mom and the Sisters of Mercy serve Thanksgiving dinner at a homeless shelter, but when I suggested that this year, since Callie seemed to enjoy it last time, she refused. When I pressed, she admitted that standing up for long periods, like she'd have to do if we helped out, had started to hurt her back. I managed to keep from commenting about that, but it made me both sad and anxious. How many other symptoms is she not telling me about?

In any case, it's just the two of us at our little kitchen table and half a turkey crown, plus a couple of vegetables. I'm not a great cook, but Callie made a sweet potato casserole, complete with marshmallow topping, and a pumpkin pie, so it feels festive, at least.

In four days, I'll find out if I'm pregnant. I know it's too early to have symptoms, but I have been obsessively checking in with my body just in case I do. Am I crampy? Do my breasts feel fuller? Was that a twinge low down, and did it mean something? Do I *want* it to mean something? I'm still not sure...

Mark and Ashley, at least, have eased off with any communication since his visit, which is a relief, because I don't have the emotional bandwidth for them right now. Ashley sent me a Happy Thanksgiving message with a smiling pumpkin GIF, and I simply responded, "You too." All we can do is wait.

"What's going on with the whole surrogacy thing?" Callie asks once we are digging into our pumpkin pie. I got out the can of squirty whipped cream and gave both our slices a generous helping.

"Well... I'm in a waiting period right now," I tell her. I'm surprised she's asked, because since this whole thing started Callie has insisted she does not want to know a single detail, which has been fine by me, because I haven't wanted to give her a play-by-play. Now, however, I feel compelled to admit, "I'll find out on Monday if I'm pregnant."

Her eyes widen as she stops with her forkful of pie halfway to her mouth. "Wait, *what*? You mean, you like... you *could* be pregnant? For real?"

I smile wryly. "Well, that's kind of the point of this whole thing, Callie."

She blushes and shakes her head. "I know, but I mean, like, how...?"

I nod toward the half-eaten turkey crown on the table in front of us. "Well... think turkey baster."

Callie makes a face as she puts down her fork. "*Ew*."

"I know." I give her a grimace in return. "But it wasn't that bad."

She is silent for a moment, her head bent as she picks up her fork once more and then toys with a piece of pie.

"This is good," I tell her, motioning to my own slice of pie. "You have mad skillz in the kitchen," I add teasingly.

"Ha, thanks." Her head is still lowered, and she isn't looking at me.

I wait, wondering what's going on. Is she wishing she hadn't asked?

"I'm sorry," Callie says at last, her voice low. "I should have been more supportive about, you know, the surrogacy thing." She's still looking down at her plate.

"Thanks," I reply, touched by the admission. "But I understand why you weren't. It's a weird concept. For me, too."

"Yeah, but..." She looks up, and to my surprise, she's blinking back tears. "You're doing it for *me*."

"I'd do *anything* for you, Callie," I tell her, and now my throat is thickening, and I'm blinking back tears, too. "I hope you know that." Because I mean it so utterly.

"I do," she whispers, and I believe her.

We smile at each other as we blink rapidly and then I break first and wipe my eyes. Calle laughs, a wavering sound.

"Dani..." she begins after a moment, and now she sounds serious.

I wipe my eyes once more before leveling her with as open and direct a look as I can. "Yes?"

"I've been thinking and..." She pauses, biting her lip, before continuing in a rush, "I want to have the surgery. I think I do need it. My back has been hurting more and I'm tired of my feet going numb, feeling like I could fall over, and just... not feeling like *me*..." Her voice breaks and she sniffs. "I'm scared, though. I was looking into and it's, like, a *really* big deal. They open up your whole back, and the recovery is intense... Plus, I mean, surgery on my *spine*." Her voice wobbles. "That's scary stuff."

I reach across the table to hold her hand. "I know," I say softly as I squeeze her fingers. "It's super scary, but I promise, I will be with you every step of the way."

"I know you will." She smiles through her tears, and my

heart aches for her, even as I am filled with relief that she has finally agreed to the surgery.

I want to jump up, do a victory dance, and then call the surgeon and schedule her surgery immediately, before she can change her mind. But first I have to switch my health insurance, fill out a million forms, arrange for a prescreening MRI... but I am so ready for this. I will do whatever it takes to help my sister.

"Is Ryan coming over later?" she asks, clearly wanting to dispense with the heavy stuff, and I tense, because I am not about to tell her that Ryan broke up with me just now. She might guess why, and, knowing my sister, it might make her backtrack on the surgery, because she'll feel guilty for indirectly causing the fallout.

"No, not today," I say as lightly as I can. "Maybe we can watch some Netflix, have a girly night?"

She beams, and once again I am filled with relief—and *hope*, something I haven't felt in a long time.

For the first time in years, the future looks like a place where I want to go.

Monday afternoon, after a lecture, I am sitting in Dr. Freedman's examining room, my sleeve rolled up and my head averted as she siphons out a vial of blood from my arm. "I'm going to send this to the lab ASAP," she tells me, "and we should have a result within a few hours."

I nod, smile. Since Callie told me she's willing to go ahead with the surgery, I know this is what I want. I *need* to be pregnant. "Great," I say.

"Of course, if it's negative, that's not necessarily conclusive," the doctor continues in a cheerful tone. "We'll test again in forty-eight hours, and then another forty-eight hours after that, just to be sure. If you get your period or experience any bleeding, you should call me right away."

"Okay."

"How have you been feeling in yourself?" she asks as she caps the vial and turns away. I start rolling down my sleeve.

"Fine," I tell her. "Normal."

"Of course, it's too early for any symptoms," she continues, saying it like a warning. "If anything, pregnancy at this stage feels pretty much the same as PMS—bloating, a little crampy, you know the drill."

"Right." I'm not sure I've been feeling any of those symptoms, either, but I'm trying not to second-guess myself too much. I'll know for sure either way soon.

Dr. Freedman peels off her latex gloves before giving me what feels like a professional smile—friendly but a little reserved. "Just so you're aware, if the lab results are positive, that is, if you are pregnant, I'll inform the agency, who will tell the intended parents first, around the same time as I tell you."

"Oh..." For some reason, I'd imagined I'd be the one telling them, and I realize I'm relieved not to. I need that little extra bit of distance.

"It's just simpler, on a variety of levels, if these types of communications go through the agency," she adds, and I nod, because I get it, I really do.

"That makes sense."

Dr. Freedman gives me a quick, understanding smile. "If you are pregnant," she continues, "then the agency will arrange a discussion between you and the intended parents, to discuss next steps, in terms of both communication and support." She smiles at me. "Just to make sure everyone's on the same page when it comes to expectations and boundaries."

I picture Mark waiting for me in this very clinic less than two weeks ago, and I'm pretty sure we will all need to have that conversation.

"I'll call you in a couple of hours with the results, regardless of what they are, okay?" She touches me briefly on the shoulder. "Try to relax and not think about it too much, if you can."

I realize I must seem jumpy, and I force a smile. "Yeah, I will," I promise, even though I know I'll be counting down the minutes until I find out.

I have the rest of the afternoon off, and while I know I should do some work, or even better, start sorting out health insurance, I feel like I need a break from all that, just for a little while, and so I end up driving twenty minutes out to Mission Trails Park to hike the Fortuna Mountain Trail. I always keep my hiking boots and some bottled water in my car, just in case, and I'm glad for both now as I lace up and strike out, over the scrubby hills, red dust kicking up under my heels, the sky a hard, bright blue as the sun beats down.

I love hiking, love the way it takes me out of myself. When I'm walking up here where the air is so fresh and clear and the whole world rolls out in front of me like a map, I feel like I can finally breathe. My thoughts, usually racing through my head, empty right out. I become a blank space, floating and free.

For an hour, I simply walk, without thinking about pregnancy or surrogacy or surgery or anything at all. The next chapter in my PhD that is due next week evaporates. Ryan doesn't exist. Callie's back isn't constantly on my mind, a worry that eats away at everything good. I just walk.

Then my phone rings.

I scrabble for it in my pocket, my heart already starting to thud. I wasn't thinking about those things, but it only takes a millisecond to have them all rushing back in. I'm so sure it's Dr. Freedman with the lab results that I swipe without even checking who is calling.

"Hello?"

"Dani?"

"Mom." My breath comes out in a whoosh and my legs are so shaky I have to lower myself to the ground. I sit right there on the dusty track as I stare out at the scrub-strewn mountains and valleys, not sure whether I'm relieved or disappointed it's not Dr. Freedman.

"Sorry, did I catch you at a bad time?"

"No, I just... I'm hiking, and I was a little out of breath."

She is quiet for a moment and then she asks in a heartfelt tone, "How are you, Dani? I've been thinking about you, with the surrogacy. Has it... progressed?"

Briefly, I close my eyes. "Actually, I thought you were the doctor calling with my lab results. I might find out if I'm pregnant today."

"Oh, Dani." I can't tell if she sounds sad or simply supportive.

Why is she even calling, anyway?

"You don't normally call me," I say abruptly.

My mother lets out a small, soft laugh. "No, because I don't think you normally want to hear from me."

"Callie does," I shoot back, and she sighs.

"I call Callie, Dani."

I know she does. I hear Callie talking to her sometimes, in her bedroom. I try not to listen.

"Why did you call today?" I ask, and now I sound belligerent; it's so hard to be anything else with my mom, because three years after she abandoned us, I'm still angry with her. I don't know how not to be.

"Like I said," she replies carefully, "I've been thinking of you. I know you said this has brought up memories about your pregnancy before. I just... I just want to be supportive."

"Since when?" I snap, and my mother is silent. I think of apologizing for my tone, but I just don't have it in me.

"I know you're angry, Dani," she says after a moment. "With me."

"You think I shouldn't be?" I demand. We've never talked like this before because I have shut down every single conversation. I simply didn't have the patience or understanding to listen to my mom's excuses, and I'm not sure I do now, but I am curious, or maybe just still so jumpy, waiting to hear, and so I'm doing what I know I do best, and picking a fight.

"It's not my place to say what you should or shouldn't feel," my mother replies, and even though she can't see, I roll my eyes hard enough to hurt. Seriously, that's the kind of pseudo self-help speak she's going to give me as an answer?

"Thanks for affirming my emotions," I retort sarcastically, and my mother sighs again, like I've disappointed her. Well, maybe I have, but she's disappointed *me.*

"I don't want to argue with you," she says. "I just called to let you know I was thinking of you."

"Thanks," I reply briefly. At least I kept myself from any number of snappy retorts I could have made—*send a text next time* or *thanks for the Hallmark message.* "I don't know if Callie's told you, but she's decided to go ahead with the spinal fusion surgery. I'm changing my health insurance this month and we can hopefully get it scheduled in January."

"Dani, that's great news!"

"Yeah, well, it's going to be a big deal. For her, I mean. Physically and emotionally." I'll have to take time off work for the week she's in the hospital; I already checked, and I can sleep in her room with her in the ICU. It's going to be intense for me as well as much more so for Callie.

"If there's a way I can help..." my mother begins, and then lets that sentiment trail away to nothing.

For a second, I let myself imagine how she *could* help, how a normal mother would help. She'd be the one sleeping with Callie in the hospital, making casseroles, googling forms of pain relief, doing all the heavy lifting. As it is, she'll be thinking of us from Arizona.

"Thanks," I tell her shortly, "but I don't think there is."

"Dani..." my mother begins, and I wait for more. Then she

just sighs. "Nothing," she finishes, just as I suspected she would. "Maybe I'll come out to visit in a few weeks?" she suggests after a moment.

"If you want to," I reply, like it doesn't matter to me, and in a way, it doesn't. Callie likes seeing my mom, but the visits are short, and they don't really change anything. It's not as if my mom acts like a mother during them, more like a slightly estranged aunt.

"I'll see what I can do," she tells me, and I wonder if she'll come. Half the time when she suggests a visit, it never happens, so I won't hold my breath.

We end the call, and I stay there sitting on the dusty ground, gazing out at the endless vista of mountain and sky. Talking to my mom churns everything up inside me—the anger, the confusion, the regret, the guilt. I know I shouldn't be so harsh with her, but surely a mother doesn't walk away from her children, whatever their ages, without a good reason? Yet she'd never explained that reason to me, but then I haven't asked, maybe because I'm not sure I really want to know.

Is there ever a good enough reason, anyway? Did *I* have a good enough reason, when I gave my own baby up for adoption without even looking in his or her face? Without even knowing whether I'd given birth to a boy or girl? If anyone's an unnatural mother, surely it's me?

I told Creating Dreams and Mark and Ashley that I wanted to redeem that experience, but aren't those just empty words? How do you redeem something that happened so long ago, that you can't ever fix? I can't find my own child even if I wanted to, and they will never be able to find me.

It was how I wanted it, how I *told* myself I wanted it, and I've kept living that lie for the last twelve years. It's only now, with this possibility of a new life inside me, that I realize what a painful mistake I might have made.

And I might be about to make another one.

As if on cue, my phone rings, and this time it is Dr. Freedman. I swipe to answer the call; all the churning emotion inside me has flattened right out, so I feel nothing when she tells me in a warm, friendly voice, "Dani? It's good news. I'm so pleased to tell you you're pregnant."

SEVENTEEN

ASHLEY

I am sitting in a hard plastic chair in the waiting room of the chemotherapy clinic at Hartford Healthcare in Plainville, hardly able to believe I'm here.

Four days ago, my mom told me she had cancer. Today, I'm escorting her to her first chemo treatment. It's all happened so fast that I've barely had time to process what this means... for my mom, and for me. She is sitting next to me, her hands clasped in her lap, her head slightly bowed. We've been waiting for twenty minutes, and we've barely spoken.

When, on Thanksgiving Day, she told me she had cancer, I simply gaped for a few seconds. "Cancer..." I repeated, dumbly. My mind was spinning. "What... how... I mean, is it serious?"

What a stupid question, I thought. *Obviously it's serious.* Cancer is always serious.

"Pretty serious," my mom said stiffly.

Mark came into the room, a look of concern on his face; he must have overheard something of our conversation. He sat next to my mom and put his arm around her.

"Nancy, I'm so sorry to hear that," he said, which is what I should have said. I would have gotten there in time, I hope anyway, but I was just so shocked.

The story came out in dribs and drabs, each fact given with my mother's usual reticence—she'd had pain in her abdomen for several months, but no time to have it checked out, and she couldn't afford the insurance co-pay, anyway. Then she'd ended up in the emergency room a week ago, after she had collapsed at work. She'd told us none of this, of course. Hadn't even let them call us when she was in the ER. A blood test showed a high white blood cell count; an X-ray showed a mass. A few more tests revealed she has stage four pancreatic cancer. She was going to start chemo next week, but she really couldn't take the time off work.

"Mom, let us help," I cried. "I can take you to chemo—"

She tsked, batting away my offer. "You have work."

"I'll take time off—"

"Nancy," Mark said, "if it's a question of money—"

"*Please* let us help you, Mom," I said quietly, and that was when her face crumpled, and my mom did something I'd never once seen her do before. She wept.

Mark put his arms around her, while for a few seconds I simply gaped. My mom had always been a tough, no-nonsense sort of person, dismissive of any kind of extra emotion, and here she was, her shoulders shaking with the force of her sobs.

She got herself under control in a few minutes, wiping her face and easing away from Mark. "I don't want to make any fuss," she said, and it felt as if my heart had splintered right in two. That's what she'd always said to me—don't make a fuss. It was her life motto, even now as she battled death.

And it *is* a question of life or death, because the survival rate for stage four pancreatic cancer is terrible. The five-year rate is only three percent; the average life expectancy is one year. I looked it all up after she'd gone, pretty sure that she must have already, as well. I felt devastated, both for the possible loss of my mother in just a year's time, and also the loss of all that had—and hadn't—gone before. I'd always wanted to be closer. Now it was almost too late.

Which was why I'd insisted on accompanying her to her first chemotherapy treatment, even though *she* insisted I didn't have to and, considering I'd just got a promotion, it wasn't a great time to take off work. Still, I'm here with her now, and I'm glad.

"How are you feeling?" I ask quietly, and she shrugs.

"Like this is a fine kettle of fish, I suppose," she says, and I almost laugh, because it's such a typical thing for my mom to say. She has what is likely to be terminal cancer, and she speaks about it like it's little more than an irritation.

"Apparently you don't feel the effects of the chemotherapy right away," I tell her. Mark and I did a crash course on chemotherapy on the internet over the weekend, using WebMD as our guide. "It's cumulative, so you won't feel it for a while, but it will get harder each time."

"Something to look forward to, then," my mother says, her thin mouth twitching into something almost like a smile.

I think it's the first time I've heard her make a joke, but I suddenly wonder if I've missed them all along, because I always took her so seriously. Seeing my mom like this, trying to be strong even as she faces the hardest, most terrible thing it's possible to face, keeping her chin up even as her eyes glitter with what I think might actually be tears... it's incredibly disconcerting. It's making me wonder if I need to re-evaluate my entire childhood. My mother, and *myself*.

"Nancy Dunning?" A nurse in pale pink scrubs comes to the waiting room door and my mother rises stiffly, chin tilted up.

"That's me."

I follow her back into the chemotherapy suite, six reclining armchairs with IV drips next to them. It all feels horribly surreal, and there's part of me that wants to hold up my hand, tell everyone to *stop*, that this can't possibly be happening. Not to me. Not to my mother.

The nurse chats companionably to my mother, who offers surprisingly friendly replies. I realize I'm seeing a side of her that I never have before. Since I left for college twenty years ago, I've spent very little time with my mom. Maybe that needs to change. Considering her diagnosis, I hope now that it will.

Within a few minutes, my mom is reclining in an armchair, hooked up to a drip that is feeding the toxic but potentially life-saving chemicals into her arm. I perch next to her on a vinyl-cushioned chair, my purse in my lap.

"You don't have to stay," my mother says. "You probably need to get back to work."

"My boss understood," I tell her. "She said I could have the day off."

My mother looks away as she presses her lips together. "I don't want to make a fuss," she says, yet again.

"Mom," I say, trying for a wry tone, "you have *cancer*. You're allowed to make a fuss."

She lets out a sound that I realize belatedly is a laugh. "Maybe," she acknowledges and then she rests her head against the back of her recliner, her eyes fluttering closed. "Maybe now it's allowed."

The words, said on a sigh, jar. "What do you mean," I ask after a moment, "*now*?"

"Oh..." A weary sigh escapes her. Her eyes are still closed. "Just... the way I grew up... and then with your father... no one liked a fuss."

I stiffen, surprised by this seemingly small admission. My mom didn't talk about her parents very much; I only saw them a few times when I was little before they died, but I knew she'd grown up strict and that they hadn't been particularly close. As for my dad? I never knew anything about him, except that he left. I think I learned very early on that discussing him was a no-go area. But now she's talking about all these people who were in her life but not in mine, and saying they didn't like a *fuss*?

Just like she used to tell me.

My brain hurts from thinking about it all.

"Mom..." I ask slowly, "what do you mean, no one liked a fuss?"

"Oh, you know..." Her voice sounds dreamy; maybe the chemo is making her sleepy, or maybe she's just exhausted from working fifty hours a week while having terminal cancer. "They just didn't."

Which explains nothing and yet everything about my mother.

I'm pretty sure she's drifted off to sleep and I sit back, my mind whirling. How can perceptions shift so radically and so fast? Or am I being fanciful, reading too much into a few drowsily spoken words?

I don't know, I can't decide, but I realize I'm glad I came today. And I'll come again. Because my mother, whether she's willing to acknowledge it or not, needs me, and that feels like something new... even if perhaps it isn't.

I sit next to my mom for an hour as she dozes and the drugs drip slowly into her arm. A few other people come and go, in various stages of treatment, taking their places in the recliners and then shuffling off again. One woman who is about my age has a bright purple kerchief tied over her bald head; she doesn't even have eyebrows. She smiles at me as she sits in the chair opposite my mother.

I feel both uncomfortable and humbled by the whole experience; I realize I've been so focused on my little life that I haven't considered other people are facing much bigger problems than whether or not their surrogate might be pregnant.

I haven't even thought about Dani or the possible pregnancy since my mom's diagnosis, but as I shift in my chair I recall that her blood test is today. I should have said something to Mark this morning, but I was so focused on my mother. Is he checking his phone, waiting for the call? I glance at my own phone; there are no missed calls or messages. I slip it into my purse, because in that moment I don't really care about the whole thing, one way or another.

It takes three hours for the chemo to finish and afterwards my mom seems even more exhausted. I drive her home and tuck her up on her worn sofa—the same one we had growing up—and turn on the TV to the QVC channel, which I know my mother likes to watch, even though she never buys anything.

Then I warm up some tomato soup and make a grilled cheese sandwich, which is what she always made me when I was sick. I can picture myself, all bundled up on the sofa like my mother is now, watching PBS Kids with my soup and my sandwich.

It's a surprisingly poignant memory. Mark is right, I realize. My mother took care of me, even if I didn't always feel loved. Maybe love isn't so much a feeling as an action, a doing rather than a telling.

"I feel like a little kid," my mom remarks with a small smile. Her eyes are half-closed, her head back against the armrest.

"Enjoy it," I tell her. "You work hard enough."

"I don't want to..." she begins, and then stops, and I smile.

Make a fuss. Well, maybe I'd like her to, for once.

I stay for another hour, until my mom is asleep.

She only picked at her sandwich and soup, and I tidy the leftovers away and then leave the TV on low, with her still tucked up on the sofa. My heart aches as I look around the shabby little apartment—a living room/kitchen and a tiny bedroom and bathroom and that's it. I don't like leaving her alone here, and I wonder how long she'll be able to stay by herself. From what I read, the chemo will really start to take it out of her.

But that's a problem for another day, I tell myself. I leave a note telling her I'll check in on her tomorrow after work, and then I head to my car. Outside, it's freezing, a metallic tang to the air that suggests snow, and even though it's only six o'clock, it's completely dark, a few faraway stars barely piercing the blackness. I am reaching for my car keys when it finally occurs to me to check my phone.

I have a missed call and text from Mark, and two missed calls and a voicemail from Creating Dreams. My stomach drops and my head feels light as I press to listen to the voicemail.

"Ashley? This is Andrea. I'm so sorry to give you this news by voicemail, as it's always much better in person, but I knew you'd want to know right away about the results of Dani's blood test." A pause that seems to swell and then: "Congratulations, Ashley. You and Mark are going to become parents. Dani is pregnant."

PART TWO

EIGHTEEN

DANI

Two and a half months later

"Dani, Dani, *wake up*."

My sister's insistent voice barely pierces my consciousness as I keep my eyes scrunched closed, my duvet pulled right up to my nose.

"Dani..." She tugs on my arm. "We're going to be late. For the MRI."

Finally, I open my eyes. Callie's prescreening MRI is finally, *finally* happening. After months of back and forth with the insurance company, filling out forms, getting on the waitlist, this day has come, the last hurdle to clear before we can schedule her surgery. Slowly, my stomach already starting to heave, I sit up.

"Okay, okay..." I tell her, half-mumbling. "Just give me a minute."

Callie regards me unhappily; I know I look terrible. I *feel* terrible. Since finding out I was pregnant ten weeks ago, the symptoms have all hit me like a bus—mainly extreme fatigue and nausea, but other weird ones I didn't even know about—a strange, metallic taste in my mouth, cramps in my calves at night that have me waking up screaming, lightheadedness at unexpected times, although that may be down to the fact that I can barely keep anything down and so I'm practically starving myself. Dr. Freedman assured me that it should get better in the second trimester, which starts next week, but so far I haven't noticed any change.

As it is, I can barely drag myself through my days. I had to miss several classes and ask for an extension for my next chapter of my thesis. I told my supervisor I was pregnant—even though I'm not showing, I looked so dreadful I think she was worried I was seriously ill—and she took it in her stride, although she seemed a little surprised, maybe even disappointed.

"Obviously taking care of a baby will affect your studies," she remarked with a little sniff. "Are you planning on taking parental leave?"

"No, I'm not keeping the baby," I replied matter-of-factly. "I'm acting as a surrogate for a couple who's infertile, and as the baby's due over the summer, I don't think it will affect my studies at all." I met her startled gaze with a direct one of my own; this wasn't the first time I'd had to trot out this line, and I knew it would be far from the last.

"Oh, I see. Well, in that case..." She nodded. "I hope you feel better soon."

Like pregnancy was an illness, and, to be fair, right now, it feels like one.

I stagger from my bed as Callie retreats to the living room to wait for me. We have half an hour before we have to be at the orthopedic clinic, and it's a good ten-minute drive. I need to hurry.

I dress quickly, drag a brush through my hair, do my teeth. I force myself to glance at my reflection—pasty-skinned, dull-eyed, lank-haired. So much for that pregnancy glow. It passed me by completely. It feels like some twist of fate, karma's kick, that after not even knowing I was pregnant the first time until I was over halfway through, I've been leveled by symptoms from the get-go this time round, so I can barely get through my days.

My phone pings with a text, and before I turn it over to check, I know who it is. Ashley, giving me her cheery morning greeting, as she has every single day since we found out I was pregnant. I don't actually mind; her texts aren't intrusive in themselves, usually just a greeting with a funny GIF or meme. It's become something of a joke between us, who can find the weirdest one, a moment of lightness in a situation that otherwise feels laden with expectation.

When I first found out I was pregnant, Mark wanted to fly out right away for a visit, maybe even schedule an early ultrasound. I felt bad for putting him off, but I was so sick, and still am, that I asked for them to wait to visit until I felt better.

He agreed—and sent me an enormous gift basket of "Beautifully Blooming" treats—ginger tea and scented candles, expensive lotion for stretch marks and fuzzy socks. It was all lovely stuff, if a little overwhelming, but that, I've come to realize, is Mark's MO. He means well, but he is full on.

Meanwhile, Ashley has taken more of a backseat; besides her daily check-ins, which are never about the pregnancy, I hardly hear from her at all. I appreciate that she's trying to give me some space, but it also makes me wonder. Is she being sensitive, or is she just not that interested in the baby? It's so hard to know.

Right after I found out I was pregnant, Creating Dreams scheduled another Zoom call for the three of us, to discuss more specifically the expectations we'd all pussyfooted around before pregnancy became a reality. Ashley was quiet, a bit withdrawn; halfway through the call, Mark explained that her mother had just been diagnosed with a serious cancer. Ashley gave me an apologetic grimace, like she was sorry for causing trouble, while I stammered through my own condolences.

Then we got down to the nitty-gritty; Mark had a whole typed list of questions. Would I be willing to take prenatal vitamins and folic acid? What about the brand he recommended? Would I refrain from alcohol during the entire pregnancy? Could I guarantee I'd get at least seven hours of sleep a night? Would I be exercising, but not too strenuously? Would I refrain from eating soft cheese—

At that point, Ashley finally intervened. "I have a feeling Frenchwomen don't give up their brie, Mark—"

He glanced up from the paper, frowning. "Studies have shown—"

"I think we've asked enough of Dani," Ashley said quietly. Her voice was firmer than I'd heard it before; I'd always got the sense, without even realizing that I had, that she deferred to Mark, especially in matters relating to this whole baby-making business. But right then, she looked like she was the one who would not be challenged.

Mark put down his paper, taking a deep breath before he said in a deliberately light voice, "Okay, I get that. I'm sorry if I'm coming across as demanding." He paused and then, seeming like he couldn't keep himself from it, added, "I just thought the point of this conversation was to explain to Dani what our expectations are." He glanced pointedly at me, and I could practically hear what was going through his head. *We're paying you sixty-five thousand dollars. I think you can take our damned vitamins.*

"It's fine." I spoke into the silence, needing to clear my throat. "It's fine. Of course I want to do what you want me to do for this baby."

Ashley flashed me another apologetic smile, and Mark, looking vindicated, picked up his paper, ready to fire off another round of questions.

It's been pretty much the same dynamic between the three of us since then. Mark arranged a subscription of prenatal vitamins and folic acid to be delivered monthly to my apartment; he also sent me the "Wellness Mama" cookbook with recipes he'd already bookmarked, *and* he texted me a link to a "Pilates for Pregnancy" YouTube channel. It was all very helpful, and I kind of understood his need to be proactive and in control, but when the morning sickness and fatigue kicked in, I found I didn't have a lot of energy—or patience—for any of it.

Dragging myself through each day was enough; I barely saw Anna or any other friends, and I'm behind on my work. I haven't talked to Ryan since that day on Marine Street Beach, although he did text me a couple of times, asking how I was and wishing me well, which felt more final than if he'd stayed silent. I miss him, even as I'm glad he's not seeing me like this, looking and feeling so wretched, although, if he was, I'm pretty sure he'd be bringing me chicken soup and rubbing my back, and that realization makes me miss him all the more.

"Dani? Are you ready?" Callie's voice sounds strained, and I can't blame her. Although the surgeon assured me the MRI is basically just a formality, it's still a big deal. She'll have to be in what's essentially a big metal tube for forty-five minutes. At least the top of her head will be out, so hopefully she won't be too claustrophobic, but I can certainly understand why she is scared.

"I'm coming." My stomach is churning, but I don't think I can manage to eat anything. Still, I grab a granola bar just in case, and I shoot Callie an apologetic smile as we head out. "Sorry for being slow," I tell her, and she just shrugs. She isn't thrilled with my pregnant self, and I can't blame her for that, either. I'm not thrilled with my pregnant self, and not just with the sickness or fatigue. Ten weeks on, my body is starting to change—my breasts are heavier and more tender, and my once toned stomach has a slight roundness that doesn't shift, no matter how hard I suck in.

Incredibly, or maybe just stupidly, I didn't really think

about how my body would change with pregnancy. I barely remember it from before; I just recall feeling miserable. Quitting school at seven months because it had become unendurable and finishing the year at home. I've blocked out everything else —the roundness of my belly, the flutters and kicks, even having to wear maternity clothes. I must have worn them, but I simply don't remember. It's alarming, really, how much about your life you can forget... if you just try hard enough.

"*Dani*," Callie prompts me impatiently. I'm sitting in the driver's seat, simply staring into space. I've become so *slow*, and it's not the way I want to be. I didn't want this pregnancy to change me, at least not any more than it obviously had to, and, the truth is, it already has.

"Sorry," I say yet again, and I start the car.

The orthopedic clinic is part of the USD Hospital complex, and the MRI machine is in its own room, looking like something out of a sci-fi movie. A nurse asks Callie to change into a hospital gown in a cubicle outside and then ushers us both in; she hangs back, though, when she sees that tubular machine that looks like a rocket.

"Dani..." Her voice trembles.

"Callie, it's going to be fine," I say firmly, a little like I am talking to a small child and not a sixteen-year-old. "Remember, this is just a medical formality, for insurance reasons. They have to do it pre-surgery, but it will be over in less than an hour."

"I *know* all that." She sounds annoyed, and so I stop. I need to stop anyway, because I really should have eaten something this morning. My near-empty stomach is now threatening to heave whatever's left in it from last night.

"Right, I know," I say, and I swallow the acid tang of bile.

The nurse looks at me in concern. "Are you all right?"

"Yes—" I clap my hand over my mouth.

Callie makes a hissing sound. "She's pregnant," she tells the nurse in disdain, just as I whirl around and head for the bathroom.

I retch miserably into the toilet, my cheek resting on the cold porcelain, my eyes closed, feeling wretched not for myself, but for Callie. I'd told her I'd be there for her every step of the way, and here I am, in the bathroom. She deserves so much better. More importantly, she *needs* so much better.

I'm supposed to be stronger than this, I think, angry with myself, and then I suddenly recall Ryan's words to me. *And then I got to know you, and I realized you weren't all those things, at least not as much as I'd thought you were. Oh, you could put it on, and most people bought it, because you're smart and beautiful, but I started to see underneath, to basically what a mess you actually were.*

I'm certainly a mess now. I haven't seen Ryan in nearly three months. I miss him, more than I want to, maybe even more than I expected to, which is equally humbling and shaming. I was both incredulous and devastated when he left, but I soldiered on, because that's what I've always done. Except for right now... when I can barely get up from the floor.

The door to the bathroom creaks open. "Hon?" It's the nurse. "Are you all right?"

"Yes," I manage as I wipe my mouth.

"I found some crackers for you. I thought they might help."

Her thoughtfulness touches me, and it also motivates me to scramble, wincing, up from the cold tiled floor. I unlock the toilet stall and come out grimacing sheepishly.

"Thank you."

"She's a nice girl, your sister," the nurse says as she hands me a packet of saltines. She nods toward my middle. "She said you were having this baby for her, to pay for her surgery, as a surrogate?"

"Yes," I say briefly, and I take a few seconds to rip open the saltines, mainly so I don't have to see the woman's expression. I never know what to expect when I tell people I'm a surrogate—surprise, bemusement, bafflement, judgment. It's usually on a spectrum of those uneasy emotions, only sometimes followed by a reluctant acceptance or rarely, approval.

"That's a kind thing you're doing," the nurse says quietly, and surprised, I look up. "For your sister. And for the couple." She pauses. "My husband and I, we couldn't have kids. We didn't have the money for surrogacy, but if we had..." She shrugs. "Anyway, your sister's ready to have her MRI."

"Thank you," I murmur as I follow her back to the room where Callie is waiting.

I put the saltines aside to help Callie climb up onto the machine. Her face is pale, her eyes seeming huge and very blue.

"It's going to be okay," I whisper. "Remember, this is just a formality."

She gulps and nods and I help her lie down. A few minutes later, the technician, a man in dark green scrubs, comes in, all brisk professionalism, and he explains everything to Callie before starting the procedure. I stand by her head; although she's entirely in the tube, I can see the top of her head and I talk to her quietly to let her know I'm there. It must feel like being electronically entombed, and it's a lot for a sixteen-year-old to take. I nibble a saltine as I keep up a steady murmur of soothing encouragement until Callie, her voice muffled, says, "Dani? Can you be quiet for a little while?"

My sister sounds like her old self, and I laugh.

"Yeah," I tell her, swallowing the last of my saltine. My stomach actually feels settled. "I'll be quiet."

An hour later, we're walking out into the balmy sunshine of a February afternoon in San Diego, having been told we'll get the results of the MRI in about two weeks. Callie is insistent that I drop her off at school for the rest of the day, and so I do, and then I head home to work on a research fellowship I'm applying for this summer. The baby is due in early August, and the fellowship is for July, so I think I can just about swing it, especially if Callie has her surgery in May, which is the hope. By July she'll be back on her feet, I'll be almost done with this pregnancy, and we'll *both* have a new lease on life. I can hardly wait.

I'm just coming into the apartment when a text comes up on my phone—no surprises that it's from Mark. He texts me more than anyone else these days.

Hey Dani, hope you're well. Just wanted to book flights for visit & ultrasound so would love to confirm that next week still works. We'd fly out on Monday, return Thursday, staying at The Fairmont Grand del Mar. We'd love to take you and Callie out to dinner.

Next week? How did I forget that?

I knew they wanted to visit as soon as I was in the second trimester, and next week I'll be almost fourteen weeks, so definitely in the second trimester. I must have agreed to the date back at the beginning, but I don't feel ready yet. I'm still so tired and sick, and I wanted to be glowing with health when they came, because I just *know* Mark is going to be checking up on me in every way possible. Just thinking about the amount of emotional energy it's going to take to host them for two whole days exhausts me. And of course they're staying at the most luxurious hotel in all of San Diego. Not that that matters, but... a sigh escapes me. Somehow it does.

I slump onto my sofa as I stare at my phone. I know I need to reply, just as I know what that reply needs to be. I can't keep putting them off. They deserve better, and they're paying for this.

Sure, Mark, those dates work. The ultrasound is booked for Wednesday, but you probably know that already! See you next week.

Hopefully that wasn't too passive-aggressive, I think as I fling my phone onto the sofa. I think about reaching for my laptop, but I end up just curling up on the sofa, hugging a cushion to me as I fall asleep.

The visit hasn't even happened yet, and already I want it to be over.

NINETEEN
ASHLEY

Our trip to San Diego feels like a mix of a doctor's appointment, a job interview, and a luxury weekend getaway. It's a jarring combination, but everything has been pretty jarring since Dani told us she was pregnant. Or, actually, *Andrea* told us, which was yet another unsettling element to this whole situation; it made Dani feel less like a friend and more like an employee, or maybe a client. Two and a half months on, I'm not sure which *I* feel like, never mind Dani.

It's been a crazy few months, what with my mother's chemotherapy and my job promotion, as well as Christmas, and that's without taking the pregnancy into consideration. The truth is, I've hardly thought about the baby that's coming our way in just over six months. It's a can I keep mentally kicking down the road, but then maybe I don't need to think about it all that much because Mark is doing it enough for the both of us.

I realized, after he sprang into action when Andrea gave us the news, that I shouldn't have been at all surprised. Mark was intense about everything leading *up* to the pregnancy, so of course he was going to go hardcore when it came to Dani's pregnancy. But even I was a little startled when he started

ALL I EVER WANTED

sending her vitamins and researching every aspect of a pregnant woman's health, including elements I was pretty sure Dani wouldn't be comfortable discussing with him. *I* wasn't comfortable with him discussing such intimate details with her.

And so I started feeling like I had to run interference, telling him that sending her three articles a week was maybe two—or three—too many; the gift basket was a nice touch but *not* to send another one of herbal supplements. I told him I would keep in touch with her via text, which he approved; I failed to mention that I never brought up her pregnancy in any of my missives. Why should I? He was doing it enough for the both of us.

"I know you think I'm being over-the-top," he told me early on, his expression a mixture of bashful and stubborn, "but this is important, Ashley. The most important thing that's ever happened to me. To *us*," he corrected quickly, flushing, and I managed not to say something hurtful back. I was starting to feel he'd been right the first time. This was all far more important to him than it was to me, not that I wanted to admit that.

"We just don't want to come on too strong," I reminded him as gently as I could. "Freak Dani out before she's even finished her first trimester."

He frowned, instantly worried. "Do you think I'm freaking her out?"

"A little," I answered hesitantly. "Just a little."

Mark's worried frown morphed into a look of hurt reproof. "Well, maybe *you* could freak her out a little *more*," he replied, and while it wasn't the cleverest comeback, I certainly knew what he meant. I wasn't showing the same level of enthusiasm as he was, no matter how much I tried. Not even close.

It's an unspoken tension that remains between us as we pack for our trip to San Diego... a trip I was reluctant to take, because I don't entirely see the point of it at this stage, but Mark was adamant that we go.

"This is about building a *relationship*," he reminds me yet again as he takes our bags out to the car.

I hold my tongue because it won't be helpful pointing out that Mark seems to view this relationship as controlling Dani's behavior, while I have been trying, in a very backseat sort of way, to be her friend.

"I just don't want her to feel pressured," I say—again—as diplomatically as I can.

"She said she was open to us visiting—"

"I know." We've had this conversation about a million times already, and having it again won't get us anywhere, so I change the subject. "The Fairmont del Mar." I slide him a teasing smile. "Looks fancy."

For a second, Mark looks like he wants to keep talking about Dani, but then he relents and smiles back. "Only the best for you, babe," he quips, and I laugh despite the nerves churning in my stomach. I'm glad we've gotten back on an even keel, even as I acknowledge to myself just how hard it is to get there these days, and how unnatural it now feels.

We arranged to meet Dani on Tuesday morning for breakfast before the ultrasound, although Mark had suggested having dinner with her as soon as we got in. I put him off for all our sakes; I think Mark and I need some alone time together, and Dani will already be visiting with us for most of Wednesday. That feels like enough time to me.

And I feel like I made the right call when we step into the sumptuous hotel with its ornate marble lobby, its pools and palm trees. Mark booked us a poolside room with a patio, a king-sized bed, and a sunken marble tub. I see a dozen long-stemmed red roses wrapped with a scarlet silk ribbon and a bottle of champagne chilling in a bucket as I step into the room.

Mark comes up behind me, resting his hands on my shoulders. "I wanted this to be special," he says, and kisses the back of my neck. "For *us*."

The tension of the last few months, never truly discussed but always present, melts away as I am reminded of just how wonderful my husband truly is.

"Me too," I whisper, and he kisses me again.

Later, as we are sprawled in the huge bed, half-drunk flutes of champagne discarded nearby, the pool glittering through the patio doors, I feel almost perfectly content. Dani—and a baby—are just about the furthest things from my mind.

Mark leans over and kisses my bare shoulder. "We have a dinner reservation at eight," he murmurs against my skin, and I smile, my eyes fluttering closed.

For a few minutes, I want to leave it all behind—not just thoughts of Dani and the pregnancy, but also worries about my mom—nearly three months on, she's on a break between rounds of chemo, but she had to be signed off work, which she hates. She's still as stoic as ever, but I can tell the chemo has taken its toll, and it makes me feel protective of her in a way I never have been before. While I'm gone, I've arranged for meals to be delivered and a neighbor to check in on her every day, but she was another reason I wasn't so keen on this trip. And work... while I love it, it's a lot more pressure and responsibility than I've ever had before, and I exist in a near-constant state of anxiety, desperate to prove myself. I'm glad I accepted the job, but that doesn't mean it's easy.

Right now, however, I'm glad we came. Mark and I needed this, like he said, for us. Just us.

He sits up in bed, shrugging off the duvet, and reaches for his phone. He draws his breath in before a sigh escapes, and already I'm tensing.

"What is it?" I ask, half-hoping it's work and not something with Dani.

"Nothing," he says briefly, and I know it's Dani.

I roll over and prop myself up onto my elbow.

"What is it?" I ask again.

Mark rises from the bed in a twitchy way. "Dani's asking if we can skip brunch and just meet her for the ultrasound."

"Okay…" I am not that sad about this. "Did she say why?"

He shrugs, his back to me as he pulls on his boxer shorts. "Just that she doesn't do well in the mornings."

"Well, she has had really bad morning sickness." Something that has concerned Mark, in case she's not getting adequate nutrition.

"I know, but…" He rubs the back of his neck. "We're only here for forty-eight hours. I mean…" He shakes his head, and I know he's disappointed, although part of me doesn't really get *why*. I mean, isn't it the *baby* we want to bond with, not the mother we'll most likely never see again? Not to be cold about it, but… that is the reality, right? At least I *hope* that's the reality.

"Well, we are still spending the afternoon with her," I remind him. Mark suggested that after the ultrasound, Dani show us her favorite sights around San Diego. "And dinner with her and her sister," I add.

"Yeah." He smiles at me, almost in apology. "I know."

I realize I really don't want to talk about Dani when I'm lying in bed, having just drunk champagne and made love with my husband. "I'm going to go out to the pool," I say abruptly, and I roll out of bed and reach for my clothes.

Outside, I position myself on a sun lounger and stare blindly at the water, sunlight glinting off its surface, hurting my eyes. I'm being unreasonable, I tell myself, far from the first time, for getting annoyed by Mark's intensity. Like he said, we're only here for forty-eight hours; this visit is *important*. Besides, I can't be jealous that Mark wants to meet Dani so much *and* irritated that he seems controlling rather than friendly. I'm a contradiction to myself, but maybe that's the nature of this situation.

Mark and I knew it would be complicated going in, but I had no idea just how much.

The next morning Mark and I drive to the clinic near the university where we're meeting Dani for the ultrasound. It's another beautiful day, the fog rising from the waterfront in gossamer threads, the sky high above a bright, deep blue. Mark and I managed to regain our equilibrium as we enjoyed a delicious three-course dinner last night; afterwards, I soaked in the sunken tub for the better part of an hour. By the time I got out, I felt better about this whole situation. Mostly.

In any case, I am determined to be upbeat this morning, to be positive and proactive about *everything*. Over breakfast, I agreed to Mark's suggestion for Dani to have ultrasounds every six weeks, even though that seems a little excessive to me. I told him an amniocentesis sounded wise, even though I'd read the procedure is somewhat invasive. I said I thought going maternity clothes shopping with Dani would be fun.

At that, he'd put his hand over mine. "I just want you to be *involved*, Ash," he said earnestly. "I don't want it to be hard for you. If you feel it's too much..."

"It's not too much," I assured him. I wouldn't let it be. "And it will be fun. Almost like shopping for myself." If there was the *slightest* edge to my voice, I don't think Mark heard it.

And now we're here, walking across the sun-warmed parking lot; I slip my sunglasses onto my forehead as we step into the clinic. Dani is already there, sitting in a chair, flipping through a magazine, which she tosses aside as soon as we step through the door.

The first thing that passes through my mind is that she looks kind of terrible—her skin is pale and pasty, her lank hair pulled back into a ponytail. I knew she'd had morning sickness, but I guess I didn't realize quite how badly.

"Dani." Mark's voice is warm, his hand outstretched. "So good to see you again."

She shakes his hand limply, manages a wan smile before turning to me. "Hi, I'm Dani. But I guess you know that."

"And I guess you know I'm Ashley." I give a light laugh as I shake her hand. "It's great to finally meet you." I'm worried I sound too formal for what is really a pretty intimate situation, but I know I could never pull off the kind of jovial familiarity that is so effortless for Mark, and in any case, I'm not sure Dani would appreciate it.

She tucks a strand of hair behind her ear. "Sorry to back out of brunch, but mornings and food haven't gone that great for me. I think I'm finally starting to turn a corner, though, thank goodness."

"I'm so sorry you've been so sick," I say, while Mark frowns. I'm pretty sure he wants to make some remark about making sure to say hydrated, but he's managing to restrain himself.

"It's strange," Dani says to me, seeming to almost deliberately ignore Mark's remark, "because last time I wasn't sick at all."

"I guess each pregnancy is different," I reply. "Or so I've heard. But morning sickness usually lessens in the second trimester, doesn't it?"

"Meant to," Dani agrees wryly.

I glance down at her middle as discreetly as I can; I don't think she's showing yet. Although she doesn't look great, she's clearly athletic and even at fourteen weeks pregnant, her stomach is probably more toned than mine is, which is a somewhat depressing thought.

"Thank you for letting us be here," I tell her, and Mark quickly chimes in.

"Yes, thank you, Dani. We really, really appreciate it." His voice is warm, and he manages a laugh. "If I come across as a little too much, sometimes, well, it's just because we're both so excited."

Dani glances between the two of us, and I can hear her thoughts as if she'd spoken them through a megaphone. *Are you both excited? Really?*

"Yes," I say a little forcefully. "We really are."

"Well, it's understandable, I guess," Dani murmurs, and then we all descend into a silence that feels more confused than awkward. It's so hard to get my head around it all—Dani is pregnant, Mark is the baby's father, I will be the baby's mother. In six months, we'll most likely never see Dani again, even though this baby is biologically hers, and so will be forever tied to her—and my husband. None of it makes sense. None of it feels like something that should be allowed to happen.

"Dani Bryson?" a nurse calls from the doorway to the examining rooms, and we all turn.

"That's me," Dani says, and she glances at us, summoning a smile. "Ready?"

"Ready," Mark sings out, and my stomach lurches with nerves as we all troop toward the door.

The room with the ultrasound machine is already darkened, and the technician is waiting, a quick, professional smile for us all as we come in.

"Welcome, welcome," she says, and gestures to Dani to sit on the examining table. There are chairs next to it for Mark and me; clearly they've been briefed.

We perch on our seats, while Dani hoists herself up onto the table.

"How are you feeling, Dani?" the technician asks, her voice all maternal warmth, her body angled away from us.

As Dani haltingly replies, I can't help but feel like an interloper, like I shouldn't be here at all. I picture the Child Catcher in *Chitty Chitty Bang Bang*, eyes gleaming with avarice as he rubs his hands together gleefully, looking for the next innocent child he can snatch. Is that me? *Us?* And yet this baby is as much Mark's as it is Dani's. I need to remember that.

"This might feel a little cold," the technician warns as she starts squirting the gel.

Dani has lifted her top, revealing a smooth expanse of golden belly, only very slightly rounded. She has a belly button piercing, a tiny diamond winking in the middle of that stretch of smooth skin. I feel like I should look away, like I'm a voyeur, but Mark is all attentiveness, his gaze on the still-blank ultrasound screen as the technician smooths the gel over Dani's belly. Her head is turned, her face averted from us, but she's not looking at the screen. I can't help but feel sorry for her; this is all so weird, for her most of all.

"All right now..." the technician murmurs, and then begins prodding Dani's stomach rather forcefully with the ultrasound wand. Within a few seconds, an image pops up on the screen. At first, it's nothing but black and white blobs, like the ink spots of a Rorschach test, only moving.

Then, slowly, miraculously, it begins to take shape. I see the nose first—tiny and snub. Then the head, and then a hand, with a thumb tucked up toward the tiny mouth. The knees are tucked up too, and I can see the vertebrae of the baby's spine, like a string of pearls. It's all there, every part of this tiny, beautiful, *incredible* human being. I catch my breath with an audible sound of wonder.

A baby.

A real, live baby. Until this moment, a baby was nothing more than an abstract concept to me, a one day what-if I wasn't even sure, in my darker moments, that I totally wanted. But now it's here, in this room, and as the technician turns the sound up on the ultrasound machine, we all hear the *whoosh whoosh whoosh* of the baby's heartbeat, like a galloping horse.

Mark wipes a tear from his eye; for the first time, I realize just how utterly emotional this is for him. Finally, he has someone who shares his blood, his DNA, his very self.

And as for me? I thought I would feel disconnected from this experience, like I had nothing to do with any of this, but already my arms ache to hold this precious little one, and my heartbeat matches the galloping rhythm of the child we're going to have, as a rush of love, visceral and overwhelming, consumes me.

Our baby. *Our baby.*

"Isn't it amazing?" Mark whispers. His voice is hushed, like he's in a church, and this moment *feels* spiritual. Holy.

I reach for his hand, and he smiles at me, still tearful.

Then I turn to look at Dani. Her head was averted before, but now she's staring at the ultrasound screen just as we were, her lips slightly parted, her eyes wide, her expression transfixed. Mark is asking the technician some questions, and she's responding by pointing out various body parts, but I can't tear my gaze away from Dani.

The look on her face, I fear, mirrored the one on my own—a look of wonder and joy.

And that sense is compounded when she moves her head, and catches my gaze, and that look of amazement on her morphs into something else, something that makes a wave of dread ripple sickly through me.

For the look on our surrogate's face then is one of uneasy guilt—and defiance.

TWENTY

DANI

I leave the clinic in a dazed blur, followed by Mark and Ashley, although, the truth is, I'm barely aware of them.

We must have exchanged pleasantries, I *think* we did, but I have no idea what I said. I do remember that after the ultrasound, the technician asked Mark and Ashley if they'd like a photo, which they both agreed to with eager alacrity. When I asked if I could have one, too, a silence descended on the room that felt... *arctic*.

Then the technician smiled at me and assured me that of course I could. When she left to get them from the printer, none of us spoke. I was wiping the cold gel from my stomach, conscious that both Mark and Ashley had been looming over me while my shirt was rucked up practically to my boobs, and in that moment... I almost *hated* them. It was a visceral feeling, almost overwhelming, even though I knew it didn't make sense. I reminded myself that they were basically paying for Callie's surgery, but... it was a hard feeling to shake.

When the technician returned with the photos placed in two separate envelopes, silently handing one to Mark and

Ashley and then the other to me, none of us opened them. I slid my envelope into my purse and wondered, when I was feeling this way, how I was going to spend the afternoon showing them the San Diego Zoo and Balboa Park.

Somehow, we made it outside, chatting inconsequentially, and then Mark suggested we leave my car at the clinic and drive together to the swanky place he'd booked for lunch, and Ashley hurriedly intervened that *Dani might like to drive her own car*, and even though I knew she was trying to stand up for me, it infuriated me that she was talking about me in the third person.

Because, I realized, that's what I was to them—the third person. The extra, unwanted one, who just happened to be having *their* baby. Not mine, no matter how much that little blob on the ultrasound screen had felt like a part of me as soon as I saw it. Him or her... a person. *My* person.

I know I can't think that way now, not for my sake and not for Mark and Ashley's. I need to make this work, and so I agree to leave my car there and drive with them. I sit in the back, although Ashley awkwardly offers me the front. Mark is being his usual jovial self, but I find him unsettlingly easy to read; all that affability can't hide those flashes of disapproval, of desire to control.

He booked a table at Coasterra, a trendy restaurant that offers "Modern Mexican" with a terrace right on the water. As I peruse the menu, I realize there's very little I'm going to be able to eat without getting heartburn or throwing up, or both. Funny how Mark can be so concerned that I'm staying hydrated yet still book a restaurant that serves only fancy tacos and spicy seafood enchiladas. I order the pear and fig salad, and when I sense Mark's concerned look, I humbly request that they omit the blue cheese.

I'm tired of this already, and it's only been a few hours. If they weren't paying for the surgery, I think, I'd be out of here.

But they are, and I know I'm being oversensitive, because this situation is so *weird*.

"So," Ashley breaks the silence after the waiter has left. "You feel you've turned a corner with the morning sickness?"

"I think so."

"That's great, Dani." She smiles at me, but I see her eyes are anxious, her fingers pleated together before she notices and places her palms flat on the table. "Seeing the baby on that ultrasound," she says suddenly, glancing between me and Mark as she nibbles her lip. "It was so incredible." She lets out a little laugh. "Until that moment... I don't think I really believed there was a baby in there." She laughs again, uncertainly.

Neither did I. I don't say it, of course. I'm pretty sure neither Mark nor Ashley wants to hear that sentiment from me. But it's true, until I saw the baby on the ultrasound—head, body, nose, lips, fingers and toes—I didn't feel at all connected to him or her as a being. Pregnancy was just feeling tired and sick, not being able to keep my breakfast down, dragging myself to work. The first time around, I never looked at an ultrasound. I never even looked at the *baby*.

This felt a lot more real than I expected it to. A baby, *my* baby. I wasn't meant to feel that way, I didn't want to, but when I saw that image on the screen... I did. A rush of wonder, of joy, of love, went through me, stronger than anything I've felt before. But was it just a moment, or something more?

I know I need some time to process what that means... *if* it can mean anything, which it probably can't, because the reality still is that I need the sixty-five thousand dollars for Callie's surgery, and besides that, I really don't need a baby in my life.

Something that I can't believe needs saying, even in the privacy of my own mind.

"Dani?" Mark's voice, slightly strident, breaks into my thoughts and I blink him and Ashley back into focus.

"Sorry, I was a million miles away there for a sec."

"I was just saying that we were hoping you would have another ultrasound in six weeks," he says. "To find out if it's a boy or a girl. We'd like to be there, as well, if that's okay."

Again?

I nod mechanically, because what else can I do? Once more, I think of Callie's surgery, and I force myself to smile. "Of course," I say. "That will be great."

A mingled look of relief and satisfaction passes across Mark's face, and he sits back, like he's finished a job. "Great." He glances at Ashley. "Shall we order champagne to celebrate seeing the ultrasound? And sparkling apple juice for Dani?"

I try not to grit my teeth. *I'm right here*, I think, *and I don't want damned apple juice.* "Sounds perfect," I practically chirp, as inside I both wilt and seethe.

The day passes slowly, so slowly. We eat lunch—I pick at my salad while Mark and Ashley share enchiladas and chili-roasted salmon, drinking the better part of a bottle of champagne between them. Ashley keeps making hesitant overtures to me, while Mark has taken on a Henry the Eighth kind of vibe, lounging back and observing me shrewdly over the rim of his glass.

Or at least that's how it *feels*. In truth, I'm pretty sure I can't trust my own judgment, because ever since seeing that ultrasound, it's been hard not to look at Mark and Ashley as nothing more than a pair of greedy thieves.

Halfway through the meal, I excuse myself to the ladies' and, in the toilet stall, with shaking hands, I take the slip of photo paper from the envelope and study the ultrasound image of the baby. *My* baby.

I whisper it under my breath, like a prayer. "My baby. *My* baby."

I release a shuddery breath, because this is so wrong. I

should not be thinking like this. I should not be *letting* myself think like this. No good can come of it, I know. And yet here I am, crouched on the toilet, studying the blurry, blobby photo of the ultrasound like it's a sacred text.

I hear the door to the bathroom open, and I tense, waiting for whoever it is to go into a stall. Then I hear a voice, soft and hesitant.

"Dani?" It's Ashley. "Are you okay?"

"Yeah, I'm fine."

I quickly flush the toilet, using the noise to cover the sound of me putting the photo away. A few seconds later, I unlock the door and come out of the stall to see Ashley regarding me unhappily.

"Sorry," I say as I go to wash my hands. "I was just feeling a little nauseous."

"I feel like maybe this isn't going as well as any of us want it to," Ashley says hesitantly, and I still for a second before I turn off the water and dry my hands. I don't know how to reply.

"It's bound to be awkward at first," I finally tell her.

"Yes, but..." She pauses. "I'm sorry if we're making it worse somehow." She bites her lip and then tries for a smile. "I feel like the champagne was a little too much."

Her honesty is surprisingly refreshing. "Maybe a little," I admit, smiling to take any sting from my words. I like Ashley; at least in a different scenario, I *could* like her. I'm not sure I do in this one.

She nods slowly, accepting. "Mark is really excited," she says in a low voice, like a confession. "As I'm sure you can tell. This means so much to him. More than you could even imagine."

"And does it mean as much to you?" I ask bluntly, and her startled gaze flies to mine before flitting away.

"Wh-what?" she stammers, flushing.

I stay silent, waiting for her reply. Is she still going to be honest with me?

"Probably not quite as much," she admits in a low voice. "Because... well, as he'd said, the... the biological aspect is so important to him. To have someone who shares his genes..."

"But this baby won't share *your* genes," I point out, and then feel a flicker of guilt when I see Ashley flinch.

"I know that, of course," she whispers, staring down at the ground. "And that's been an issue for me—not... not because I wanted to have my own baby, although I did, but just because the way it all happened made me feel really distanced from everything. I struggled to connect with any aspect of it."

I nod slowly in acknowledgment. That's how she's come across, not that I'm going to tell her that now. She's been put in a hard position... just as I have.

"But, Dani..." Ashley looks up, and her dark eyes are luminous, her pale face flushed, so for a moment she looks otherworldly, like a dark-haired Madonna, the light of heaven beaming down on her. "All that changed when I saw that image on the ultrasound screen. That's what I was trying to say earlier, but I don't think it came across very well. I was just... I was so excited to *be* excited, if that makes sense. I felt connected, really connected, for the first time since this whole thing began, and that was amazing."

So did I, I think, just as I did before, and this time I almost say it. I *want* to say it, I want Ashley to know. I want to know what she thinks about the fact that we're both bonding with this baby in a way neither of us expected to.

A smile trembles on her lips as she blinks at me, everything in her so clearly yearning for me to—what? Offer my blessing?

Yes, I realize that's exactly what she wants.

And so that's what I do.

"Ashley, that's so great," I tell her. "That's just what I

wanted to hear." If my voice sounds wooden, she doesn't seem to notice. "I really want you and Mark *both* to bond with the baby," I continue. I feel as if I am reading from a script, playing a role—*the saintly surrogate*. "I get why it might be a little harder for you," I tell her as she blinks back tears. "That's totally understandable. So it's great that the ultrasound really made a difference."

"It really did," she whispers. "Thank you, Dani. You really are giving us such a... such a gift."

Well, not really a *gift*, I think. More like merchandise. Very expensive merchandise that will pay for my sister's surgery.

All I have to do is keep remembering that. Over and over again.

Ashley and I head back into the restaurant together, and Mark smiles to see us together. I tell myself he's not the enemy; that his intense level of involvement is both expected and understandable. And really, he's paying for the pleasure of having me drink sparkling apple juice and not eat blue cheese. I need to remember that, too.

"Hey." I retake my seat, smiling at him. "Sorry about that. Still feeling a little queasy."

"I'm sorry to hear that," Mark murmurs, his forehead puckering in concern. "Maybe I shouldn't have picked a Mexican restaurant. I'm so sorry, Dani. That was thoughtless."

He sounds so genuinely remorseful that I find it easy to let it go. "I love Mexican," I reassure him. "And the salad was delicious. Trust me, I'm feeling a lot better than I was last week."

"That's good to hear."

We finish our meal, keeping the conversation light. Mark asks me about my PhD, and I do my best to explain about bacterial pathogenesis in layman's terms. To his credit, he understands more than the average person and even asks a few intelligent questions. The antipathy I was feeling earlier has definitely receded, which can only be a good thing.

After lunch, we head to Balboa Park, which is where every tourist goes in San Diego. It's a combination of nature trails, parkland, and seventeen different museums, along with the world-famous San Diego Zoo. We can't see it all in the space of a single afternoon, and so I suggest a stroll through Zoro Garden, a former nudist colony turned butterfly garden, and then a zip around the San Diego Museum of Art. After that, I know I'll need to go home and put my feet up before meeting Mark and Ashley at the Fairmont for dinner with Callie. This day feels like it will never end.

We keep the conversation desultory as we tour the museum, strolling through the various galleries.

"Do you like art?" Mark asks me at one point, sounding genuinely interested, and embarrassed, I shrug.

"As much as the average person, I guess. I'm more of a science person, really."

He nods, seemingly approving, and I wonder if he's hoping this baby has my scientific genes.

I pause in front of a portrait, *Esther Fortune Warren and her daughter Hester*, by Thomas Sully. It was painted in 1811 and it's of a young woman with dark curly hair—a little bit like Ashley's, actually—holding a baby to her. Clutching the little girl, really, her chin resting against the baby's forehead protectively. The baby is golden-haired and rosy-cheeked, oblivious to the look on her mother's face, which is watchful, a little sad, maybe even a little scared. Or am I being fanciful, reading my own emotions into the face of this long-dead woman?

Mark comes to stand next to me. "Beautiful, isn't it?" he says quietly. "Poignant."

Yes, poignant. Poignant with the upcoming loss, because that's how I know I need to think. I need to prepare myself for what is coming, what *has* to come. I think Mark senses some of my emotion, or maybe he feels it himself, because he doesn't say anything else and I don't reply, so we both simply stand in front of the painting and let it soak into us.

A minute later, Ashley comes over to join us. I hear her quietly indrawn breath and when I glance at her, her face is pale as she stares at the painting. The moment, which felt poignant and profound, has suddenly become painful.

I move onto the next painting without a word, staring blindly at *Still-life with Peaches*, waiting for the moment—and the feeling—to pass.

At four o'clock, the Weirs drive me back to my car and I leave them with relief; I'm exhausted, and we're meeting up again for dinner in just three hours, which I kind of can't believe. I just want this day to be over.

Callie is sitting on the sofa, my laptop propped on her lap, as I come into the apartment.

"Hey." Her eyebrows lift. "How was it all?"

I hesitate, realizing I should have prepared for this moment. I'd told Callie I was meeting the Weirs and having the ultrasound, so I should have expected her to ask. I just don't have a reply ready—at least not one that I can pull off convincingly, not when all my emotions are so jumbled up and intense.

"It was about what I expected," I finally say as I go to the sink to get a glass of water.

"Good or bad?" Callie asks, and I shrug.

"Both, in a way. I don't know."

I glug my water while Callie slowly closes the lid of my laptop, regarding me thoughtfully all the while. I don't think I'm going to stand up under her scrutiny.

"Are you okay?" she asks.

I put my glass down. "Yeah."

"Dani..."

"Yeah, I'm okay, Callie," I say more firmly. I'm getting my equilibrium back. "It was just a long, emotional kind of day."

"The baby's okay? You saw it on the ultrasound?"

And just like that I'm back to being near-tearful. "I did," I confirm, and my voice sounds a little clogged.

Callie is immediately alarmed. "Dani—"

I hold up a hand. "I'm okay, Callie, really. It's just... been a really long day."

Her expression softens. "Are you feeling sad?" she asks softly, and I have to wipe my eyes.

"A little." I force myself to rally. "I mean, that's to be expected, all things considered. It's part of the process." I think of the counseling I still need to have. Maybe I'll book my first session, because I know now I'm going to need more help to get through this than I thought I would.

My phone starts buzzing and wearily I slip it out of my pocket, wondering if it's Mark or Ashley. It feels like they can't leave me alone for five minutes, which I know is unfair, because they're here for such a short time.

But it's not Mark or Ashley. It's the office of the surgeon who is meant to do Callie's surgery. I swipe to take the call.

"Hello?"

"Is this the guardian of Callie Bryson?"

"Yes, Dani Bryson, her sister."

"Hello, we'd like to schedule an appointment for you to come in and discuss her recent MRI results."

"Okay... is this normal procedure?" From the corner of my eye, I see Callie frown and I shake my head, try to smile. "I mean, because the MRI was just a formality, I thought," I tell the receptionist.

"I'm afraid I can't comment on individual results, only that Dr. Maier wanted to speak with you and Callie personally. Would next week work?"

"Yeah, sure, fine." We arrange an appointment for Monday,

and I end the call, just as Callie comes up to me, her face pinched with anxiety, her hands clenched into fists.

"What was that about?" she demands.

"They just want to discuss the MRI results," I say as casually as I can. "No big deal." But instead my insides are tightening with fear, because what if it *is* a big deal?

What if this changes everything?

TWENTY-ONE

ASHLEY

"So, tell me what brought you here today, Ashley."

The counselor's voice over the Zoom call is warm and inviting, but I am too tense to let it relax me. I know there are people who like talking about themselves to strangers, but I am not one of them. The only reason I arranged this counseling session was because I had to, and also because of that ultrasound last week, which feels like it changed everything for me. I went from being negatively ambivalent about surrogacy to wanting this baby with a desperation I wasn't sure I'd ever feel, and it's alarming and exciting in equal measure.

I'm not sure how to say any of that to this woman, or even if I want to.

"Well..." I say nervously, smoothing my skirt, "I think you probably know why, since Creating Dreams recommended you." I glance around; I'm in one of Kennett's conference rooms during my lunch hour, and the floor-to-ceiling window facing the hallway is making me feel exposed.

"Yes, of course," the counselor, Margaret, replies easily. "Everyone who goes through surrogacy is required to have counseling during the process." She leans forward, her dangly earrings—they look like little chandeliers—swinging against her neck. "But *beyond* that, Ashley. What has this experience so far brought up for you that you'd like to discuss? Because counseling isn't meant to be just something to check off, as I'm sure you appreciate. It's meant to help you come to terms with your emotions, whether negative or positive or ambivalent... I've found this whole process stirs up a lot of big feelings." She smiles, an invitation to emote.

"Well..." I clear my throat. "Yes, I suppose it has. I must admit, I started this whole process feeling pretty... unsure." As soon as I say that, I wish I hadn't, because it feels too revealing, but Margaret is nodding in seemingly sympathetic understanding, and so, emboldened, I continue. "I just felt left out, as in a way I was the only one who wasn't directly involved. But beyond that..." I swallow, sifting through the feelings I haven't yet wanted to examine too closely. "Part of me wasn't sure I even *wanted* to be a mother." I think of that ripple of relief that went through me when Dr. Bryant told me I couldn't get pregnant. I haven't been able to shake it... until now. "But then," I continue hurriedly, "everything changed." I really don't want Margaret to think I'm still in that negative space of not wanting a baby, because I'm not. I'm really not.

Margaret leans back and crosses her legs. "Tell me about how it changed," she says, and so haltingly I explain about the miraculous magic of a single, grainy ultrasound image.

Even just picturing that barely-visible baby makes my heart swell with helpless love. She was so *real*. I know I can't possibly know for sure, but she feels like a girl to me. A perfect little girl.

"That's wonderful," Margaret says warmly. "It's amazing how technology can connect us to these lived moments."

I nod, although I'm not exactly sure what she means, simply because I want to go with it, but then she cocks her head and floors me with the next question, stated in such an innocent yet knowing tone.

"So, tell me more about how reluctant you felt before. What do you think that was about, Ashley?"

"Well, I... That is... I don't..." As ever, I stumble over my words in my attempt to sidestep and prevaricate.

Margaret simply waits, a small smile hovering about her lips. I fall silent. I don't want to keep skirting the issue, I realize. I want to get to the bottom of what I feel and why, because I know I could never say anything about this to Mark.

But I can say it to Margaret.

"When I found out I couldn't get pregnant," I blurt, "I felt relieved."

To her credit, Margaret's expression doesn't change. She simply says in her calm, warm voice, "Tell me more about that."

"It came as a surprise," I admit. "I thought I wanted children. I mean, I *do*—" She stops me by holding up a hand.

"Ashley, there is no judgment here. And nothing I say is reported to Creating Dreams or anyone else. This isn't some kind of psychological check to make sure you're a suitable parent. This is for you, and *only* you." She punctuates this statement by sitting back with a little sigh and smile. "So take your time. There are no right or wrong answers here."

I nod, thoughts and feelings fluttering through my mind in an emotional kaleidoscope. And then I find myself saying slowly, "I never wanted to make a fuss." Margaret's eyebrows lift, but otherwise she simply sits and waits. "That's what my mom always said to me, growing up," I continue. I'm not looking at Margaret, or at anything; I'm turned inward, picturing my childhood in a grainy montage of shabby apartments and tinny-sounding television. "My dad walked out when I was a baby, and she had no help. She worked two jobs to keep a roof over our heads, and she was *amazing*." My voice throbs with this newly discovered, heartfelt sincerity. My mom was—and is—amazing, and that is something I've only just learned—and appreciated.

"But she always—well, *often*—told me not to make a fuss," I continue. "Probably because she was so maxed out she couldn't handle anymore. In any case, I never did. And I think, growing up, and even as an adult, that's been my MO. Don't make a fuss. Don't rock the boat. So when Mark—my husband—said he really, really wanted children, I said I wanted them too. Of course I did." I fall silent as I consider all this. I've never said anything like this out loud before. I've never even thought it.

"And when you told him you did, how did you feel about that?" Margaret asks after a moment has passed.

I'm fully aware that she isn't doing all that much, just finding neutral-sounding ways to get me to keep talking. But the truth is, that's enough, because I want to talk. I *need* to, because since this whole surrogacy thing started, my emotions have been all over the place.

"I don't think I even thought how I felt about it," I tell her. "I just went along with everything because it felt like the right thing to do. But, deep down, I had this fear that I wouldn't be a good mom." The words are spilling out, coming from a deep, wounded part of me I didn't even know I could access. "That I *couldn't* be, because of the way I grew up. Because I didn't feel my mom was a good mom, and frankly, most of the time she didn't seem like she could be bothered to even pretend to be maternal. At least, that's how it felt at the time... but looking back, I've realized she was an amazing mom. She worked so hard, and maybe she wasn't this cuddly, emotional, super-supportive type, but she was *there*. You know?"

Margaret, smiling faintly, simply nods.

My tone turns fierce. "She was *great*, and I accept that now, and appreciate it, and I also realize that moms can be different. There's not one-size-fits-all for being a good mother. And when I saw that ultrasound... I realized *I* could be one... whatever that looked like." The realization is like a sunburst, spreading light through me, giving me hope and even joy. I have to wipe my eyes. "It's possible. Maybe I'll be a great mom." My voice throbs. "Why shouldn't I be?"

Margaret smiles and nods. "Exactly, Ashley," she says, like I've given her the right answer to the riddle of the universe. "Why shouldn't you?"

By the time the session finishes, I feel limp with emotional exhaustion, and I have to drag myself back to my desk.

Since getting my promotion, I've loved work. I love talking to people on the phone, sounding so confident and self-assured. I love flipping through my calendar, looking for dates I'm free to meet or talk, because I am so very busy. I love the way my heels click on the kitchen floor as I go for a coffee refill of the designer travel mug Mark got me as a promotion present.

I know that these are little things, that I've always liked the trappings of work rather than the work itself, but that's okay, because it turns out I'm good at it. I might have been nicknamed "the Mouse," but when it comes to clinching a deal on the phone, my inner lioness comes out roaring.

But this afternoon, after my counseling call, I feel too jumbled up inside to do much of anything, and so I end up doing a lot of mindless admin simply to stay busy. Since we returned from San Diego a week ago, Mark and I have been in a fever of excitement. He wants to pick paint colors for the nursery, and I'm only one step behind him, lagging only because I'm afraid to trust that this is really going to happen. Dani is only fourteen weeks along. There's a lot of time between now and her signing her baby over to us.

Part of me wishes, savagely, that we'd gone with an egg donor like we'd originally planned. Then we wouldn't have this uncertainty, this *fear*, because we could have had a birth order already signed and stamped. The baby that we saw on that ultrasound screen would be, most definitively, *ours*.

But that's not the case and so we have nearly six more months of limbo, which at this point is utterly terrifying... and there's nothing I can do about it.

I haven't spoken of my fears to Mark, mainly because I don't think he could handle them. He has the desperate light of a zealot in his eye; our whole trip to San Diego felt tense because Mark was, at turns, trying so hard to either impress or influence Dani. When I asked him, gently, to tone it down just a little, he looked hurt, and then annoyed.

"We have a lot on the line here, Ashley," he'd whispered, when Dani was in the bathroom at lunch. "Not to mention that, including medical costs, we're paying upwards of a hundred grand to her to have this baby. So I think it's not too much of an ask, to expect her to refrain from some blue cheese."

I agreed with him, in theory, but it still made me cringe, and I could tell it was irritating Dani. I did what I could to mitigate Mark's controlling impulses, but I'm not sure I was very successful.

Dinner, at least, seemed to go well; Callie was a sweet kid, and Dani clearly doted on her, and we steered clear of any pregnancy conversation, which I think was a relief for all of us. But I haven't heard from Dani since we left, and I feel uneasy.

I really, really want this to work now, and while I trust my about-face, I'm not sure I trust Dani... even though I want to.

I leave work an hour early to visit my mom, who is about to start her next round of chemotherapy. Three months after she started, she's holding steady, but there hasn't been as much improvement as either of us longed for, although my mom was, as ever, pragmatic about it. Still, I tell myself there's still time, even as I suspect there isn't.

As I let myself into her apartment—she gave me the key a few months ago—I see that my mom is, as usual, asleep on the sofa. She hasn't been able to return to work and Mark and I are paying her rent, something I know she resents and appreciates in equal measure. It's only been a few days since I last saw her, but I am jolted by the sight of her asleep on the sofa—her hair is lank, her body frail, her skin papery and thin. She looks old, and she also looks ill. I told myself she was holding steady with the chemo, but right then I wonder, and that scares me.

She has a CT scan next week to see if the tumor has shrunk, and I am semi-dreading the news, even as I hope for the best.

"Mom...?" I call gently, and her eyes flutter open before her face creases into a smile.

"Ashley." She reaches out one claw-like hand, and I thread my fingers through hers, something we never did when I was growing up, but I think we're both grateful for the physical affection now. "How are you?"

"Good." I perch on the chair next to her, still holding her hand. "More importantly, how are *you*?"

"Oh, right as rain." She lets out a soft, tired huff of laughter. "Can't you tell?"

I smile; this is another new discovery, my mother's sense of humor. "Well, don't run any marathons till next week," I joke back, and she smiles as her eyelids flutter closed.

My heart aches to look at her. I feel as if we missed so much time together, and yet I don't think we could have had that time before she got cancer. Why is it, that hardship and even tragedy is what forces us to wake up and realize what we're about to lose? Why can't we have those realizations earlier, so much earlier?

I slip my fingers from my mom's and go to the kitchen to make her some dinner—her usual tomato soup and grilled cheese that she'll only pick at, but I try, and so does she. I feel a heaviness inside me, along with a hope, the two twined together. There is something new starting, just as something else is slipping away. How can it all happen so fast?

As I return to the sofa with her dinner tray, my mom's eyes open and she smiles at me. "You're so good to me, Ashley," she murmurs as she tries to sit up.

"It's no trouble, Mom." I put the tray next to her as I sit down. "What would you think," I ask, "about moving in with us, at least for a little while?" It's something I've been thinking about for a few weeks, as I've seen my mom get weaker and weaker. And while I know she would have resisted such a notion back at the beginning of her cancer treatment, I'm hoping she can see the sense of it now.

"Moving in with you?" She draws back a little, like she's going to resist.

"It would be easier for you," I tell her, "and for us. But mainly for you." I don't want to pressure her into this, but I'm worried for her—and driving to New Britain several times a week is challenging, not that I'd admit that to her.

My mom rests her head against the sofa and closes her eyes as a small, sad smile curves her lips. "I'm not going back to work, am I?" she asks softly.

I know how much it cost her to admit that. "You never know, Mom," I say gently, "but maybe enjoy the break, if you can? You've worked all the hours God has given you for your entire adult life. Now you finally have some time to rest."

She opens her eyes as her smile widens. "Some break," she remarks dryly.

I nod in agreement, managing a small smile in return. "Yeah. Some break."

We are both silent, and then my mother nods slowly. "All right," she says on a drawn-out sigh. "If you're sure." She straightens, alarm flashing in her eyes. "But what about your baby? I'll be in the way..."

I don't know if my mom will even be here in six months, when we bring our baby home, although I certainly hope she will.

"We have three bedrooms," I tell her. "You won't be in the way at all. And I'd... I'd like to have you there."

"You would?" She pauses, her gaze sliding away. "I haven't been as good a mother to you as I wished I had," she says quietly, a confession. It's the first time she's ever said anything like that.

"Mom..." I begin, although I'm not sure what I'd even say. What I feel, besides sorrow that this is only happening now.

"I was just so *tired*," she whispers. "All the time. Like a weight dragging me down." A sigh escapes her, long and low. "And the truth is, I didn't know if I had it in me, after your father left. I loved him so much, you know. I shouldn't have, because he wasn't worth it, but I did." She sighs again, as she shakes her head. "I was young. So young."

"Oh, Mom." I've never heard her talk this way, with so much regret and sorrow. "None of that matters now," I tell her as I reach for her hand. "I mean, for me. I'm just glad you're here, and I'm here, and that Mark and I can help you."

She nods, sniffing, and then she smiles. "Tell me about your beautiful baby again," she says. I told her about the visit to San Diego when I saw her over the weekend, but I kept it low-key because now that I want this so much, I'm afraid to jinx it. Afraid to trust, to believe. But for my mom's sake, I decide I need to.

"The baby is healthy and perfect," I tell her. "And we don't know for sure, but I *think* she's a girl. I just have a feeling, you know? And look." I reach for my purse, where I still keep the printout of the ultrasound scan. Mark has his own copy. "I didn't show you this before, because, well, I guess I felt like I was pushing my luck. But here she is, Mom. Or he. Trust me, I wouldn't be disappointed if it was a boy."

I show my mother the scan, and she blinks at it, slowly making sense of the shapes. I know on first glance it looks like a bunch of blobs, but it really is a baby. And then she sees it—him or her—and a slow smile dawns across her face, spreading like a tide. "Oh, *Ashley*," she whispers. "Oh, Ashley, she's gorgeous."

"Or he," I tease, but I am smiling, full of pride. It's only an ultrasound scan, I know it's still so early, but I feel proud and hopeful and full of love all at once.

I stay with my mom as she picks at her dinner, barely eating any of it, and then falls back asleep. Outside, it's gotten dark, the first stars coming out in the sky as I pull the blanket up over my mother's shoulders and gently kiss her cheek before tiptoeing out of the house. Tonight I'll talk to Mark about having my mom come and live with us. I know he'll agree, but I'm also wondering if he'll mention using the second bedroom as a nursery, and whether it will be "too much" for me to care for both a baby and my mother.

I'm just getting into the car when the phone pings with a text. I assume it's Mark, asking when I'll be home, but it isn't.

It's Dani, and it's the first time her text hasn't been a response to one of my smiley GIFs or memes. It's just three stark and terrifying words.

Can we talk?

TWENTY-TWO

DANI

In an instant, everything changed. On Monday morning, four days after Mark and Ashley left, Callie and I sat in front of the surgeon's desk while he gazed at us somberly and told us in a matter-of-fact tone the news I never expected to hear.

"I'm sorry, but the MRI showed severe stenosis in more of Callie's vertebrae than we had originally anticipated. It's partially why she's been experiencing so much numbness, but unfortunately it makes her ineligible for the surgery, as she'd lose too much flexibility if we were to fuse all the affected vertebrae. Her quality of life would be severely compromised."

I stared at him blankly, some part of me refusing to accept what he'd stated so plainly. "But you can fuse *some* of them," I finally said. It was not a question.

"Such a procedure would compromise the stability of the vertebrae that were not fused," he explained. "I'm afraid I can't recommend such a procedure at this time." He shook his head, regretful but resolute. "The best treatment for Callie would be physical therapy and steroid injections. With those, I think her pain could be effectively managed." He smiled, like he'd just given me good news, but I was reeling.

Callie couldn't have the surgery. *Callie couldn't have the surgery.* There I was, nearly fifteen weeks pregnant with a baby I hadn't had to have, because I no longer needed sixty-five grand. And Callie wasn't going to get any better.

I felt numb, and yet I wanted to howl.

"There's no way for me to have the surgery?" Callie finally asked quietly, while I simply sat and stared, struggling to get my thoughts together. "I mean, no possibility of any kind of spinal fusion at all?"

"I'm afraid not," the surgeon said firmly. "But, Callie, your condition can be managed more aggressively, with injections and physical therapy. This isn't the end of the road, treatment-wise, trust me." He smiled at her, effectively ignoring me. "It's just closing the door on surgery, which, frankly, is a relief for a lot of people, because having this surgery is no small endeavor."

"No." Callie gave a small smile back. She sounded relieved. "No, it isn't."

We left fifteen minutes later, having been given the names of physiotherapists and orthopedists who could help her manage her condition. I'd barely spoken during the whole appointment.

"Dani?" Callie asked once we were back at the car. "Are you okay?"

I swung around to stare at her. "Are *you* okay? After all this..." I shook my head. "I really thought the MRI was only a technicality."

Callie shrugged. She seemed remarkably unfazed, unlike me. "I guess it wasn't."

"But, Callie, your *symptoms*..."

"I know my symptoms, Dani, and they suck. But you heard what he said." She nodded toward the office as she slipped into the car. "It can be managed. I haven't been all that consistent with the physio, and I haven't had a steroid injection in months. Maybe I can find ways to make this work. And maybe that other doctor was just really pro-surgery or something, because right now I'm choosing to believe there are more options than we thought."

I didn't reply as I started the car. *I* was the one who had been pro-surgery, I knew. I'd wanted the quick fix, the absolute solution rather than an ongoing, laborious road of injections and therapy, a halfway house that might have Callie in constant or chronic pain, a struggle she always had to face, and I would have had to face it with her. I hadn't wanted to consider such a prospect, and so I'd put blinders on, focused only on fixing my sister.

And now I found she couldn't be fixed.

"Dani…" Callie's voice was gentle. "It's okay, you know. I don't mind as much as I thought I would. I mean, the prospect of having to deal with this for my whole life is a lot, and I know I'd decided I wanted the surgery, but… it still scared me. A lot."

"I know it did." My voice sounded scratchy, like I had a sore throat. I felt as if I could cry, except I was too numb.

"I feel like you had your heart set on it, though," Callie said. "Are you disappointed that I can't have it?"

"I…" I shrugged helplessly. How could I possibly explain how I felt? "Yes, I am, but I get that you're relieved. It's just…" Tears pricked my eyes. I blinked them back. I wasn't about to explain to Callie what a mess I was in, with this surrogacy. That had been my choice, not hers.

But my sister was smart, and it didn't take her long to figure out what was going on. "The baby," she said quietly. "You didn't have to do that, Dani."

"Well…"

Too late now. I couldn't make myself say the words.

"You still don't need to," she continued, her voice growing stronger. I turned to stare at her, trying to find the humor, even though inside I still felt devastated… on so many levels.

"Um, Callie?" At least I managed to sound sort of wry. "You might have noticed that I'm already pregnant."

"Yes, obviously," my sister said, starting to smile, "but, Dani, now you can keep the baby"

Callie's words, so innocently, so *naively* spoken, reverberate restlessly through me for the rest of the day, and then the day after that.

You can keep the baby. So simple. So easy.

Or not.

First of all, I tell myself, I'm in no position to keep a baby. I don't have the resources, the life setup, the *will*. I told myself I wasn't maternal, and I'm not. Except... for three years, I've been acting like a mother to my own sister. Why not to my own baby? The baby whom I looked at on that screen and in that moment *loved*?

Of course there is the money I'd have to give back. Sixty-five thousand dollars, except I haven't spent much of it. And I've only received twenty thousand dollars so far, and all of that, minus the co-pay for the MRI, is still in my bank account, earmarked for the surgery Callie is now not going to have. There are my medical expenses, which are significant. An ultrasound, the regular checkups, plus I might be on the hook for Mark and Ashley's expenses, coming all the way to San Diego, staying at the Fairmont... Who knows? If I was to consider this, I realize, I'd need to consult a lawyer. Mark and Ashley will want to, as well.

But of course I'm not really considering this, because the overwhelming reason *not* to keep the baby is Mark and Ashley themselves. They'd be devastated, *both* of them, and in any case, this baby is as much Mark's as it is mine—something that is unsettling in the extreme. He has parental rights too, rights I'm pretty sure he wants to claim, no matter what, which could have us all ending up in a messy, protracted legal battle I will likely lose.

No, there are far too many reasons for me *not* to keep this baby... And yet, day after day, I keep thinking about it. And thinking about it. And wondering if maybe somehow I *could*.

At night, I dream not of this baby, but of the twelve-year-old somewhere in the world, a boy or girl, who is living their life with no knowledge of me. In one dream, I have a dark-haired boy with deep, chocolatey eyes. In another, a slim, freckle-faced girl who looks like Callie. I wake up aching, my face damp with tears, my hands cradling my barely-there bump.

The morning sickness has finally abated, and I have energy again, but I am still dragging myself to class, to work, because I feel so heavy inside. It's been only a week since the Weirs left, but it feels like an age, a lifetime, and in a way it has... the life of this child, that I now care about, that I tell myself I can't and yet I do.

Because I know I can't talk to Ryan or Anna about this, I end up calling the one person whom I never go to for advice, but maybe I should. My mom.

"Callie can't have the surgery," I blurt as soon as she answers the phone. "I feel like everything I did was for nothing."

"It wasn't for nothing," my mother replies calmly, as unflappable, or maybe just as indifferent, as always. "Callie knows how much you'd do for her. How much you love her."

"Well, yay for that lesson learned," I reply, with some bitterness. "I feel like there could have been an easier way to show her. Bake her cookies, maybe?"

"Maybe," my mother agrees, and I find myself letting out a huff of laughter.

"Mom..." I say suddenly, asking the question I've been too

angry to ask her before, "why did you leave? I mean, *really* why? Because you never explained, and I know I've never asked. I never wanted to know the answer, because I knew it couldn't be good enough."

"And now?" my mother asks after a moment, her voice quiet.

"Now I don't know, and I want to," I reply honestly.

My mother is silent for a long time, and I simply wait. I feel weirdly calm, like there's nothing she could say that would shock or upset me now, although maybe that's not true. Maybe I'm just feeling numb, the way I so often do, to protect myself.

"I suppose it felt like the only thing I could do," my mother says at last. "I was so shocked by your dad's death, the debt, the complete loss of the life I'd worked so hard to build. I just couldn't see the point of trying anymore, if it can all collapse like a house of cards. And I was fifty-one, Dani, which you might not be able to understand, but it felt like I was staring down the barrel of old age and this was my last chance to do, to *be* something different, and the truth was, I didn't know how to be myself anymore. I didn't know who that person was."

She lapses into a silence, and I can't think what to say. On one hand, it all sounds like a bunch of touchy-feely mumbo jumbo. On the other, I can understand it.

"But beyond that," she resumes, "I don't think I even had the capacity to make a conscious decision. I felt like I was existing outside myself, watching the decisions I made like I was a spectator to my own life. And I think I knew on some level that I couldn't care for Callie in that state, that she'd be better off with you. I didn't feel I could even care for myself, which is how I ended up at the Sisters of the Mercy. They understood and they took care of me." She sighs. "That probably sounds like a lot of excuses, and I know you've been angry, and I understand that, but I am glad that you finally asked me that question and seemed to want to genuinely hear the answer, whatever you make of it now."

"I did want to hear it," I tell her quietly. "And I'm glad, too, that I asked and that you answered." Because when she was speaking, I realized she could have been talking about me, when I was pregnant. The numbness, the lack of choice, the shutting out and cutting off... I did it all, too, so how could I possibly blame my mother?

But I don't want to be that way this time. This time, I want to be different. I want to be different with *my* child.

"I think... I think I want to keep this baby," I suddenly blurt out.

"Then keep it," my mother says simply. "And let me help."

When I get off the phone with my mom, I pace the apartment, restless and anxious.

Callie is out with a friend, although she said she'd be back by seven. Outside, the sky is just darkening, the first stars coming out over the ocean. My stomach is in knots, and I feel like every nerve is flaring painfully to life, so everything both hurts and feels wonderfully alive. What am I going to do? *What am I going to do?*

I snatch up my phone and before I can overthink it, or even think at all, I text Ashley. *Can we talk?*

Then I fling my phone onto the sofa as a shudder goes through me. I don't want her to reply. I'm not sure I want to flip this switch, push this button, and see where it leads, because already I know it will send the three of us down a road I don't think I'm ready to go down... And yet...

My phone pings with a text. It's from Ashley, two words. *Yes. Now?*

Another shudder goes through me. This conversation is

going to be like a detonation, upending everything, and yet some part of me knows it has to happen, one way or another.

My thumb hovers over the screen. Then, my finger trembling, I type, *If you're free*. And wait.

Just a few seconds later, a request for a video call comes through. Biting my lip hard enough to hurt, I swipe to accept the call. Ashley's face comes onto the screen, pale and tired, with dark smudges under her eyes. It takes me a moment to realize she's in a car, the night dark all around her, her winter coat pulled up almost to her chin.

"Dani? Is everything okay?" she asks. I can't tell if she can guess where this is going; her voice is strangely flat.

"Yes... I mean, with the baby, yes. No emergency there." I sink onto the sofa. I'm not sure I can do this.

"What did you want to talk about?" she asks in the same flat voice. She tucks her hair behind her ears, her gaze sliding away from mine.

"I... I found out that Callie can't have her surgery," I tell her. "The MRI showed she wasn't eligible, because of the condition of her vertebrae... Anyway, I hadn't realized that not being able to have the surgery was even a possibility. I assumed she'd be able to go ahead."

Ashley's face softens momentarily into sadness. "I'm so sorry, Dani. That must have been really hard to hear." I can tell she hasn't yet connected the dots the way Callie did, the way *I* have. "What are you going to do?" she asks. "I mean, what is Callie going to do? Is there another possible treatment?"

"She'll have to manage with physical therapy and steroids. She's okay about it, because she was nervous to have the surgery, but we'll see how it goes." My voice is getting faster and higher, so I'm stumbling over the words. "The doctor says he thinks the steroids will help with the numbness, and maybe it could improve in time, but it's hard to say..." I shrug helplessly, because there are still so many unknowns, and I don't want there to be. "I don't know exactly how it will all work out," I confess. "I was so fixated on surgery that I didn't really consider anything else, which I am only now realizing was pretty blink-ered of me." A rueful sigh escapes me, because I don't know how I feel about that. If I hadn't gone ahead with the surgery option, I wouldn't now be pregnant. And I want to be pregnant now... *don't I?* At least, I want to keep this baby.

Don't I?

"I don't know what to do now," I confess quietly, and for a few endless seconds Ashley simply stares at me blankly. Then, realization dawns, like a shadow passing over her face, and her mouth gapes before she snaps it shut and, for a second, some-thing like hatred flashes in her eyes. I can't blame her.

"Tell me what you mean," she commands huskily.

"I... I was thinking that maybe I... maybe I..." Even now, it's so hard to say it. I can't make myself say the words.

"Are you thinking of keeping this baby?" Ashley demands in a low, throbbing voice. "Is that what you're thinking?"

Wordlessly, feeling miserable yet also defiant, I nod.

A shudder rips through her, and she sits back in her seat, shaking her head, her gaze on something I can't see. "I knew it," she whispers. "I knew it when I saw you look at the ultrasound screen. I saw it on your face."

I nod; I remember that moment, too. We both were experi-encing the same incredulous wonder, and only one of us should have, at least in that way. Like a mother.

"I'm sorry," I whisper.

Ashley is silent for a long moment. "It's not that simple, you know," she says suddenly, her tone turning sharp. "Legally you *may* be able to keep this baby, but you'll owe us, Dani, all the money we paid you? Can you even repay that, *ever*—"

I can't help but recoil at the sudden savagery of her tone. "I know I do," I cut across her. "I haven't spent that much of the money. I was saving it for Callie's surgery."

"Of course you were." The anger has seeped out of Ashley's voice, leaving only despair. She rests her head back against the seat and closes her eyes. "I've been waiting for this to happen," she whispers. "All along, some part of me was waiting. I think that's why I didn't want to believe that we were really going to have a baby. To trust, or to hope, until just a few days ago, when I saw that image on the ultrasound and I couldn't help but believe, *hope*... but I just *knew*." Her voice spikes with anger, and she lifts her head as she wipes her eyes. "I just knew it was all too good to be true. Something had to go wrong."

"I really wasn't expecting this," I insist. I need her to believe me. "I wasn't planning—"

"But you have the luxury of being able to change your mind," Ashley snaps. "And we don't." She shakes her head, anger flaring once more in her damp eyes. "You know this baby is still Mark's, whatever you feel right now?" she tells me. "He will have rights, too, even if you keep the baby. Parental rights, and let me tell you, I know for a *fact* he will enforce them. So think about that while you're spinning your little happily-ever-after." And on a sob, she abruptly ends the call, plunging my phone screen into blackness, the room into silence.

I drop my phone onto the sofa and let my head fall into my hands.

What have I done?

I close my eyes. I knew pulling the trigger on this would be complicated, but already I am filled with regret. This hasn't *become* complicated; it always was. And, I realize, it doesn't end happily for *anyone* now, no matter what.

How can it? We'd all already lost something, before we even began.

TWENTY-THREE

ASHLEY

The worst part is, I am not even surprised. I knew this was coming. I *knew* it.

And so I seethe with anger all the car journey home, my mind both racing and filled with fury at the trick Dani has played on us, even if she didn't mean to. Of course, this is what happens in plenty of adoption stories, according to the message boards I've perused. The birth mom is on board until the last moment, and then she decides she wants to keep her baby. But this is meant to be different, I tell myself, because this is *Mark*'s baby, too. Dani doesn't have exclusive rights. Mark has equal right to their child.

In fact, the only person who doesn't have any rights in this scenario is *me*. Still, I tell myself, that doesn't matter so much, because I am married to Mark. Dani can't ride into the sunset with her little bundle of joy the way she might be picturing. Not without a custody battle, anyway... Yet is that really the route we want to go down? A protracted legal battle where we wrest a newborn away from its mother's arms?

A groan escapes me. I don't want any of this. I never did. And I'm so angry with myself for allowing Mark to convince me that traditional surrogacy was a sensible option. That I was okay with him having a baby with the surrogate *I* stupidly picked out. That it all made sense and seemed normal and risk-free and *good*, because Mark—and Mark only—got what he wanted.

None of it was good. *None* of it. And now I'm the one who has to tell Mark that it's all gone to hell. Why me? Why did Dani call *me*, and not Mark? Did she think I'd be more amenable? Was she afraid of Mark's reaction? *I'm* afraid of Mark's reaction, and yet I'm still so angry—not just with myself for being such a pushover, but with Mark. He was so blinded by his need for a biological child of his own that he basically hung me out to dry.

At least that's what it feels like right now, and, if I'm honest, it's felt that way all along. Yes, I was glad to get on board with the whole idea when I saw that image on the ultrasound. And yes, I'm devastated that now Dani might be keeping the baby after all.

But still, the biggest emotion I feel right now, is fury. Fury at my husband for having brought us to this place at all. Fury that he railroaded me into it.

I pull into the space in front of our townhouse. I need a minute to calm myself before I face Mark, but I don't take it. I yank my car keys out of the ignition and storm into the house like a ship in full sail, letting the door slam behind me.

"Ashley?" Mark doesn't register the slam, or what it might mean, as he comes down the stairs. "I was just looking at paint colors for the nursery. I was thinking yellow or green, depending on whether we go with a Noah's Ark or Beatrix Potter theme..." He stops when he sees my face. I don't even know what my expression is, but I feel like I could *ignite* with the force of my anger. "Ashley...? What's wrong?"

"Dani wants to keep the baby," I spit.

"What?" Mark stares at me in incomprehension for a full

ten seconds before he slowly shakes his head. "No. No, she can't…"

"You know as well as I do that she can," I snap. "Because she's a *traditional* surrogate. If she wasn't, she'd have no parental rights. As it is, she *does*, and whose fault is that?"

Mark's face pales. "Ashley…"

"*Whose fault is that, Mark?*" I practically scream.

I wheel away from him and storm to the kitchen. I feel as if I'm vibrating with fury and hurt, and I know I need to calm down. *Mark and I never argue*, I think, and then I wonder if that's been part of the problem all along. Maybe we should have argued before now. Maybe we should have argued a *lot*.

"Ashley, there is a solution to this," Mark says, his voice calm again, as he comes into the kitchen. "We can sue for custody. It's been done before. I did look into the legal ramifications when we first decided to go down the traditional route—"

"*We* didn't decide anything," I tell him, pointing a shaking finger at his chest. "*You* decided. *All* of it."

"That's not true," he states with quiet dignity, his face flushing. "I know I was the driver in this, I can take full responsibility for that, but I did my utmost to make sure you were with me every step of the way, and, Ashley…" He flings his hands out in appeal. "I thought you *were*." This isn't said as an accusation, but it feels like one, and I'm not having that. He might have convinced himself I was on board, but he knew how I always caved so easily. I know he knew that, and now we might lose the chance of our own child, after all this time and effort and *emotion*…

"You *knew* I wasn't," I say quietly. "On some level, Mark. Be honest. *Please.*" I take a shuddering breath. "I mean, how could I be," I continue, my voice rising, "when this is your baby but not mine? How would that ever work out for me?"

He pales, his eyes widening. "Is that really how you saw it?"

he demands. "I did everything I could to make you a part of things—"

"What, pick out paint colors? Be with you in the room while you donate sperm? Do you honestly think those things make a difference?"

He shakes his head, looking torn between anger and something like grief. "I didn't realize the biological factor was this important to you—"

"But it was so important to *you*!" I cry, my voice high and wild. "How could it be so important to you, and not to me?"

"Ashley, you know why." Mark's voice has risen too; we've never fought like this before, both of us filled with hurt, practically vibrating with anger. "I'm *adopted*—"

"Oh, and that's your trump card yet *again*?" I practically sneer. "I never knew my dad. I wasn't close to my mom. I have one other relative in the whole world. You're not the only one with a sad story, Mark, even if you like to act as if you are. And besides, you had two loving adoptive parents who saw you through your whole childhood, who unequivocally accepted and supported you. They paid for your college and the down payment on your first apartment. Honestly," I spit as I shake my head, "you had a lot more than I did growing up."

"It's not the same," he says after a moment. The anger has left him; now he just sounds sad. "But I don't even know why we're arguing like this," he continues. "We shouldn't be fighting each other, Ashley."

He sounds so desperately earnest, and I know he's right, in a *way*, but what is he implying? "So we should be fighting Dani?" I ask wearily.

"Not fighting," he amends, "but addressing this situation. What did she say exactly?"

I can barely be bothered to go through it all again. He doesn't get it, I know. He doesn't realize this isn't even about Dani, *or* the baby. "That she found out Callie isn't eligible for the surgery," I tell him in a monotone, "and so that's made her think about keeping the baby."

"Okay. Okay." Mark nods thoughtfully.

I feel so incredibly tired all of a sudden, as well as defeated. I push past him to go to our drinks cabinet, where I pour myself a stiff gin and tonic and toss back half of it in one burning swallow.

"Let's sit down," Mark suggests, and now he's all gentle coaxing. "Let's sit down and talk about this sensibly."

"Fine." I feel flat, and too exhausted to object. Besides, Mark will do most of the talking, anyway. He'll just want me to listen.

When, I wonder as I curl up on one corner of the sofa, *did I get so cynical?*

Mark comes into the living room with a glass of Scotch, poured probably in solidarity with my gin and tonic. He sits on the other end of the sofa, gazing at me with a puppyish eagerness.

"We can figure this out, Ash. I know we can. *Together.*"

I shrug and take another sip of my drink. Mark, like he's in a drinking game, takes a sip of his. The silence between us stretches, settles. Outside, it's fathomlessly dark; we're in the depths of winter, everything cold and barren, which suits my mood perfectly. Which suits *me*, because that is what I am, and I don't care as much as I thought I would.

Yes, I let myself hope for our would-be family, I got excited about a baby because I knew how much Mark wanted it and it felt like the right thing to do. And yes, part of me—a big part— *did* want this baby. Dani's baby. But now that she's said she wants to keep it, and I've sifted through the wreckage of my own disappointment, I realize what I feel at my core.

A treacherous little flicker of relief, just like I did at the doctor's office all those months ago.

But the far bigger and more important emotions are the

anger and resentment I feel toward Mark. I let him be blinded by his need for a biological child, and I let it blind *me*. I'm as much to blame as he is—or almost—but right now I don't know where we go from here—not as the potential family of three he so desperately wants us to be, but simply as a *couple*.

And I absolutely know he doesn't see that. He doesn't understand how precarious our marriage feels to me in this moment. All he's thinking about is how we can get Dani's baby back.

Sure enough, the first thing he says is, "I can contact our lawyer tomorrow morning about this, but I also think we can take a longer, more reasoned view. If Dani only just found out that Callie can't have her surgery, her visceral and under-standable reaction might have been that the surrogacy was pointless. But in time, with a little distance, she might realize that sixty-five thousand dollars could still help both her and Callie quite a bit, and, of course, she wouldn't want a protracted legal battle. Nobody wants that, obviously." He nods, seemingly satisfied with this argument, before taking a sip of his Scotch.

I don't bother replying. I feel empty inside, like I am about to tip over into a swirling devastation that I can't bear to think about. So instead I completely change the subject and announce, "I want my mom to come live with us."

Mark looks understandably startled. "I thought we were talking about Dani..."

I lean forward, belligerent as well as a little drunk. "We're *always* talking about Dani," I tell him. "Enough. I want to talk about my mother. She's getting weaker and she's lonely on her own. I want her to live here, with us."

He raises his eyebrows. "Even though you work all the time?"

"Oh, *now* the claws come out," I can't help but sneer. "I *knew* you resented my promotion. You've wanted me barefoot and pregnant in the kitchen, but of course I can't be pregnant now, so you'll settle for the other two, I guess?"

"*Ashley*." Mark, quite suddenly, looks stricken by my change in tone, the ugliness of my words. "What's happening to us?" he asks, sounding bewildered.

"What do you *think* is happening to us?" I demand. I really am drunk, I realize, and I don't care. "What did you *think* would happen to us, when you introduced another woman into our marriage?"

"Now that is blatantly false, as well as absurd—" Mark begins, sounding like he's working himself up into a self-righteous fury.

"It's how it felt to *me*, Mark." My voice is quiet, and suddenly I feel stone-cold sober. "I don't mean romantically; I was never truly threatened that way, but..." I pause for only a millisecond before plowing on resolutely, "Having a biological baby felt like it was more important to you than I was. Than our marriage *is*. And you can deny it now all you want, and I know you will, but that's how it felt to me all along." It feels both painful and a relief to finally say it all out loud.

Mark is silent, and I finish my gin and tonic, the ice cubes rattling in my glass.

I put my glass down with a clink, and the silence settles on us like a shroud. Is this the death of our marriage? I wonder numbly. It's lasted all of seventeen months.

When I force myself to meet Mark's gaze, I can't gauge his expression at all. His lips are pursed, his gaze distant. "I wish you'd shared these concerns with me earlier," he finally says, and he sounds like a lawyer.

"I tried," I reply, "but maybe I should have tried harder." I hesitate, and then decide it's time for a total emotional bloodletting, however gruesome it gets. "I never wanted to make a fuss," I explain haltingly. "My mother used to say that to me—'Ashley, don't make a fuss.' And my dad used to say it to her, along with her parents. Like making a fuss was the worst thing a woman could possibly do, and should be avoided at all costs." I shake my head slowly. "And so, when it came to us and our relationship, our *marriage*, I never wanted to make a fuss with you. Ever."

I swallow, my throat sore with the effort of holding back my tears. "I felt so lucky that you chose me, you know," I choke out. "That's how it always felt—like you chose me, rather than the other way round, and I was so *glad*." My voice wavers, breaks, and then I make myself continue. "And I never wanted you to regret your choice, not for one minute, so I never made a fuss about any aspect of the surrogacy, but I know I dragged my feet about it, and you noticed and then tried harder, which probably made us *both* resentful."

I can't bear to look at him as I admit all this, but I hear the anguish in his voice as he says, "*Ashley...*"

"I know it's been a massive disappointment to you that I can't get pregnant," I force myself to state. "And I know you've never actually said that, and you've been amazing in so many ways..." I make myself look up at him; his eyes are bright with tears, which just about undoes me. "But I still felt like I'd failed you," I finish. "And the fact that you didn't even think to let go of this dream for one *second*, but just tried to figure out a way to still get what *you* wanted..." I trail off, because I wonder if I am being unfair. Mark was upfront from our very first date that having a baby was important to him. And he did offer to let go of it all, if only halfheartedly, back at the beginning. "Maybe this is all my fault," I whisper. I draw my knees up to my chest and press my forehead to their tops. "I don't know," I whisper, so quietly I don't know if he can hear it. "Maybe this was never going to work." I don't even know what I mean by "this"—the baby or our marriage.

Mark is silent for a long moment. I keep my forehead pressed against my knees, both because I don't want to see the expression on his face and, worse, because I'm afraid there's no point in trying to make him understand. We've reached an impasse, and I have no idea how we can navigate it. Even with the best will in the world, we can't change our very selves... can we?

"You've given me a lot to think about," Mark finally says quietly. "A *lot*. And I want to think about it all properly and give your concerns the time they deserve. I mean that, Ashley." I don't so much as lift my head, because I sense what is coming next. "But," he continues, just as I feared he would, "for right now, can we deal with the pressing matter at hand? Shall I contact our lawyer tomorrow and see what our options are, if Dani does decide she wants to keep the baby?"

I would laugh but I can't dredge up the energy. Wearily, I lift my head. "Sure, Mark," I say in resignation. "Why don't you do that?"

Mark nods, looking re-energized, before he gives me a guilty, half-apologetic look. "I'm not disregarding what you said, Ashley, I promise. It's just... this is urgent, and..."

I'm not.

I don't bother saying it. I just take my glass and walk out of the room to get another drink.

TWENTY-FOUR

DANI

For two whole weeks after my call with Ashley, I hear nothing from the Weirs. Not an email, not a phone call, not so much as a text. It makes me very uneasy. Are they giving me space to change my mind, or are they assembling their legal team? Maybe both.

And meanwhile I am trying to figure out if I really *do* want to keep this baby... and if so, how I could possibly manage it. Callie is, as I'd expect her to be, buoyant with possibilities. "I can babysit, like, *all* the time," she insists. "And she can share my room! I'll get up with her in the night, I don't mind—"

"We don't know if it's a *she*," I remind her. "And, Callie, you have a life—"

"Not that much of a life," she dismisses. "Dani, I want to do this."

But do I?

I am trying to imagine teaching a class with a newborn. Finishing a thesis on no sleep. Getting my first job with a toddler in tow. It all feels impossible... and yet I can't deny that there is something exciting about it, too. I envision a hazy future where I'm attending Callie's graduation with a baby on my hip;

making sandcastles on the beach with a towheaded toddler; strolling through La Jolla with a sassy six-year-old, and I feel an ache deep inside me, both of longing for what could be and sorrow for what I never had with the first child I gave up.

This, I can't help but think, would be *true* redemption. And yet, at the same time, it would be horribly unfair to Ashley and Mark. Can I live with that? With myself, for making such a selfish choice? And what about Mark's parental rights, as Ashley said? A long, drawn-out legal battle that I might very well lose is enough to have me composing an email to them late one night, saying I've changed my mind and that I don't want to keep the baby.

Before I press send, I delete it all.

I live in this limbo for two weeks of uncertainty in myself and radio silence from Ashley and Mark before I finally break and reach out. Not to them, but to Ryan, whom I haven't spoken to since he broke up with me, although we've exchanged a few friendly-ish texts. I've missed him, more than I ever thought I would, and he's the person I want to talk to when I'm feeling like I don't know what to do, which is probably telling.

I text him, because I'm too cowardly to call. *Could we meet up? I'd like to talk.*

He replies six agonizingly long hours later, just two words. *All right.*

We arrange to meet at Liberty Public Market at Point Loma's Liberty Station, the former home of San Diego's Naval Training Camp, and now a trendy hub of artisanal bakeries, boutiques, coffee shops, and restaurants. Ryan is standing outside the entrance of Pure, a juice bar we both like, when I arrive five minutes early. Clearly we're both nervous.

I've taken care with my appearance; fortunately, I don't look like something the cat dragged in anymore. Now that the nausea is gone, I'm getting a little bit of that pregnancy glow. My hair is shiny and thick, and at nearly seventeen weeks, I don't quite yet need maternity clothes, although I chose a loose top to hide the slight swell of my stomach.

Ryan looks great, as he always does, with effortless indifference. His hair is rumpled, and his jade-green polo shirt matches his eyes. He smiles faintly when he sees me.

"You look good," he tells me as he steps forward to kiss my cheek. I can't tell from his tone if he's pleased about this or not, but at least it didn't sound grudging.

"Thanks, but you should have seen me a few weeks ago," I reply, stepping back. I have to resist the urge, at least for now, to lean into him. "I looked pretty rough then," I say with something of a laugh.

He frowns. "Did you have morning sickness or something?"

"Yeah, and a lot of tiredness. But I'm doing better now. Physically, I mean." Because the truth is, I feel like I'm falling apart emotionally. If Ryan thought I was an emotional mess before...

Ryan nods toward the juice bar. "Let me get you something."

He's being so nice, all things considered, that I feel like I could burst into tears. Got to love those pregnancy hormones.

I order a protein smoothie, and he gets a kombucha. Then we sit at one of the outside tables, an umbrella shading us from the abundant March sunshine as people stroll by, enjoying San Diego's amazing weather.

"So why did you want to talk?" Ryan asks as soon as we've sat down. Clearly he's not up for pleasantries, but that's okay, because I'm not either.

"I've missed you," I blurt. It wasn't what I'd expected to say. "More than I thought I would, if I'm honest."

He lets out a huff of soft laughter as he raises the bottle of kombucha to his lips. "That sounds about right."

"I wasn't fair to you, Ryan," I tell him, surprising myself yet again. This is really not where I thought I was going with this conversation. I was going to tell him about how I was considering keeping the baby, and whether he had any legal advice. Not that he's a lawyer, but I feel like he'd know the legal ins and outs more than I would. Or maybe I just wanted a semi-sympathetic listening ear. Truth be told, I don't know *what* I wanted, but I realize I'm glad I'm telling him all this, because it needed to be said... for both our sakes.

"I kept a distance between us, and you were right, it was for all the reasons you guessed: my dad, my mom, the pregnancy I had before..." I shake my head slowly. "But that doesn't make it right, maybe just understandable. But I'm sorry... for hurting you."

He is silent for a moment as he squints into the sun, before turning to look at me. "So, is that all you wanted to say?" He doesn't sound angry or even annoyed; if anything, he sounds curious and a little sad.

"No," I admit. "I mean... I didn't totally realize I was going to say all that in the first place, but I'm glad I did." He waits for more, and haltingly I continue, "I just... miss you. And not just for the movies or the nights out or even the sex." I give an embarrassed laugh. "I miss you being you. With me. If that makes any sense." I try for another laugh, but this time it comes out like a croak. "I guess I just wanted you to know that," I tell him in little more than a whisper. I'm feeling less like I needed to say all this and more like a complete fool, because Ryan is simply staring at me without any expression at all.

The silence between us stretches on, and for want of anything better to do, I take a sip of my smoothie, and the sound of me sucking it up through the straw is a loud gurgle that makes Ryan's mouth quirk up in a tiny smile.

"I've missed you too," he finally says, and I am lightheaded with relief. "I tried not to," he adds matter-of-factly. "Tried my best to get over you. Even went on a couple of dates, which all basically sucked."

I suppress the sting of jealousy his candid admission gives me. While he was going on dates, I was hanging over a toilet, throwing up my breakfast. "I can't blame you for that," I half-joke. "I would have tried to get over me, too."

"Oh, Dani." He sighs and shakes his head, sounding more wistful than sad. "Where does that leave us, though?"

"Before I attempt to answer that question, I need to tell you something else." The real reason—or at least what I thought was the real reason—for meeting up at all. "I'm... I'm thinking of keeping this baby."

Ryan's jaw drops as he stares at me silently for a full ten seconds. "You... you *are?*" he finally stammers. "But... how? And what about Callie's surgery..."

And so I explain, about her surgery, or lack of it, and about my own changing feelings. "I know it's not fair to Ashley or Mark," I finish. "And Mark would have parental rights of some kind, so... it all feels really messy." A sigh escapes me as I admit something I haven't before. "I never should have agreed to this," I tell Ryan in a low voice. "And I'd be sorry I did, except there's an innocent life involved and I'm not going to ignore that—or him or her—the way I once did, with my first pregnancy. But, I don't know, maybe I shouldn't use one difficult situation to redeem another. Maybe I need to let them *both* go." My voice cracks and I look down at the table, blinking rapidly to stem the sudden tears. "Honestly, I don't know what the right thing to do is."

"Oh, Dani." Ryan reaches over and rests his hand on top of mine. I like the feel of it there, solid and warm. "I don't know what the right answer is," he tells me. "I don't know if there even is a right answer, just a lot of different ones that feel various degrees of wrong."

"Yeah." I manage a shaky laugh. "That's exactly how it feels."

"So, maybe in the end," he says gently, "you need to think

not what you want, or what Ashley and Mark want, but what is actually best for the baby... whatever that is." He squeezes my hand. "Whatever you decide, I'll support you."

I glance at him, still tearful but also surprised. *Support me...?* What exactly does he mean by that?

He must see the unasked question in my eyes because he laughs softly and squeezes my hand. "Remember when I said I loved you? I don't always know why I do, but it hasn't changed."

"Oh, Ryan..." My throat is thick with tears as I realize I am finally ready to say the words I'd resisted saying—and feeling—for so long. "I love you, too."

"You do?" He feigns surprise, or pretends to. "Last time I said so, you weren't sure."

"I know, and I wasn't. But being apart from you... it made me realize how great you really are. I mean, I always knew, but..." I trail off guiltily, because I fear I'm making things worse. If there's any chance that we might get back together—and to be honest, until now I didn't think there was—I really don't want to blow it now. "I am sure now," I tell him firmly. "But if I did keep this baby..." I shake my head. "That's a lot for you to have to consider. Would you be okay with that?"

He is silent for a long moment, giving the question the serious consideration it deserves. "I hope I would be," he says finally. "I mean, I'd certainly try to commit to... to loving this baby, and raising it as my own, if... if that's the direction we were headed in." He ducks his head, clearly feeling vulnerable from that admission, and I love him all the more for it.

"Thank you," I whisper.

We remain silent, our hands still linked, as we both consider a future that right now, at least to me, feels entirely unknowable.

Over the next week, as Mark and Ashley maintain their now-ominous silence, I try to figure out what Ryan suggested—that is, what is best for this baby. And so I ask the people in my life, few as they are.

Anna definitely has strong opinions. "Dani," she says when we're having brunch at Snooze, a breakfast place on Fifth Avenue, "*why* would you keep this baby? I'm not trying to be callous, but I just can't see it." She shakes her head as she reaches for her Bloody Mary, complete with celery stick and slice of tomato. "You have everything ahead of you—your doctorate, your career, a really good relationship, now you're back with Ryan—and you have a couple who aren't just ready but *desperate* to welcome this baby as their own and can provide for it way better than you can. I mean, I'm sorry, I just don't get it. To me, it's an absolute no-brainer."

"Well," I joke feebly, winded by all her arguments, "when you put it like that..."

"I'm not trying to be unkind," Anna says earnestly as she leans forward, drink in hand. "And I can totally see how this has become emotional for you, especially since it's your biological baby." Something that had horrified her when I'd reluctantly told her. "But nothing's actually changed," she continues, "except now you can use all that money in another way—a deposit on an apartment, better therapies for Callie, your *wedding*..." She waggles her eyebrows, trying for a laugh.

It makes so much sense, I know it does, and yet some elemental part of me resists.

Anna drops her smile as she puts down her drink to reach for my hand. "When something is hard," she says quietly, "that doesn't make it wrong. Often the opposite."

"I know." I reach for my own drink, a passionfruit and coconut virgin cocktail. Right now I'd rather have a Bloody Mary. "I know," I say again, because I do, and I don't have any other words.

. . .

Three days later, my mom comes to visit. It's now been three weeks since I've heard from the Weirs, which feels not just ominous, but weird. No smiley memes or funny GIFs from Ashley. No pointed check-in emails from Mark, with links to helpful articles on vitamins or Pilates or playing classical music to your baby while in utero. No vitamin delivery, even though I was due one.

Surprisingly, I find I miss these communications, as much as I resented them all before, even the kindly meant messages from Ashley. Being cut off so abruptly and deliberately, no matter that I may deserve it, feels hurtful. And meanwhile, I have no idea what Mark and Ashley are thinking... or doing.

I consider calling Andrea to alert her to the situation, but that feels like hurling yet another grenade into an already explosive situation, especially when I haven't yet decided what I'm going to do.

My mom offers her own wisdom. "I feel like I pressured you before," she tells me. We are curled up on the sofa in my apartment with mugs of herbal tea in a way that feels weirdly cozy; Callie is at school. "To give up the baby. I just was so scared for you, and I felt like you had all this life before you... but I should have given you more choice. I should have supported you either way, and so that's what I want to do now. I know it's all kind of late in the day..." Her smile wobbles as she continues, "But I am trying, Dani. At least, I'm trying to try. And I thought... if you do decide to keep this baby... maybe I could move to San Diego."

"What?" I can't help but goggle. That is not something I ever expected my mother to suggest.

"I think it's time," she tells me. "Either way, whether you keep the baby or not, I want to be more involved in your and Callie's lives. Maybe I should have before... No, I *know* I should have before," she corrects, pressing her lips together, "but I just didn't have it in me. I'm sorry for that... and I want to do better now." She lifts her chin, flinching slightly as if waiting for my barrage of disdain, which I once might have determinedly given. "And if you do keep the baby," she offers, "I could help with childcare. I'd really like to be able to do that." Now she sounds shy, and I am completely and utterly gobsmacked.

Here, at last, is the mother I remember from my childhood, whom I loved. The mother I ran to when I got hurt, who stuck my preschool drawings onto the fridge, who was at every track meeting I ever went to and cheered for me even when I came second to last. Why did it take so much heartache and hardship to get her back—and can I really blame her for not returning sooner? Truth be told, have I been any better?

"I'd like that too," I finally say, my voice choking a little bit, and my mother smiles.

It's now been nearly four weeks since I've heard from the Weirs. I'm nearly halfway through this pregnancy, and my ultrasound—the one where I can find out if it's a boy or girl, that Mark and Ashley said they wanted to attend—is tomorrow. I am bewildered by their silence now, have no idea what it means. I never expected it to go on this long.

Part of me wonders, in a surreal sort of way, whether I'll ever hear from them again. They've disappeared so completely from my life, and yet surely they still want this baby. And if they didn't, wouldn't they say so? I have no idea what to think about any of it, and so, when my phone pings with a text on a Monday afternoon in late March, when I am about to get into my car to head home from a class, shock ripples through me as I see who it's from—Ashley.

But that's nothing compared to the shock that slams into me when I read what she's written.

I'm at San Diego Airport. Can I see you?

TWENTY-FIVE

ASHLEY

The morning after our big discussion—that's what Mark calls it, *not* an argument—he consults our lawyer, and I move out.

I don't phrase it like I'm leaving him; I tell him I need to stay with my mom for a few days, for her sake rather than mine, but, the truth is, I need some space. Mark is fooled, maybe because he wants to be, but my mother is not.

"What's going on?" she demands from her habitual place on the sofa, after I've been with her for three days, her voice papery, her face gray with fatigue and pain. Her next round of chemo—and maybe her last, if it isn't effective—starts tomorrow. "Why aren't you with your husband?" Her mouth twitches in a wry smile. "I thought I was meant to be moving in with *you*."

Once, I might have put her off. Lied, or at least joked back. But no more. "Because we fought over the baby," I tell her. And I give her the unfortunate highlights—Dani wanting to keep the baby, Mark insisting on consulting a lawyer, how this isn't even about the baby, *any* baby, but our marriage. My mother is silent as I speak, her face screwed up into a thoughtful frown.

"I can see why you're upset," she finally says, which is

another first for us. "But, Ashley…" She smiles then, her eyes lighting up with a wry humor I'm still in the process of discovering—and appreciating. "Don't throw out the baby with the bathwater."

I laugh in spite of myself, shaking my head. "And in that saying, is the baby the *actual* baby? What's the bathwater?"

"Your marriage," she replies quietly. "Mark is a good man. I know, because I know what a not-so-good man looks like." She sighs. "But, more importantly, you love him. You can both get past this. I know you can."

"I can," I tell her, "at least I think I can. But can he?"

"If you let Dani have the baby," my mother says slowly, "what about Mark? That's his child, too."

"I know." Which is why I wish, so very desperately, that we'd never gone down this route. Mark said at the heart of every adoption was brokenness, but it seems to me it's the same for surrogacy. Someone will have to suffer loss… it's just a matter of who it is. "I don't want a big legal battle," I tell my mom. "That doesn't seem right, or good, for anyone. But just walking away…?" A heavy sigh escapes me. "I know that's not fair to Mark."

"Maybe he could have some visitation rights?" my mother suggests. "Or partial custody?"

"From birth?" That hardly seems like the best thing for the baby… and really, we should be thinking about what the kindest and safest thing is for this little life we all agreed to create. But what is that? To be in a stable home—at least financially, if not emotionally—or with the biological mother whose life is a little chaotic and who said she didn't want a baby in the first place?

Is there even a right answer? The trouble is, the more I consider the question, the more I think there isn't. By going down this tangled route, we created a situation with no right answers… which means there are only wrong ones.

Mark, meanwhile, texts me to tell me he is in discussions with our lawyer. She advises us not to talk to Dani for a while; maybe this will blow over, but in any case we want to have our legal case watertight before we make a move.

The language of the lawyer that Mark uses both depresses and alarms me; he's strategizing for warfare, and I already want to give up. I feel bad for essentially ignoring Dani; I have a feeling she didn't love my daily texts with the funny memes, but the absence of them could appear hostile in a way I don't feel or want to seem. And what about the lack of communication from Mark? Admittedly, I always tried to keep him from messaging her too much, but he did shoot off an email at least once or twice a week, with some "helpful suggestions."

Now there's nothing but silence.

But in that silence, I find I am coming back to myself. I can breathe easier; I can live my life without being in a constant state of tension, although considering the state of my marriage, maybe I should be. Still, I am enjoying my job; Lila even offered for me to work from home two days a week, so I can spend more time with my mom.

Our evenings are quiet, usually a small meal in front of the TV, watching *Jeopardy* or the QVC channel; my mom's dry remarks about the quality of the merchandise make me laugh out loud.

"A set of three rechargeable lighter wands," she remarks, musing. "*With* gift bags, and in such lovely pastel colors. Now that's clearly a must-buy."

"Don't forget the set of three compact jar openers," I remind her. "Also with gift bags."

"Well, that's Christmas sorted." She leans her head back against the sofa and closes her eyes. "That is, if I'll be here at Christmas." She opens her eyes to gaze at me with a strangely peaceful bleakness. "I don't mind dying so much," she tells me quietly. "It's just that I'll miss you." She gestures to the space between us. "And this. I wish we'd had this so much sooner."

"So do I," I whisper. *So much.*

Several weeks pass, where I focus on my job and my mom and I more or less ignore the texts from Mark, fobbing him off with pithy replies that he accepts. I'm too busy with work and helping my mom out, I text him, to come back to our condo. He says he understands.

I know we need to talk, and, more importantly, we need to talk to Dani. She must be wondering what on earth is going on... as I am. Is Mark planning something? Do I really want to know?

And then I find out. Three weeks after my phone call with Dani, Mark calls me.

"Can you meet me in Hartford on Monday morning, at Donna's office?" Donna is our lawyer, a six-foot-tall tigress of a woman who scares me even though she's on our side. "Eight o'clock, before you head to work. We need to discuss the case."

"The *case?*" Even though I've been expecting something like this, I'm shocked by his choice of word. "Mark, we don't even know if Dani is still thinking about keeping the baby. We haven't communicated with her—"

"And she hasn't communicated with us," he retorts swiftly. "Telling, don't you think?" His voice is sharp, focused; he's in lawyer mode, and I feel as if I barely recognize him.

"Do you really want to sue for custody?" I ask quietly. "Is that what you're considering?"

"Ashley, this is *my* baby," he tells me, his voice rising, like I don't know that already, haven't had it drilled into me. "My only biological relative that I know of, in the entire world. What do you think I want to do?"

"Your baby," I am compelled to point out. "And not mine."

"You've made it pretty clear that's how you think," he shoots back, "so why shouldn't I, too?"

There seems to be no acceptable answer to that, and so I agree to meet him, with foreboding, because I already know this is a route I don't want to go down, not even one step.

Donna and Mark are already in the law office's conference room when I am ushered there by a secretary, offered coffee or tea. I refuse both, stepping into the room with a nod rather than a smile.

I haven't seen Mark in three weeks, and he looks pretty terrible. His skin is slack; he's lost weight, and while he always said he needed to lose a few pounds, it doesn't suit him. But worse than that is the air about him, of frenetic energy, manic focus. I have *never* seen my husband like that, like he's being eaten up from the inside out.

"Ashley." Donna stands up as she sees me. She is dressed in a magenta power suit, her iron-gray hair cut short, her eyes already narrowed. I have a feeling Mark briefed her that I might not be as on board with this course of action as he so obviously is. "How are you?"

"I'm..." I find I don't know how to answer that, and so I cut to the chase. "What's going on here? I feel like I might have missed a few meetings."

I glance at Mark, who looks away, and I realize I have been deliberately naïve, enjoying my job and my time with my mother, the respite from *all this*, while hoping that Mark was just trundling along. I knew he was consulting our lawyer, but I didn't envision this kind of deliberate, coldhearted plan he so clearly has already set in motion.

We all sit down, and Donna goes through it, point by point, while I listen numbly, the realization dawning that my marriage ended sometime when I was watching *Jeopardy* with my dying mom. Donna tells us—although I'm pretty sure Mark has heard this all before and believes it with the fervor of a zealot—that we have a strong case for total custody of this baby. That our stable home life—*ha*—and financial situation would make this a clear-cut decision for any judge. That Dani's history of having already given up one baby for adoption could be used against her—Donna's actual words—and Mark's paternity rights cannot be ignored. She goes on and on, but at some point I stop listening.

When she pauses for breath, I turn to Mark. "Is this what you really want?" I ask him.

He stares at me, determinedly nonplussed. "Ashley, you know what I've wanted all along," he replies. "I never made a secret of that... unlike you."

"Let's keep focus," Donna murmurs. Clearly she realizes any signs of marital disharmony are not good for our case.

"And you want to take this baby from Dani?" I demand, my voice rising. "Even though she's the baby's biological mother?"

"*I'm* the baby's biological father," Mark returns swiftly. "Are you saying I don't have the same rights?"

"You seem like you want to have *more* rights," I point out. "You want total custody, even though Dani, as the baby's biological mother, wants to keep her own child." I shake my head, overwhelmed by how dogged he is about this. "Mark, imagine your own mother, if someone had treated her this way. Imagine if she gave you up because she was *forced* to, even though she'd wanted to keep you. How does that seem fair?"

"Obviously feelings are running high," Donna interjects smoothly. "Which is understandable. And total custody isn't the only option here. We could certainly consider offering the biological mother some visitation rights, even generous ones. A weekend a month, maybe, once the child is of an age where he or she can understand the complexity of the situation?"

"Which would be when?" I ask in disbelief. "Six, seven

years old? And meanwhile Dani never gets to see her own child?"

"Or *I* never get to see my own child," Mark points out in a lethal tone.

"My sense is that Dani might be open to this kind of arrangement," Donna remarks carefully. "Based on her own life situation. The fact that you haven't heard from her in several weeks... that could suggest she's rethinking her rash conversation with you, Ashley."

Maybe this is meant to make me feel better, but it doesn't. Too much has happened, has been said and felt, for us to go back to an and-now-it's-all-okay scenario.

"Maybe someone needs to reach out to her," I say finally. "Without," I add pointedly, "an agenda."

Donna and Mark are both silent, and I realize what the obvious answer is.

"I'll talk to her," I say heavily. "In person. I'll visit her in San Diego." Even though it means leaving my mother at a time I really don't want to. This, I know, is important. For Dani's sake... and for my marriage's, if there's even anything left to save.

"To tell her what?" Mark counters, sounding belligerent. "That she can have the baby, free and clear? I want to be there—"

"I don't think that's a good idea, at this juncture," Donna intervenes once again. "When feelings are running so high."

Mark falls silent, chastened and a little peevish. I feel like I have no idea who my husband is anymore, and yet didn't I see flashes of this obduracy right from the beginning, on our very first date? Maybe I shouldn't feel as surprised, as *devastated*, as I do.

"I'm not going to tell her that," I tell Mark wearily. "But neither am I going to threaten her with some massive legal case, which wouldn't help matters." Something in me twists, breaks, and I turn to my husband, ignoring Donna. "Mark, don't you remember what you said at the beginning? How this was a journey, a *relationship*? We were meant to be supportive of Dani. Of *Dani*, and not just her having the baby. I know how much this baby means to you. Trust me, I have always known that." I take a wavering breath. "But this is bigger than what either one of us wants. We have to think what's best for the *baby*—"

"I *am*!" he cries out, before falling silent. For the first time, I see something like doubt enter in his eyes, a flickering shadow as he looks away. Could he possibly be reconsidering, even just a little?

"Let me talk to her," I urge. "Just to see where she is with all this. Maybe she has reconsidered. If that's the case, we want to be a support, not antagonize her."

"Do you even want this baby anymore?" Mark flings at me brokenly, his voice catching on the words.

"I don't know what I want anymore," I reply honestly, because that much is certainly true. "But right now I want to do what's best for Dani, a single woman whom *we* have put into a vulnerable situation."

Everyone is silent for a long, tense moment and then Donna gives her verdict.

"Mark, I think this is probably a good idea," she says, effectively ignoring me. "We need to feel Dani out in terms of her thinking, and Ashley is best placed to be supportive. Besides, nothing that she says in a private conversation is legally binding." She turns to give me a measured look. "I hope you realize what's at stake, Ashley, and you can act with discretion."

I don't bother to reply.

Four hours later, I'm on a plane.

The sunshine and heat roll over me in a wave as I step out of the airport.

I didn't tell Dani I was coming, which might have been a mistake, but there wasn't time, between arranging leave from work and cover for my mother, and, more to the point, I didn't want her to have the opportunity to refuse. So here I am, waiting for an Uber and texting her that I'm already at the airport. She is, I know, going to be shocked, and maybe, understandably, hostile.

Her reply to my text comes just seconds later. *Now?*

Yes, I text. *If that works for you.*

Let's meet somewhere. Balboa Park's Trails Gateway on Park Boulevard is ten minutes from the airport. I hope you have sneakers.

I almost smile at that, and I text back my agreement. Then I step into the Uber that has pulled up to the curb.

Fifteen minutes later, I am standing by the Trails Gateway sign, having changed into sneakers, my travel carry-on by my feet. I feel surprisingly *not* nervous, which I didn't expect, considering how much is riding on this conversation, and I don't even know what I'm going to say yet. Above me, the sky is a hard, bright blue, and the air is a balmy and perfect seventy-five degrees. Balboa Trails is a verdant oasis of bright green, manicured lawn and swaying palm trees. I almost feel like I'm on vacation.

Dani pulls up in her car, her face a pale oval behind the window. As she gets out, I can't help but notice how much better she looks than she did a mere month ago. And how much more pregnant; she's wearing a fitted T-shirt and there is a defined roundness to her stomach, a fullness to her face.

"I can put that in my car for you," she says by way of greeting, with a nod toward my bag, and I murmur my thanks and heft it myself, so she doesn't have to.

Neither of us speaks as we walk back to her car and put away the bag. Then we head back to the trail head, where several walkways branch out.

Dani glances up at the sun, which is just starting its lazy descent in the still-bright sky. "We can do the mile and a half before it gets dark," she says. "Is that enough time for you?" The question isn't hostile, but it's tense.

"A mile and a half sounds good," I answer, and she strikes out, leaving me no choice but to follow her.

We walk in silence for a few minutes as a variety of pedestrians pass us by—middle-aged power-walkers, with weights strapped to their ankles and wrists; someone ambling along with her dog; a fearsome rollerblader.

Eventually, as we round a corner, we are alone—or as alone as we are ever going to be in a public park. It's time for me to say something.

"I'm sorry," I venture, "for the silence on our part."

"Yeah," Dani remarks after a moment, her gaze straight ahead. "It's been pretty weird."

"You look well," I offer. "Like you've got that pregnancy glow."

She glances at me sharply, as if suspecting some hidden innuendo or even threat in my words, and then she nods. "Thanks," she says, and resumes staring straight ahead.

We walk in silence again, the minutes stretching on as I struggle to think what to say. I am wondering why I came here, and what on earth I hoped to accomplish.

"I think I freaked out a little on the phone, when you told me you were thinking of keeping the baby," I tell her finally. "I'm sorry."

Dani glances at me again, this time in wary surprise. "Well, I'm sorry for telling you like that," she answers. "I totally get that that's the last thing you want to hear, as the intended parents." She sighs. "It's the last thing I expected to feel," she confesses. "I hope you believe that."

"I do." I hesitate and then ask carefully, doing my utmost to keep any judgment from my voice, "What are you thinking now? Do you feel the same way?"

Dani stops walking, and so I halt next to her as she stares up at the sky for several seconds. I have no idea what's coming next.

"Honestly?" she answers, sounding weary and hopeless as she turns to look at me. "I have no idea."

TWENTY-SIX
DANI

It's kind of surreal to have Ashley here, looking so worn out, but also so calm. I could tell as soon as I saw her that she wasn't here to threaten me or give me the hard sell. What she *does* want, I have no idea, just as I have no idea what *I* want, either. Maybe, I think wryly, we can figure it out together.

"Well, it's understandable you'd feel... ambivalent," Ashley tells me. "To be honest, I've felt pretty ambivalent about this whole thing from the beginning."

Her honesty surprises me, but I'm glad for it.

"I kind of suspected that," I admit as we keep walking. Neither of us is looking at the other; I think it's easier to say these things that way. "It always seemed like Mark was driving the whole surrogacy thing."

"Yes, you could say that." She is quiet for a moment. "It's proved to be pretty difficult for us," she confesses finally. "In ways we didn't expect."

"I'm sorry." I genuinely mean it. I like Ashley, and I respect her, maybe more than Mark, although that might be unfair. He's been all solicitude and consideration to me, even if it's felt kind of oppressive at times.

"I don't know where we go from here," she continues. "I think we're all in the same boat of not knowing what to do." She lets out a tired laugh that wavers. "What the best thing to do is, not for us or for you, but for the baby." She stops to turn to look at me. "But I don't want you to feel pressured, Dani, about any of it. I really don't."

"And if I said I was keeping this baby?" I ask, feeling curious rather than aggressive.

"Mark is this baby's father," she states after a brief pause, not that I need the reminder. "That counts for something, certainly. But how much, I don't know."

"I've thought that the baby might be better off with you two," I admit, somewhat reluctantly, because I'm afraid she—or maybe Mark—will use this against me. "You're financially stable, you both want this baby, in a committed relationship..." I trail off because something in Ashley's expression makes me wonder if those things are still true. "Aren't you?" I finish uncertainly.

"I don't know what the state of our marriage is," she admits, glancing down at the ground. "Like I said, this whole thing has been more difficult than we expected. And yes, we're financially in a better position... but, God knows, money isn't everything."

"And do both of you want this baby?" I ask, because that's the one part of the equation she very much hasn't mentioned. And so, just to be clear, I stop walking, turn to face her straight on and ask bluntly, "Do *you* want this baby, Ashley?"

She stares at me for a long moment, and then her face crumples. "I've wanted to want this baby," she says, her voice coming out on something close to a sob as she holds her hands up to her face. "I really have. And sometimes... like when I saw the ultrasound... I did want this baby, *so much*. And I've been so afraid to be a mom, but now, with the way things are with my own mom... I'm not anymore, and that's a big deal for me." She lowers her hands as she wipes at her eyes. "I know I'd like to be a mother. I'd like to have a child. But do I want *this* baby? Yours and Mark's?" She is silent, her expression turning distant, resolute, the tracks of her tears still visible on her face. "I'm not sure I do."

It's hard to know where to go from there, and so we are both silent as we resume walking.

"I didn't come here to say all that specifically," Ashley tells me, her voice still sounding like she's holding back tears. "I came here mainly to ask how you were feeling, and to be supportive. And..." She blows out a shuddery breath. "To tell you that, at the moment, Mark is considering a legal battle."

I spin around to face her, her words reverberating through me. "*Mark* is?"

She shrugs. "Like I said..."

"Things have been difficult," I fill in, my mind whirling. "Are you guys even together anymore?"

Ashley presses her lips together. "I don't know."

If Ashley doesn't support Mark's custody claim, does that mean I have a better chance? But, heaven help us all, I really don't want to take this to court. That will be messy, painful, expensive. I rest one hand on my belly, my fingers spreading over my bump. In the last few days, I've started to feel little flutters. They seem magical to me, like kisses from inside my body. Ashley, I realize, will never know how that feels. I feel a twist of pity for her, as well as a surge of admiration. She has been remarkably resilient and compassionate throughout this whole process.

"I have my ultrasound tomorrow," I blurt. "When I find out if it's a boy or a girl, get to see all the fingers and toes. Why don't you come?"

She goggles at me, clearly not expecting this. "Are you... Dani, are you sure?"

I nod. For once, I am completely sure I am doing the right

thing. This is what we both want, and what feels good. "Yes," I tell her. "I am totally sure."

The next morning, we meet at the clinic. Ashley found a hotel near the airport while I returned to Callie. My mind and heart both felt too full to explain to her what had happened, and so I didn't mention that Ashley was here. I did text Ryan about it; I've finally learned not to keep things from him. My guardedness hasn't been fair to either of us.

He called me immediately, as I knew he would. "She came all the way to California?" he exclaimed as I stepped out onto our balcony so Callie wouldn't overhear. "Is she pressuring you?"

"No, pretty much the opposite." Briefly, I explained what had been going on. "I asked her to come to the ultrasound tomorrow."

"You did?" He sounded a little hurt, and belatedly I realized that maybe Ryan had wanted to come with me. If I really was considering keeping this baby, he needed to be a part of this process, too—something I am still needing to learn and remember.

"I want you to be there too," I said quickly. "Of course I do. I'm sorry I didn't ask you before. But if you want to..."

Ryan was silent for a moment. "I do want to be there," he said at last. "But I think maybe this time it should just be you and Ashley."

I loved him all the more for understanding that, because I knew he was right.

And so here we are, heading into the clinic as we exchange well-meant but uneasy smiles, because this feels so strange and surreal and yet, also, in a way I cannot explain even to myself, right.

Just like before, we are ushered into a darkened sonogram room. I hoist myself up onto the table as Ashley perches nervously on a chair near my head. The technician, all professionalism, greets us both warmly and doesn't ask where Mark is, although I'm pretty sure that it's noted on my file that he's meant to be here.

She squirts the cold gel onto my stomach and then starts pressing the wand into my bump, hard enough to make me wince.

"Are you okay?" Ashley asks quietly and I manage a smile.

"Yeah. Just a little tender." It doesn't help that I had to have a very full bladder for this procedure. Hopefully I won't pee myself.

"All right, here we are," the technician says, and then, just as before, an image appears on the screen—first just blobby black and white shapes, and then, wonderfully, miraculously, a baby.

Our baby.

I see that now; I feel it. We've been tussling over this baby like it's a much-treasured toy, but it's not like that at all. At least, it doesn't have to be. I still don't know what the way forward is, only that if we try, we might be able to find one.

I turn to look at Ashley, and I see she is, very discreetly, wiping her eyes. I have a feeling she wants this baby more than she was willing to admit, maybe even to herself. But perhaps that's the endlessly complicated nature of this whole scenario.

And *this*, here, now, is how it—and us—can be redeemed.

"Do you see the nose?" I ask gently. "I think it might be Mark's?"

She lets out a wavery sound. "It is kind of snub like his, but those long arms and legs are totally yours."

"Maybe we have another runner in the family," I say by way of agreement.

The technician continues with her poking and prodding, measuring the growth of the limbs, the chambers of the heart that is steadily beating away. Ashley and I simply gaze at the screen, lost for a few blissful moments in wonder, with no need to speak.

Then the technician does. "Would you like to know if it's a boy or a girl?" she asks, and I hesitate. This feels like edging toward a precipice, letting ourselves fall. Will finding out make a difference, one way or another? It feels like it might.

"It's your call, of course," Ashley says quietly.

But there's no *of course* about it, I realize, because I wouldn't be here without Ashley, without Mark, without the money they so generously gave me. If I hadn't gone on this *journey*, I wouldn't have found out that Callie couldn't have the surgery; she wouldn't now be seeing a very good physiotherapist with already improved results. I wouldn't have reconciled with my mother; I wouldn't have the strong relationship with Ryan that I now do.

"Would you like to?" I ask Ashley. "I don't know if it makes a difference to either of us, but... I want to know what you think."

"Oh..." Her voice trembles as she tries to laugh. "I suppose... I suppose I would."

We both glance expectantly at the technician, who answers with a smile, "I'm pretty sure it's a boy."

"*Oh...*" This from me, a tremble of sound, of wonder, because for some reason, I'd always pictured a girl. I'm not disappointed, though, just amazed.

"Dani, that's great," Ashley says firmly, and I know in that moment what she's decided. Whether it's the right decision remains to be seen.

We are silent as the technician prints out photos for each of us; our baby is sucking his thumb, knees tucked up to his chest. I'm still reeling from the fact that it's a boy. Knowing that much more has made a difference, but I'm not yet sure how.

"Let me take you out to lunch," Ashley says when we're

walking out to the parking lot. "If you want to, and you have the time, that is…"

"Let me take *you* out to lunch," I counter. "You and Mark have given me so much already. And now that I'm not nauseous anymore, I want to show you what real Mexican food tastes like."

She laughs and nods, wiping the corner of her eye as discreetly as she can. "That sounds fabulous," she says.

I take Ashley to Las Cuatro Milpas, a bare-bones kind of place that is one of the most authentic Mexican restaurants in the city.

It's a far cry from the seafront terrace of Coasterra, where Mark took us; it's located on Logan Avenue in the downtown area, and the food is delicious and cheap. I order rice and beans and tamale, and Ashley asks for a burrito. We take it to go and walk over to Chicano Park, just beneath the San Diego–Coronado Bridge, to sit on a park bench and eat our lunch. I'm not letting myself think further than that, although I'm aching to take the envelope out of my purse and study that printout of a little boy I think we might both love.

"Well, that was intense," Ashley says, finally breaking the silence. "Mark would have loved to have been there." She sounds sad, and a little wistful. "I think I might have been unfair to him," she confesses. "About all this." She lowers her head as she slowly unwraps her burrito. "It all got so emotional… I felt like he lost perspective, but maybe I did, too."

"Maybe we all did," I offer. As wondrous as seeing that ultrasound image was—*again*—I'm not sure it changes anything after all. We're still in the same predicament, maybe even more so, because no matter what she says, I could tell by the way she reacted to that image that Ashley wants this. At least some part of her—maybe a really big part—does.

She sighs as she looks up again. "How did you feel, seeing that ultrasound? Knowing it's a boy?"

I let out an uncertain laugh. "I think maybe the way you felt," I tell her, but already Ashley is shaking her head.

"No, I don't think so," she says quietly. "I can't deny I was emotional... and part of me..." She trails off, shaking her head some more, seemingly lost in thought. After a moment, while I pick at my rice and beans, she starts again. "I feel like we can work something out, Dani," she says, sounding more determined than pleading. "I think we can find a way forward with this. With Mark having some kind of parental right... or visitation... something. But I think... I think this little boy belongs with *you*."

To hear her say it out loud, so definitively, causes something warm and tight to bloom in my chest. I didn't realize until she said it, but I agree with her. Even if it doesn't make sense. Even if I have no idea how I'll manage a PhD, my sister, my *life*. Somehow I will. Ryan and I will, together.

Ashley smiles at me. "You know I'm right," she says, and I let out a shaky laugh.

"Ashley... I don't know what to say." Or even what to feel. I'm grateful, and moved, but also sad for her... and for Mark. We can't forget about him in this scenario, and whether he'll agree to any of it. "You're being very generous," I say at last. "Thank you."

Ashley smiles again and touches my hand. "This is the way it's meant to be," she says, and I wonder how she can be so certain, when I still feel so scared. I also wonder how she'll convince Mark.

We eat the rest of our lunch without, amazingly, talking about the baby. Instead, we talk about our lives, something we never really did before, during that trip back in February. I tell Ashley about Ryan and how we're back together, and how relieved my sister is not to have the spinal surgery, although I'm still worried for her. In return, Ashley tells me about her new job and how much she loves it; her mom, and how their relationship was never that great, but now it feels stronger than ever.

"Just as I'm about to lose her," she finishes wistfully. "It doesn't feel fair, but I don't think it could have happened any other way, and I'm just trying to be grateful for the time we do have together."

I think of my own mom as I nod. "Sometimes that's how it has to happen," I agree. "I wish it wasn't like that, but I don't know if we can learn any other way." I certainly couldn't.

We finish our lunch and stroll through the park, admiring the Chicano murals that gave name to the park, painted in the 1960s and 1970s as a response to police brutality. The day is getting on, and I need to return to work, but I find I don't want to shortchange Ashley. I'm enjoying this time with her, far more than I would have expected to.

After about an hour, her phone buzzes and she slips it from her pocket, her mouth going slack in surprise as she stares at the message.

"What?" I ask, anxiety clenching my insides hard. Has Mark started legal proceedings? Has something made Ashley change her mind?

"It's Mark," she says faintly. "He's in San Diego."

TWENTY-SEVEN

ASHLEY

Mark texted me from the airport, just like I texted Dani yesterday.

All he wrote was: *I'm here in San Diego.* I have no idea what it means, if he's come here as a penitent, or with guns blazing. I'm afraid it's the latter. In fact, as I head to the airport to meet him, having left Dani with a promise to be in touch later today, I'm pretty sure it must be. Twenty-four hours can't change a person that much, surely.

He's waiting outside as I pull up in an Uber. I'm not sure where we go from here; my flight leaves this evening. I climb out, let the car go, and stare at my husband. He has no luggage, and he's unshaven, with bloodshot eyes and a tormented expression. I have no idea what any of it means.

"Ashley..." he says, and then stops.

"Why did you come?" I ask. I sound wooden; I feel desperately tired. There has already been a lot of emotion for one day, and I'm not sure I can take anymore, especially if we're going to fight. If Mark is going to tell me how he's lawyered up...

"Because I love you," he says, which is about the last thing I expected.

"Mark..." I stop, still having no idea what to say.

"Let's not have this conversation on a curb," he tells me with one of his old, wry smiles, the kind I haven't seen in a long time.

"Would an airport Starbucks be better?" I ask, and his eyebrows lift.

"Marginally, I'd say."

I feel as if I'm getting my husband back, but I'm not remotely ready to trust it. *Him.* Still, I let him lead me into the airport, and to a coffee shop. He orders a latte for me and an espresso for him and takes both to a table in the back. We sit and sip, both of us silent. Maybe we're both afraid to begin.

"I think," Mark says finally as he stares down into espresso, "I got a little crazy."

"Not crazy," I say quickly. I am determined to be fair. "Focused, maybe."

"All right, very focused." He sighs and stares up at the ceiling; I see tears in his eyes. "I let having a baby consume me. Being connected to someone... something bigger than myself... but I had that all along, Ash. With you."

"Oh, Mark." Now I am blinking back tears too. "I understand why you did. And why you still are. You have a baby. A child. We can't ignore that." I hesitate and then admit, "Dani had the ultrasound today."

"*Oh...*" Mark's eyes widen as his expression goes soft. "Did you find out...?"

I nod. "A little boy."

"Oh. Oh, wow." He blinks rapidly as he shakes his head. "Wow," he says again, softly.

We both fall silent and it takes several minutes for me to work up the courage to say, "So, in terms of suing for custody...?"

His expression turns resolute, but not in the way I recognize from before. "Does Dani still want the baby?" he asks.

"Yes, very much so, I think, although she's scared about it all."

"That's understandable." He is silent for another long moment, and I wait it out, knowing this is too important, and too painful, to press. "What you said to me back at Donna's..." he finally says slowly, "that hit home. About adoption. About what if it was my mother. I felt like I could stand outside of myself for a second and actually see what I was doing. Acting like. And I realized that is not who I want to be at all. But..." His voice wavers and he wipes his eyes. "I'm going to have a *son*."

"I know," I whisper, wiping at my own eyes.

"I wish... I wish we never went down this route," he confesses in a low voice. "I wish I'd considered just how complicated it would be."

"And yet good has come of it," I remind him, surprised I am the one who has to say that, and yet I know it's true.

"Still..." He shakes his head again. "It was so hard for you especially. You're right, I did know you weren't as on board with it as I was. Not even close, and yet I pretended, for my own sake."

"As did I," I tell him, another reminder. "We're both to blame in that regard, Mark."

He reaches for my hand, threading his fingers through mine. "Ash... can you forgive me? For all of it?"

I shake my head as I squeeze his fingers. "Whatever happened, it was down to both of us. But yes, I forgive you, Mark. Of course I do." As I say the words, I know that they are true. My mom was right. Mark is a good man, and I love him. We said vows, and finding a way through this is part of that. As to what that's going to look like... "I told Dani that if she kept the baby," I venture hesitantly, "that you had parental rights. We had to find some way forward, where you could visit... be involved, have a relationship..."

I trail off, because, as I say it, I realize how little it is, compared to what Mark wanted. What he should have had—his own child, in his home, in his arms, in his *life*. Instead he'll have to make do with—what? A weekend a month, if that? The occasional weekend that trickles down to Christmas cards and birthday presents? He won't be this little boy's dad, not in the way he wanted to be. Not even close.

None of it feels right, or fair.

"Thank you," he says, and squeezes my fingers back. I hear grief in his voice, but also acceptance. We might have found a way forward, but that doesn't mean it's easy or painless, far from it. I have a feeling it will be just as complicated as everything that went before, as well as messy and painful, and both less and more than what we all wanted. But at least it's a way forward.

"I love you," I tell him, and he gives me a watery smile.

"I love you, too."

There doesn't seem to be much more to say than that.

We fly home that night, after texting Dani that we'll be in touch, that we'll find a way to make it all work. We're both too fragile for a protracted wrangling session about what that will look like, in the long term. There is plenty of time to work it out later.

Returning to our gray condo feels like a homecoming, but also a mourning. There will be no green or yellow nursery. No Noah's Ark or Beatrix Potter theme. No baby.

No baby.

The realization slams through me, as if for the first time, and I feel a grief akin to Mark's, freshly agonizing. I chose this, I made it happen, but even so, it hurts.

That night, we lie in bed, our arms around each other. Although we're exhausted, I'm not sure either of us sleeps. We are both grieving, and it is a process that we have to let happen. Eventually, toward dawn, I drift into a doze.

The next day, I move my mom into our place. She comes

willingly, making the wry comments I now love, about how we need to add some color to the place, if she's going to live here or she'll feel like she's already dead. My mother, I realize, has come into herself in a way she never dared to before. Finally, at the end of her life, she is making a fuss, and I love it.

We celebrate her arrival with champagne, and she falls asleep after just a few sips, curled up on the sofa. I put a blanket over her and then Mark puts his arms around me.

"This was the right thing to do," he says as he rests his chin on top of my head. We stand there for a moment, simply breathing, being, finding a poignant joy in the loss.

Later, when my mother is up in her bedroom asleep and we are getting ready for bed, I text Dani a GIF. It has the words "so exciting" over Snoopy doing his classic Snoopy dance. I add another one, from *Jerry Maguire*, of Renee Zellweger saying "you had me at hello." I hope she gets the double message—Mark and I are willing for her to keep the baby, and that we're back together.

She responds almost instantly with a GIF of her own—a woman in tears with the words "I'm not crying, you are" underneath. I laugh out loud, just as Mark joins me.

Silently, I show him my phone. He smiles faintly at the exchange, and then he takes my phone, types three words, and shows them to me. I nod, and he presses send.

The text was simply: *Thank you. Mark*

It's the final part of letting go, and he puts his arms around me as I turn my phone off and take Mark by the hand, reaching up on my tiptoes to kiss him softly.

"Thank *you*," I say.

Neither of us knows what the future holds, or how difficult or challenging it will be, but right now we have this moment, and I am going to let that be enough. Right now, it is.

TWENTY-EIGHT

DANI

Seventeen months later

It's Toby's first birthday, and we're having a party. I'm as nervous as I am excited, because Mark and Ashley are coming, and while this is far from the first time they've visited, it still feels new and sometimes a little uncomfortable, but I think we're all learning to accept that that's okay.

We worked it all out in the end, in painful fits and starts. First, of course, was the issue of custody and the prospect of visitation rights. Mark asked if he could see our child—because, yes, that's what Toby is—once a month. It felt like a lot, but I suspected a judge would grant him even more, not that anyone was talking about legal battles any longer. I said yes, because it felt mean and even wrong to deny Mark such a simple and heartfelt request. Of course, we had to go through all of it, put everything into writing— his son visiting him when he's older, a trust fund formed, letters and emails and texts exchanged, in due course.

Ashley might have said this little boy belongs with me, but it started to feel like he would be spending an awful lot of time with Mark. But Ryan was okay with it, saw the sense of it even, and eventually I did too.

Ashley and Mark agreed not to be present at the delivery; Ryan was, and this time it wasn't a pain-filled blur, mainly because I had an epidural, and after Toby was born, Ryan sneaked in tacos. Callie and my mom came right after, and we all celebrated. All in all, it was a wonderful experience. I might even do it again one day.

Mark and Ashley visited when Toby was two weeks old; I'd already sent plenty of photos and videos, sometimes so much that it started to feel a little overwhelming, at least to me, but I knew Mark was desperate to be part of it all, and it was a small enough way to let him. When they came to visit, he brought a big blue teddy bear that I duly put in Toby's crib, as well as enough clothes and toys to outfit an orphanage. I got it; he was thrilled, and he was also trying. They only stayed for two days, and that felt like long enough, but I didn't begrudge Mark any of it. I couldn't.

By all rights, this baby should be his. I'd given back the money, of course, every last dime, but when I offered to repay the medical costs of the first four months—with Ryan's help— Mark and Ashley refused. It was generous of them, and I accepted.

And that's how it has been all along—this tentative push and pull, a gentle tug of war of managed hopes, expectations, and realities. Sometimes Mark has sent something—a remote toy Jeep that's almost as big as a real one, and hardly appropriate for a child who is not yet walking—that I've put away without showing to Toby. Sometimes he's asked to have a video call when Toby is fractious and I'm tired, and I say yes. And so it goes.

Now it's our son's first birthday, and we're having a party. Nothing too big, I know Mark will provide plenty of over-thetopness, so it's just a cake, some snacks and lemonade, and a picnic blanket in Balboa Park. That's enough.

Ryan hoists Toby onto his shoulders as I spread out the blanket and my mom and Callie arrange the food. Callie still has chronic pain, but it's better than before, and there's a new procedure we're investigating, experimental and expensive, but possible in time. My mom moved to San Diego right before Toby's birth; she lives in a little rented condo in the hills, works part-time at a yarn store, and takes care of Toby when I'm at work. I'm taking an extra year to finish my PhD; after that, maybe a career in pharmaceutical research. Ashley convinced me to look into that field. She loves her job so much, and maybe I will, too.

Ryan has taken to fatherhood just as I knew he would, enjoying every moment. He really doesn't mind that he's not related to Toby by blood, or that Mark is. In fact, they've developed a surprising bromance that I really don't get, but I'm willing to go with it, as is Ashley.

She's been more tempered with Toby, mainly for my sake, because sometimes, during their visits, I've seen a longing in her eyes, and I wonder if she occasionally regrets the choice I know she made. If she hadn't said what she had back when we found out he was a boy, the outcome might have been very different. I know I could have been convinced otherwise, and I'm pretty sure Ashley knew it, too. I'll always be grateful to her.

I am just checking on the cake in its white bakery box when I hear Ryan call out a greeting and then Toby squeal, his chubby arms outstretched to Mark, which is about the best birthday present ever... for Mark. I see the delight on his face as he reaches for his son, and I know this will always give me a little twist of—something, I'm not sure what. Not quite sorrow, or anger, or regret. Just... something. I know Ashley feels it too, by the way she smiles at me, her expression wistful and wry, and I wonder if it will always be this way. If it is, I think we can all live with it. We'll have to.

"Great to see you guys," Ryan says as Ashley comes over to give me a hug. It's been six weeks since we last saw them, for a weekend visit, and as always it feels both familiar and awkward. Mark is beaming, Toby hoisted on his hip.

"He's loving this," Ashley tells me with an affectionate glance at her husband. "But I want you to know we're going to be taking something of a step back."

"You are?" Based on Mark's delighted reaction to Toby just now, I'm surprised, to say the least. And not altogether displeased, it has to be said.

"Yes." Ashley nods, resolute. "It was Mark's idea. You know if he could, he'd be here every weekend. But he recognizes that he needs to let you guys be a family. And..." She pauses as she takes a breath, a cautious but proud look coming over her face as a light dawns in her eyes. "We need to be a family, too."

The import she gives to the words has me doing something of a double take. "Ashley...?"

"We've been approved to adopt," she explains with a shy smile. "And we've started the process with a little girl. She's three years old. Her name is Ciara."

"That's wonderful—"

"It's going to be challenging," she continues quickly. "Mark always said there is brokenness at the heart of every adoption, and that's true here, too. Ciara's had a difficult start in life. She's got some issues, but we're working through them, and we want to help her. We love her already, and so does my mom." I know Ashley's mom is still living with them, in a new house in the suburbs, an old brick Colonial that Ashley has always loved. Amazingly, her mother responded to her last round of chemo and while the outlook still isn't good, they're treasuring every moment they have with her.

"Oh, Ashley." I give her a quick, tight hug. "I'm really, really happy for you."

"And I'm happy for you, too." She nods toward Mark, who is blowing raspberries on Toby's tummy while he shrieks with laughter. "I know this has been… well, challenging."

"We all knew this would be challenging, going in," I remind her. "That doesn't make it wrong."

"No, but…" She pauses. "Mark will always want to be involved," she states carefully. "As I will, and that's right. That's good, I hope. But… we all need a little space, I think. For now. And that's okay, too."

"Yes," I agree, knowing how much she means it, how much this still costs all of us. "It is."

We both stand and watch as her husband continues to dance around with my son. Maybe this is how it will always be, the flows and eddies of a relationship that might not be natural but which we're all committed to making work. Maybe that's the best you can do with anything in this fractured, painful, messy, wonderful thing that is life.

Mark puts Toby on his hip once more as he smiles at me. "I think this boy wants his mama," he says, and, still smiling, he hands him over.

I put my arms around my son as his chubby hands fist in my hair and his soft round cheek brushes mine. Mark puts his arm around Ashley, and Ryan smiles at me.

My heart is both light and full as I kiss my son's plump cheek and he squeals in delight, while all of our mingled laughter floats away on the breeze.

A LETTER FROM KATE

Dear reader,

I want to say a huge thank you for choosing to read *All I Ever Wanted*. If you enjoyed it, and would like to keep up to date with all my latest releases, just sign up at the following link. Your email address will never be shared, and you can unsubscribe at any time.

www.bookouture.com/kate-hewitt

I've always been intrigued by surrogacy, and how emotionally and ethically complicated it can seem. I hope I've given the issue a fair treatment in exploring both Ashley's and Dani's sides of the story. It's always my aim to explore any issue from both sides and find empathy and understanding wherever I can.

I hope you loved *All I Ever Wanted* and if you did, I would be very grateful if you could write a review. I'd love to hear what you think, and it makes such a difference helping new readers to discover one of my books for the first time.

I love hearing from my readers—you can get in touch on my Facebook group for readers (facebook.com/groups/Kates Reads), through Bluesky, Substack, Goodreads (goodreads.com/author/show/1269244.Kate_Hewitt) or my website.

Thanks again for reading!

Kate

katehewittbooks.com

 x.com/author_kate

ACKNOWLEDGMENTS

As ever, there are so many people who are part of bringing a book to see the light of day! Thank you to the whole amazing team at Bookouture who have helped with this process, from editing, copyediting, and proofreading, to designing and marketing. In particular, I'd like to thank my editor, Jess Whitlum-Cooper, as well as Imogen Allport, and Sarah Hardy, and Kim Nash in publicity, Melanie Price in marketing, Richard King and Saidah Graham in foreign rights, and Alba Proko and Sinead O'Connor in audio. I have really appreciated everyone's positivity and proactiveness!

Thank you also to my new writing friends in the US. We're just starting to get to know each other, but it's great to be building up a new network after moving from the UK. Writing can be a lonely profession, and I am so grateful to those who make it a little less so.

Lastly, thanks to my husband Cliff and my five children, Caroline, Ellen, Ted, Anna, and Charlotte, and also my new and wonderful son in-law, Jacob! So, so grateful for all of you, and how you help with the family business!

PUBLISHING TEAM

Turning a manuscript into a book requires the efforts of many people. The publishing team at Bookouture would like to acknowledge everyone who contributed to this publication.

Audio
Alba Proko
Melissa Tran
Sinead O'Connor

Commercial
Lauren Morrissette
Hannah Richmond
Imogen Allport

Cover design
Alice Moore

Data and analysis
Mark Alder
Mohamed Bussuri

Editorial
Jess Whitlum-Cooper
Imogen Allport

Copyeditor
Jade Craddock

Proofreader
Tom Feltham

Marketing
Alex Crow
Melanie Price
Occy Carr
Cíara Rosney
Martyna Młynarska

Operations and distribution
Marina Valles
Stephanie Straub
Joe Morris

Production
Hannah Snetsinger
Mandy Kullar
Ria Clare
Nadia Michael

Publicity
Kim Nash
Noelle Holten
Jess Readett
Sarah Hardy

Rights and contracts
Peta Nightingale
Richard King
Saidah Graham

www.ingramcontent.com/pod-product-compliance
Ingram Content Group UK Ltd.
Pitfield, Milton Keynes, MK11 3LW, UK
UKHW042107140425
5472UKWH00002B/161

9 781835 252710